SO-CEZ-213

full stop

full stop

Joan Smith

FAWCETT COLUMBINE • NEW YORK

Copyright © 1995 by Joan Smith

All rights reserved under International and Pan-American
Copyright Conventions. Published in the United States by
Ballantine Books, a division of Random House, Inc., New York, and
distributed in Canada by Random House of Canada Limited, Toronto.
Originally published in Great Britain in 1995 by Chatto & Windus Ltd.,
Random House UK Ltd., London.

Library of Congress Cataloging-in-Publication Data
Smith, Joan, 1953–
Full stop / Joan Smith.
p.   cm.
ISBN 0-449-91048-2
1. Lawson, Loretta (Fictitious character)—Fiction.   I. Title.
PR6069.M4944F85   1996
823'.914—dc20   95-50471
                                                        CIP

Manufactured in the United States of America

First American Edition: April 1996

10   9   8   7   6   5   4   3   2   1

FOR LEE CHESTER AND CLAIRE HARMAN,
WHO CONTINUE

Author's Note

One of the people I most wanted to read this book was Charlie Stramiello, who died before I was able to finish it. Charlie didn't realise, when he loaned me his apartment and showed me round Manhattan in May 1993, that he was also handing me the setting for this novel. Short friendships sometimes have as much impact as lengthy ones and I think of Charlie with fondness and regret.

full stop

1

The heat was so intense that Loretta felt it on her skin like an invisible presence, folding her unwilling body in its damp embrace. She had been in the taxi for only a few minutes but a patina of sweat was already forming on her bare arms, while a remorseless wave of heat seemed to be directing itself to the back of her neck. The taxi was old and cramped, with black plastic seats; Loretta felt as though she were trapped in a small room with a fan heater going full blast, yet without any possibility of turning it off. She had paid no attention when her Californian friends had warned her that July was the worst time of year to visit New York, knowing that if she did not stop off there on her way home from San Francisco she was unlikely to get another chance for months, if not years. Brushing their objections aside, she had booked an air ticket whose only condition was that she had to spend a Saturday night in New York before continuing her journey to Heathrow, and deliberately avoided the weather section in the *San Francisco Chronicle*. She found out what she had let herself in for a few minutes before her plane came in to land, when the pilot welcomed his passengers to New York and reeled off some alarming statistics; it was ninety-two degrees in the city, he announced cheerfully, with 75 percent humidity.

"I hope you guys like it hot," he finished as the FASTEN SEAT-BELTS sign came on and the cabin staff patrolled the aisles checking that hand luggage was stowed away and seatbacks were in the upright position. Loretta didn't know much about humidity but she guessed that 100 percent was rain, and that 75 percent was much higher than she had become accustomed to in breezy San Francisco.

She took out the money to pay the bridge toll and lay back in her seat with the folded dollar bills in her hand. Her eyelids fluttered and closed, swollen from lack of sleep and the recycled cabin air which had dehydrated her skin and irritated her sinuses. Within a couple of minutes she was in a fitful doze, half aware of where she was but also experiencing hallucinatory snatches of conversation from the previous evening when she had attended a farewell party in San Francisco thrown by her colleagues at Berkeley. She was still in this waking dream when an overtaking car gunned its engine and her left foot shot out, frantically seeking the brake. For a few panicky seconds she trod air and it was relief when her shin collided with the hollow plastic bench seat in front, jerking her back to reality. Her heart beating wildly, Loretta took a deep breath and sat up straight, forcing herself to stay awake for the remainder of the journey. She had slept a little on the plane, not as much as she would have liked because the man next to her got up to go to the loo or summoned a member of the cabin staff with some trivial request every time she settled down. Halfway through the flight she had considered offering to change places with him, giving up her aisle seat in return for an hour or so's uninterrupted rest, but then a baby began to grizzle in the row behind, its thin but persistent wail putting sleep out of the question.

The taxi slowed as the traffic got heavier, giving Loretta time to read a poster suspended from a bridge: "We haven't suffered enough!" it announced enigmatically. "Re-elect Cuomo." The taxi swerved into a faster lane and her bag slipped off the seat, disgorging its contents onto the floor. Loretta leaned forward with a "tut" of annoyance and saw that her purse had come open, sending nickels, pennies and dimes in all directions. It took her a while to retrieve them all and when she sat up the car had left the expressway and was bowling along a high-sided suspension bridge. With an inkling of what she was about to see, Loretta turned her head and got her first, heart-stopping view of Manhattan.

The familiar skyline floated in a light mist, defying her knowledge that she was looking at solidly made constructions of steel, glass and concrete. Loretta's tiredness evaporated as she stared in wonder and delight, trying to make out landmarks like the World Trade Center and the Empire State Building. One skyscraper blended into another, creating a jagged line which appeared resolutely two-dimensional—like the studio backdrop of Oxford used in TV current affairs programmes, she thought inconsequentially. The image was so over-used in films and on postcards that she could hardly believe it retained its power, yet what she felt, winding down the window and craning her head to get a better view, was an almost sexual charge of excitement. She marvelled at how compact and shining the island was even as she experienced the illusion that it was rushing towards her, individual buildings becoming solid and visible through the heat haze. She guessed she was on the Triborough Bridge, whose right-angle course into the city she had followed on a map of New York a few minutes before coming in to land. The only one she had previously heard of was the Brooklyn Bridge, familiar because she had recently seen a revival of *A View from the Bridge* in San Francisco, but she now knew that LaGuardia Airport was in Queens and linked to Manhattan by the Triborough. She reached in her bag for the map, wanting to get some idea of how long it would take to get from here to Toni's apartment, and recalled as she did so that the taxi driver had merely grunted when she gave him the address at the airport. She felt a momentary flare of anxiety, a familiar but unwelcome reaction to the fact that she was travelling alone in a foreign country, even an English-speaking one, and dismissed it with the common-sense observation that there couldn't be a single cab driver in New York who hadn't heard of Riverside Drive.

She had an uneasy sensation that she was being watched and her eyes flicked up to the rear-view mirror just in time to catch a fractional movement of the driver's head as he returned his gaze to the road. She frowned, recalling the other warnings she had been given by her Californian friends when she had announced her intention of stopping over in New York. They had talked endlessly about the soaring crime rate, about teenagers who carried guns to school and shoot-outs between crack dealers, until a weekend trip to Manhattan began to sound about as safe as a guided tour of the headquarters of a Colombian drug cartel. One woman, a history lecturer at

Berkeley, had graphically described an encounter with a psychopathic cab driver who sped off in entirely the wrong direction when she asked him to take her to a conference at NYU; the cab screeched to a halt, she said, only when she flung open the passenger door in heavy traffic at considerable risk to life and limb.

Loretta told herself she was being silly, that the driver was probably just checking that she was all right; she knew she was paler than usual, having caught a glimpse of herself in a mirror in the airport loo, her features flattened by tiredness and her pallor accentuated by the washroom's harsh strip lighting. She wished she hadn't stayed so late at her farewell party the night before, leaving herself very little time to finish packing, but she had hung on in the vain hope that Sean would arrive. Their affair had lasted only a few weeks and it had been comfortable rather than intense, an agreeable summer diversion, but she was dismayed when he told her he had to work late on Wednesday night, and if he got to the party at all it would only be towards the end. Loretta was as cross with herself as she was with Sean when she finally accepted that he wasn't going to appear and took a taxi home to Cow Hollow. Her bedroom looked like the aftermath of a burglary, clothes strewn in piles and every pair of shoes she owned sitting on the floor waiting to be stuffed with tissue paper; she had had to make a hasty, late-night decision about what to take with her and what to leave for her landlord, Alberto, to airfreight to England after her departure. The problem was that she had no idea how long the box of books and her trunk would take to arrive, and she needed several of the books for an article which had to be finished within two weeks of arriving in Oxford.

Trays of food had circulated at the party but all Loretta had managed to grab was a couple of chewy white parcels which tasted faintly of prawn and some *focaccia* smeared with roasted garlic. The garlic had left a peculiar taste in her mouth and she also had an uncomfortably furry sensation on her tongue caused by drinking too much wine on an empty stomach. She was no longer used to over-indulgence, having become accustomed after three months in San Francisco to raised eyebrows every time she poured her second or third glass of alcohol, and she still remembered the expression on Alberto's face when she had arrived home from her first trip to Safeway with a case of red wine. It had crossed his mind, he admitted when he got to know her better, that the charming English academic with perfect references to whom he had rented his spare bedroom was secretly a lush.

Loretta moistened her lips, longing for a cool drink or, even better, a cup of tea. She became uncomfortably aware that the driver was watching her again, his eyes in the rearview mirror as cold as stones, and she had to suppress a childish urge to stick her tongue out at him. Instead she turned sideways, resting her arm along the back of the seat, and stared out of the rear window, simulating close interest in the long expanse of bridge stretching behind the cab. Her ears picked up an odd noise, like the beginning of some large industrial process, and a moment later she realised it seemed to be emanating from two sinister figures on bikes who were rapidly gaining on her cab. The noise rose to a roar, puzzling Loretta until she realised that the heat haze around the riders concealed the fact that there weren't two bikes but a dozen, riding in two-by-two formation and taking up as much of the road as the stretch limos she had seen waiting in line at the airport. The big machines gleamed with chrome, their riders' arms spreadeagled to grasp handlebars bristling with wing mirrors, and Loretta observed their progress with involuntary fascination, intrigued by a display of masculinity which was at once menacing and comically absurd. Suddenly the lead riders broke formation, fanning out to surround her cab like a cloud of buzzing, malignant flies until the noise level was unbearable; as Loretta lunged to wind up the open window, which was admitting acrid fumes as well as the ear-splitting roar, she remembered reading somewhere that the Hell's Angels habitually ripped the exhaust cylinders off their Harley-Davidsons precisely to achieve this intimidating effect.

"Uh," she gasped, falling back against the seat. The bikers stared unnervingly ahead, close enough to touch and pacing their engines to the speed of the taxi without acknowledging its existence. Loretta thought of the rock stars who used to arrive at open-air festivals with a similarly alarming escort, the Rolling Stones and Janis Joplin, and her mind leapt effortlessly to Altamont, and the murder of a member of the audience by a gang of Angels. Her earlier anxiety returned, focused outside the cab this time rather than inside it, and her hand grew clammy on the forgotten dollar bills.

"What?" she demanded, leaning forward as the cab driver muttered something unintelligible. "What did you say?"

Instead of replying he put his foot down on the accelerator, a hopeless gesture as the old car had nothing like the speed of the big bikes. Loretta clutched her bag to her, thinking of her credit cards, her air ticket, her passport—not that they could do much with that—and the sizeable sum in dollars she had withdrawn two days ago from her bank in San Francisco to see her through the weekend. Apart from anything else, getting it all replaced by Sunday evening, in time for her flight home, would be a nightmare. She turned and glared at the man immediately to her left, her fear overlaid by a healthy burst of anger, and at once her expression changed. Uncertainty flick-

ered across her face, followed by astonishment and then outright amusement: the biker was *old*, grey-bearded even, more
ZZ Topp than *Easy Rider*. Wispy hair straggled under the rim
of his helmet, curling over the collar of his ancient leather
jacket, and Loretta almost laughed out loud at this proof that
even the Hell's Angels were subject to the laws of time. His
companions were of a similar vintage, she now saw, and their
uniformly senescent appearance made her wonder what had
happened to their children—whether they were busily re-
belling against their parents by getting Harvard MBAs and
working on Wall Street. As if they had picked up her silent
ridicule, the front bikes abruptly accelerated, signalling a rapid
advance and leaving the yellow taxi to rattle on its way unmo-
lested for the remainder of the journey into Manhattan.

"The mother-fuckin family," Loretta read as they streamed
past, and a line of smaller letters which announced that the
bikers belonged to the LI—which she took to stand for Long
Island—chapter of Hell's Angels. Feeling a small professional
irritation at the omission of the final *g*—the mother-*fucking*
family, she wanted to call after them, or at least point out the
need for an apostrophe—she did not catch the clipped remark
her driver suddenly flung over his shoulder. A moment later
she realised it was not an attempt at conversation, simply a request for the bridge toll, and she handed over her three dollars
with relief. They headed into the city, somewhere in East
Harlem she supposed, and she began looking at the buildings
with real interest although they were for the most part modern
and undistinguished. Her driver had relapsed into silence,
concentrating on the heavyish traffic, and Loretta wondered
how long it would take to get to the Upper West Side; from
previous visits she recalled a road through Central Park but she
had no idea whether it came out anywhere near Toni's apart-

ment. The cab stopped at a red light and a black woman swung across the road, banging her fist on the bonnet of Loretta's taxi as she passed.

"Bitch," the driver said under his breath, without real force, as though it was the sort of thing that happened all the time. Although the woman couldn't possibly have heard she turned and made an obscene gesture, revealing the legend on her shrunken T-shirt: I WANNA SEX YOU UP. Loretta gave her head a disbelieving shake and leaned forward as the taxi moved off, reading the driver's name on the laminated licence on the dashboard—it sounded French, confirming her impression that he was from Haiti—before reminding him of her destination.

"Riverside Drive and Seventy-third," she said on a faintly interrogative note, and he grunted exactly as he had at the airport. Loretta sat back in her seat and wiped sweat from her forehead, deciding it was even hotter in the city than it had been on the expressway. Her eyebrows were wet, not just damp, a phenomenon she had never encountered before. She thought of the play she was going to see that evening with Toni, she had forgotten what it was called, and hoped that the theatre would be air-conditioned. Her original suggestion, David Mamet's *Oleanna*, had fallen through because the play was no longer on in New York.

"You haven't missed anything," Toni had told her on the phone, "the guy's blown it this time," and Loretta had left the choice of a substitute to her. Through the car window she saw that the cross streets had declined from the hundreds to the nineties, and by craning her neck she was able to get a view of distant treetops which might, she thought eagerly, be her first glimpse of Central Park.

•

"Loretta! How was your flight?" Toni surged forward as Loretta turned the corner from the lift, hugging her and firing off half-a-dozen questions without giving her time to answer. She looked just as Loretta remembered her, slender and elegant with dark blonde hair pulled back from a face which was just too gaunt to be beautiful. Toni's paternal grandparents were Italian immigrants from Reggio-Calabria who arrived in New York at the turn of the century; her father, who was born in the city, still ran his own restaurant in the East Twenties. Loretta had never eaten there but she had read a carping review of it in her guidebook, which complained that the food was old-fashioned and the portions too large.

"Did you take a cab from LaGuardia? You didn't have a problem with the traffic? I didn't expect you yet"—she glanced down at the watch on her bony wrist—"but it's fine, come inside." She slipped an arm round Loretta's shoulders and walked her towards the open door of apartment 15G. "You've never been here before, huh? I warned you it was small. Down, Honey, *down*."

This last remark was addressed to the ugliest dog Loretta had ever seen, a thick-set animal which appeared, at first sight, to be made of concentric circles of bulging doggy fat.

"*Honey,*" Toni exclaimed, pulling the dog away from one of Loretta's shoes which it had begun to worry with ferocious growls. "It's OK," she went on, hauling the animal into the apartment by its collar, "she has a thing about leather. She's only a pup and she gets kind of over-excited."

Loretta followed nervously, not at all reassured, and hovered just inside the door.

"Honey, on the couch, *good* girl. Come on in, Loretta. Are you in a hurry to go somewhere?"

"No, of course not." Loretta put down her weekend case

and glanced round the L-shaped room, immediately perceiving that there was nowhere to sit. The room looked like a simulacrum of her own the night before, with clothes everywhere and a dress spilling out of a brown paper bag which Loretta recognised as from Bloomingdale's. The dog lumbered up onto the sofa, collapsing onto a green silk blouse and panting with its jaws gaping open. Toni pulled the blouse from under the dog, not before the soft fabric had become spattered with saliva, swept a pile of clothes off the only armchair in the room and motioned to Loretta to sit on it.

"Sorry," she said distractedly, "I haven't finished packing."

Loretta surveyed the room, taking in the wide double bed which filled the alcove formed by the short bar of the L. It was at least cool in the flat, although the air-conditioning unit set in the bottom of one of the windows was irritatingly noisy. Toni seemed to be feeling the heat, flopping down on the bed and brushing back wisps of hair from her face. "What a *day*," she exclaimed.

"I thought you weren't going till tomorrow," Loretta said, wondering why Toni was getting ready for her trip to Long Island a day early. She had already noticed that the sofa's deep red cover, an oriental design which echoed the rugs hanging on the walls, was thick with dog hair and crumbs of soil; it was just as well, she thought, looking down at her chair, that she had travelled in jeans. Suddenly the dog sat up on the sofa, apparently taking a slight movement on Loretta's part as an invitation, and Toni murmured its name warningly. Shooting her a reproachful glance, it subsided into panting rolls of flesh.

"She's so affectionate," Toni assured Loretta, still sounding distracted. "Are you OK with dogs? I recall you kept a cat in Oxford. She's a full English bulldog, I wanted one for years and Jay got her for my last birthday. I'm sorry about the mess," she apologised again, looking helplessly at the untidy heaps of clothes. "Term's over but I had to rush out and see one of my graduate students one more time before he went home to Kansas. He lives in midtown so we generally meet up in a café instead of trailing all the way up to Columbia." She leaned back on the bed, supporting herself on outstretched arms. "This kid," she said, still not answering Loretta's original question, "he's very bright but he will *not* concentrate. It's all free association, if we go on like this he's gonna turn in the first stream-of-consciousness thesis. One week he tells me—OK, this is how I do my first chapter, then I take up this point, then I go here . . . Two weeks later it's like the whole conversation never happened."

"What's his subject?"

"Huh, you tell me. I mean, Carver, that's the one thing we're all agreed on . . ." She sat up straight. "Loretta, can I get you a drink? You like tea, right? Or maybe you'd prefer something cold? How's everyone at St. Frid's?" It was a while since Toni had spent a term as a visiting fellow at St. Frideswide's, the Oxford college where Loretta taught part-time, and she was still trying to work out who had left or published books or done anything else of note when Toni got up. "Kitchen's in here," she said, crossing the room and pushing open a door, "bathroom's next door. I put out some clean towels, and I changed the sheets on the bed."

Loretta heard a tap being turned on, presumably Toni filling the kettle. She got up and went to the window, stooping to examine the air-conditioning unit. It was turned up high and Loretta wondered if there was any setting which would keep the room cool without making such a din; there were several dials and buttons, and she would ask Toni later. She straightened and looked out of the window at a modern building across the street—not much of a view, she thought, relinquishing her fantasy of looking out on to the Guggenheim Museum or the Art Deco spire of the Chrysler building. The flat was fifteen floors up, high enough to make her slightly queasy as she looked down on to a broad avenue jammed with almost stationary traffic. Loretta wondered which it was, vaguely remembering names on the Upper West Side from her map—Columbus, Amsterdam, West End Avenue.

"What street are we on? I mean, what avenue?" she asked, moving away from the window as Toni came back into the room carrying a mug.

"West End. Riverside Drive's over there," she added, pointing towards the door of the apartment. "You take sugar?"

Loretta shook her head.

"I didn't think so. Listen, Loretta." She put the mug on the coffee table in front of the sofa and went back to the bed. "I hate to do this to you on your first night. What it is, Jay . . ." She paused, and Loretta remembered that Jay was Toni's boyfriend. She knew he played tenor sax in a jazz band, but nothing else about him. Toni said rapidly: "Jay totaled his car two nights ago, he was driving back from an out-of-town gig in New Jersey." She saw Loretta's expression and hurried to reassure her. "He's fine apart from a whole lot of bruising. But it's messed up the weekend, I don't have a car so we're gonna have to take the jitney to Long Island—"

"The what?"

"The jitney. The bus. And it's full tomorrow, all booked up, so we have to leave this afternoon. The other thing is, now we don't have the car, Honey isn't so used to people that I totally trust her. Not for three hours, which is how long it can take to the Hamptons at this time of day. All you need to do is walk her twice a day, her food's in the kitchen—"

Loretta stared at her. "You mean you want me to look after . . ." She turned to the animal, realised how rude she must have sounded and tried to retrieve the situation. "I mean, of course, does she have any special . . . No, *stay*." She put out a hand as the dog heaved itself to its feet and began plodding across the sofa towards her, its paws sinking into the cushions. It sank back onto its haunches, giving Loretta the same reproachful look she had seen a few minutes before, and it crossed her mind that at least it seemed to be obedient.

"She won't be any trouble, really," Toni said pleadingly. "I'm sorry to dump this on you at short notice, I called the theatre and they said maybe you could sell my ticket. It's near the end of the run but there are always a few people who show up on the night—"

"Oh God, the theatre," Loretta exclaimed, too worried about the dog to have thought of it before.

"I'm *sorry*, Loretta. Didn't you say you had a friend in town? Maybe he could—"

"John Tracey," Loretta said quickly. "My ex-husband. He's flying up from Washington tomorrow."

Toni grimaced. "Shit. I booked a table for dinner after the show and I was hoping . . ." She went to a cupboard, her voice muffled as she yanked open the door and hauled a holdall into the room. "I feel so bad about this but there isn't anything I can do. Jay fixed it with his parents weeks ago—"

"His parents?" Loretta hadn't realised that this was the purpose of the trip to Long Island.

Toni seemed mildly embarrassed. "His father's a minister, I only met him once but he's big on family." She laughed nervously. "Jay's parents, they go to church like you and I go to the *bathroom*. They have a sign in the yard—you know, it lights up at night. 'We want to share God's love with you.' "

"You mean he's an *evangelist*? Like Jim Bakker?"

Toni shrugged. "Don't ask me, I was raised Catholic. I don't know much about these Protestant sects."

Loretta said: "You really have to go tonight?"

Toni held out her hands, palm up. "I'm *sorry*, Loretta."

"It's my fault," Loretta said generously. "I should have given you more notice. I'll be all right."

Toni gave her a regretful smile and changed the subject. "Is Christopher meeting you at Heathrow?"

"Christopher?" Loretta sipped her tea, realising Toni was out of date about her love life. "That finished ages ago, before I went to California. He wanted us to live together and I really couldn't . . . I just don't *want* to live with anyone. You know the old saying—you start off sinking into his arms and end up with your arms in his sink? Every relationship I've had starts as an affair and ends up with a row in Sainsbury's on Saturday morning. You know, those stupid arguments about what to have for dinner and whose turn it is to put the rubbish out. I've had it with domesticity," she finished, suddenly and unexpectedly feeling better about Sean.

"You're not scared of being lonely, Loretta? I mean, it makes a lot of sense in principle . . . But what about when you're old? Really old, I mean?"

Loretta smiled. "Older than I am now? I have lots of friends, and you can be even lonelier in a bad relationship. I was amazed how much better I felt when my marriage ended."

"I hear what you're saying," said Toni, "but . . ."

"But what?"

"What about children?"

Her voice was suddenly strained. Loretta shrugged and said lightly: "It's not an issue for me."

"Really?" Toni sounded unconvinced, as though she was

about to say something else, but instead she got up and began folding clothes. "Do you mind if we—I don't find it easy to talk about it."

"Of course," said Loretta, baffled. She hadn't brought up the subject.

"It's not easy at this age," Toni blurted out, her back to Loretta. "I mean, you think there's still time and then . . ."

Unable to think of anything else to say, Loretta asked: "How old *are* you?"

"Coming up to forty," Toni said crisply. "Listen, Loretta, I have to meet Jay at the bus stop in an hour. It's on Sixty-ninth and Lex and with this traffic . . . What time's your flight Sunday?"

Loretta tried to picture the flight coupon. "Nineish, I can't remember exactly. Nine *P.M.* I mean."

"So you can walk Honey Sunday night? I asked Denny, he's my next-door neighbour, to take her out first thing Monday. I'll give you the spare keys and you can drop them through his door when you leave—15H. I told the guys on the desk downstairs you were staying, if there's any problem tell them to look in the book."

"What book?"

"It's the building security system, you have to tell them who's staying and for how long. Oftentimes they forget to tell the next guy on shift, so they write it in a book. Let me get you those theatre tickets, where did I put them?" She went back to the closet, disappeared inside and returned with them in her hand. "If you can't get rid of it, just cut me a cheque for yours."

Loretta said: "I was going to give you the money for them. It was going to be my treat—"

"And I messed it up, I know. Here they are."

As Loretta took the tickets she glanced at the price and her eyes widened. At forty dollars each, it made sense to try and find a buyer for the spare. With a twinge of anxiety she added: "Did you say something about a restaurant?"

"Yeah, I booked a table at Dad's place so there's no problem about cancelling. But he'd be very pleased to see you, I told him I was bringing a friend. Did I tell you he still makes his own pasta?" She hesitated, taking an off-white linen dress from the Bloomingdale's bag and holding it against her. "What do you think?"

"Great," lied Loretta, who thought the proportions were all wrong. American women seemed to be a different shape, either worryingly thin or rather too plump; she had bought hardly anything all the time she was living in San Francisco, relying on the summer clothes she had brought with her from Oxford. Toni's new dress was short and very formal, with padded shoulders and a double-breasted fastening at the front.

"You really think so?" Toni held the dress away from her. "I wonder if it's too short . . . Oh well, it's too late now." She folded the dress and eased it into the holdall, placing a bra and three pairs of pants on top. "You'll need to get a cab to the restaurant," she said over her shoulder, finishing her packing. "I'll call Dad and tell him the meal's on me."

"Where is it exactly?"

"East Twenty-sixth and Lexington." She zipped her bag and turned to face Loretta. "You haven't been to New York in a while, right? I don't know what your plans are but if you use the subway, make sure and hide your jewellery. Like this," she explained, tucking the necklace she was wearing inside her shirt. "And it's safe to walk in the parks in daylight, but not when it gets dark. Not even at dusk, OK? I'm not trying to scare you but you have to be sensible—stay away from the obvious places, I mean, there's no reason why you should want to go to Harlem or Alphabet City—"

"Alphabet City?"

"You know, Avenue A, Avenue B, the Lower East Side. It's a big drug area, there's a lot of people down there out of their heads on crack." She checked her watch again, becoming visibly anxious. "I don't want to be late, let me show you where I keep Honey's food and the poop-a-scoop."

Loretta had been about to launch into a slightly forced speech thanking Toni for allowing her to borrow the flat. "Poop-a-scoop?" she repeated disbelievingly.

"It's no sweat, really." Toni went into the kitchen, explaining over her shoulder the city ordinances on animal feces. "Loretta?" she called when her friend didn't move. "Could you come in here, please?"

Loretta turned to the dog and wrinkled her nose, revolted by the idea of obeying Toni and getting a rundown on its toilet arrangements. Dog shit, she thought, I'm going to spend my weekend picking up dog shit . . .

"Coming," she said reluctantly, and followed Toni into the windowless kitchenette.

2

The dog would not let go of her shoe and Loretta was rapidly losing both her temper and her balance. "You stupid, *stupid* animal," she hissed, hanging on to the heel, the only part of the shoe she had been able to grasp when she came out of the bathroom and saw it in the dog's mouth. "You've been for a walk, what more do you want?" The towel she had wrapped round herself when she got out of the bath slipped down, exposing her naked back to the uncurtained windows, and Loretta glanced over one shoulder in an inconclusive attempt to check whether the building across the street was close enough for anyone to see her.

"Oh, for God's sake," she snapped, turning back to face

the dog, which had begun a new tactic of shaking its head violently from side to side to make her relinquish the shoe. Loretta, who hadn't anticipated this problem when she undressed for her bath, could not help thinking what a ridiculous figure she must make if anyone was watching the apartment, the bath towel clutched ever more ineffectually in her free hand as the dog redoubled its efforts. Suddenly the phone rang or, more accurately, emitted a long, muffled burr. Loretta abandoned the shoe and fumbled with the towel as she waited for Toni's answering-machine to cut in; when it didn't, she turned and made a swift check of the area near the double bed from which the sound seemed to be coming. The phone wasn't on the bedside table, nor on the high shelf which seemed to contain Toni's night-time reading, and it took Loretta a moment to realise that the reason for the muted sound was that the handset was actually under the bed. She lifted the cover and groped underneath, her hand colliding with the receiver as the phone rang for the tenth or eleventh time. Dragging it out, she said breathlessly: "Yes? I mean—hello."

She glanced round the unnaturally tidy room for a pen and paper but couldn't see anything like a desk. It crossed her mind for the first time that there was nowhere in the apartment for Toni to work; surely she needed to bring books and essays home from time to time? Or did she keep everything in her office at Columbia?

"Sorry," she said, vaguely aware of a man's voice at the other end of the telephone line. "Are you ringing for Toni?"

"Toni?" said the voice, friendly and laconic. "This is Michael."

"Michael?" It meant nothing to her so she added: "I'm sorry, Toni's not here. She left a couple of hours ago. She's gone away for the weekend."

There was a longish pause. "OK. Who am I talking to?"

"Um—my name's Loretta Lawson. I'm a friend of Toni's."

"Hi, Lor—Loretta, did you say?"

"That's right."

"Hi, Loretta—nice name. Toni's not there?"

"No," Loretta said firmly, beginning to sweat again as the cooling effect of the bath wore off. "Would you like to leave a message?"

"Sure. You English, Loretta?"

"Yes. Hold on a minute while I find some paper." She checked the room again, smothered an impatient sigh and went to kneel beside her weekend case, still talking into the receiver. "I've only just got here, I don't know where Toni keeps pens and things." Belatedly she remembered the cupboard on the other side of the room from which Toni had produced the theatre tickets, but by now her hand had closed on her own spiral notebook and she was flipping it open at a clean page. "She's gone to . . . to Long Island, but she'll be back on Monday."

"Great. You say you're a friend of hers, Loretta?"

"Yes. What shall I—"

"Funny, I don't recall she ever mentioned you. Tell me what you look like, Loretta."

"What I look like?"

"Yeah, like . . . are you an English rose?"

She gave a puzzled laugh. "I haven't heard that expression for years. No, I think I can safely say I'm not an English rose."

"OK. Tell me what colour hair you have."

"My hair? What for?"

He was immediately contrite. "I'm sorry, Loretta, have I offended you?"

"Um—" She made a sound halfway between a laugh and a

gasp. "I thought you wanted to leave a message for Toni. I mean, what's my hair colour got to do with anything?"

"You're blonde, right?"

"Well—"

"You *are* blonde. I truly believe I can tell a whole lot about a person just from hearing their voice and you had to be blonde."

Loretta had come across a lot of wacky theories in California, people who consulted crystals before changing their lovers or their jobs, but she had never encountered this one. She pulled a face, hoping he wasn't going to give her a lecture on astral waves. "All right, I'm blonde," she said curtly, "but what do you want me to tell Toni? Listen, Michael—you did say your name was Michael? I've just got out of the bath and I'm going to the theatre this evening, I really ought to get dressed—"

"You just got out of the tub? You mean—you're not wearing any clothes?"

"What is this?" cried Loretta, pulling the towel tightly round her and glancing uneasily at the windows. "I mean, if you're a friend of Toni's—"

"Sure I'm a friend of Toni's. Hey, Loretta, cool it, all I asked was what you're wearing. The temperature drops pretty fast at night and if you're standing there without your clothes you might catch a chill."

This was so obviously preposterous that Loretta was about to protest when a thought struck her: how did he know she hadn't answered the phone sitting down? A shiver ran down her spine as he pressed on. "Are you *naked*, Loretta? I'm picturing you in Toni's apartment with your long blonde hair and without your clothes . . . You know what I'd like to do, Loretta? I'd like to come on over and—"

"Shit," she exclaimed, not quite believing what she'd heard, and slammed the phone down. She stared at it, her heart thumping and her breath coming in gasps, half expecting Michael—if that was his real name, which she doubted—to call back. When he didn't she began to breathe more easily, telling herself there was nothing to be frightened of, that the flat door was securely locked and anyway a stranger was unlikely to get past the porter on the ground floor. Even so she felt vulnerable, as if the caller really had seen her without her clothes—he seemed to know she had *long* blonde hair—and she realised how unwise she had been to undress without doing something about the windows. She edged towards them, fumbled with the cords to release the Venetian blinds and let out a sigh of relief as the plastic slats tumbled down and blanked out the building across the street. Loretta thought it was an office block, in which case most of the employees would already have gone home, but she felt safer with the blinds shielding her semi-nakedness.

Could it have been someone across the street? Someone who had been watching Toni's apartment? If so, it seemed a remarkable coincidence that he should choose this of all evenings to call for the first time, catching Loretta so soon after she arrived in the city. Yet if he had phoned before, had been making these calls on a regular basis, wouldn't Toni have warned her before she left? Loretta folded her arms across her chest, over the bath towel, and tried to remember how the conversation had begun. She had supplied both names, her own and Toni's, she was almost certain of that, but had he said anything that suggested he knew who he was talking to? Getting her hair colour right was probably just a lucky guess, either that or he was fixated on blondes; Loretta shivered, not wanting to visualise the possibility that Michael, whoever and wherever he was, had been masturbating while he talked to her. She had read Arthur Miller's autobiography immediately after seeing *A View from the Bridge* and vividly recalled his description of seeing a man, a total stranger, jerk off as he watched Marilyn Monroe browse in a bookshop.

From the other side of the room, next to the front door, the dog let out a long rumbling snore. Loretta turned to see her shoe, which she had completely forgotten, lying abandoned close to its jaw. "Oh well," she said, trying to make light of what had happened, "I suppose you do have a use after all." Even if Michael had been watching her, even if he knew Toni's address and succeeded in getting past the building security system, there was always the dog to protect her. Still trying to reassure herself, Loretta returned to the cramped bathroom, hung the damp towel over the shower rail and sprayed perfume on her wrists and the backs of her knees. In the living-room she wriggled into a sleeveless black body, snapped the poppers together between her legs with practised efficiency and stepped into slingback shoes with two-inch heels. Her skirt, which she had absent-mindedly left on the sofa, had acquired a light coating of dog hairs which she brushed off with her hand before fastening it round her waist.

Loretta looked at her watch and saw she had twenty minutes to spare before she needed to set off for the theatre. She frowned, thinking there was no point in ringing the number Toni had left, she probably hadn't even arrived in Sag Harbor yet, and a mildly obscene phone call was hardly a reason for dialling nine-one-one. But she wanted to talk to *somebody*; she fastened a necklace, pulled a long scarf from her weekend case to cover her bare arms later in the evening and picked up her notebook. The number she wanted was scrawled in biro at the top of a page and she knelt by the phone, dialling a Washington, D.C., number.

"Reception. How may I help you?"

"I'd like to speak to one of your guests, he's called John Tracey."

"Do you have Mr. Tracey's room number?"

"No, sorry."

"One moment."

Tracey answered on the first ring, his tone immediately conveying to Loretta that this was not a good time to call. "John, it's me. Are you busy?"

"Mmm. Where are you? Can I call you back?"

"New York, Toni's flat, but I'm about to go out."

"So am I. Where'll you be later on this evening?"

"At the theatre."

"Oh. Sorry, Loretta, can it wait till tomorrow?"

He sounded harassed and she remembered how uncommunicative he had been when he called from London to say he was flying to Washington on a story. He had muttered something about Whitewater, the failed Little Rock loan company which was causing the Clintons such trouble, and Loretta had been surprised by his sudden interest in American politics. They hadn't talked for long and Loretta concluded that the assignment had been forced on him by the new regime at his newspaper, the *Sunday Herald*. It had recently been taken over by a French media tycoon, a chic blonde businesswoman in her late forties who was unaffectionately known in London as *la belle dame sans merci*. Loretta had seen a newspaper picture of Mme Paroux stepping from a plane at the City of London Airport in what the caption described as a Lagerfeld suit, en route for the *Herald* office in Docklands where she was said to be drawing up a hit list of employees to sack. Tracey seemed to be hanging on but Loretta was anxious on his behalf.

"Of course," she assured him, not wanting to add to his burdens. "You are still coming to New York?"

"I'm looking forward to it," he said, spoiling the effect by adding: "There's some showbiz story they want me to follow up—we're not allowed to go anywhere without a reason these days. Give me your number and I'll call you when I get to my hotel."

Loretta rang off and remained where she was on the floor, kneeling by the phone. After a moment's thought she tried another number, in San Francisco this time, and her expression darkened when she heard the click of an answering-machine.

"Hi, this is Dolores del Negro. I can't take your call right now but—"

Loretta tutted and cut off the rest of the message. Dolores was her closest friend in San Francisco but it was the long vacation and she could be anywhere—in her office at Berkeley, working in the library or just out shopping. Loretta got up in search of a telephone directory and, when she couldn't see one, finally pulled open the door of the cupboard she hadn't yet investigated. It turned out to be a cross between a walk-in cupboard and a box room, furnished with a small desk and Toni's clothes hanging from a rail. Loretta located a New York telephone directory in a desk drawer, took it over to the bed and looked up the word "Police." The entry was brief, giving the emergency number and referring Loretta to another part of the directory.

It took her a while to find the right section, a separate set of blue pages listing official departments, and then she had to decide which precinct was most likely to cover the area Toni lived in. The 20th, based on West Eighty-second Street, was the nearest geographically but when Loretta tried it she was immediately put on hold. Eventually a woman came on the line, listened to the beginning of Loretta's story and abruptly transferred her to a harassed male detective who suggested she should ring the telephone company.

"Say the guy calls back, and most likely he will, they can give you counselling—"

"Counselling?" repeated Loretta.

"There's no charge," he began, mistaking the cause of her astonishment.

"I don't want *counselling*, I want you to trace his number. I'm reporting a *crime*—I assume it is against the law to make obscene phone calls?"

"Sure, but we just don't have the manpower—"

"The least you can do is take my name and number. Or don't you have the manpower for that either?"

With obvious reluctance he wrote down the details, mishearing her name the first time, and telling her again it was really a matter for the phone company. Then: "Sorry, I have a call coming through on another line," and the phone went dead.

"Great, thanks. I feel *so* much better," snapped Loretta, and reached for the directory again. Sure enough, there was a long section on how to deal with obscene, harassing or threatening calls, even though most of the advice was blindingly obvious—of course she would have hung up as quickly as possible, Loretta thought, if she'd realised earlier what was going on.

"Don't talk about these calls to anyone outside your family," the advice continued, "not even to a best friend. In the majority of cases the caller knows either the person who takes the call or some member of the family. If the caller hears about your anxiety and concern, either directly or indirectly, this is encouragement to continue."

Loretta frowned, wondering again about Michael. Was he a friend of Toni's, someone with a warped sense of humour who had decided, for reasons best known to himself, to play an unpleasant practical joke when an unknown woman answered her phone? According to what she had just read, it would be a mistake to tell Toni about the call but how else was she to rule out the possibility that he wasn't a complete stranger? Loretta read on, discovered the existence of an Annoyance Call Bureau and was about to dial its number when she read that the service was available only between nine A.M. and four P.M., Monday to Friday. Michael had called between six and six-thirty, she wasn't sure of the exact time, but Loretta was willing to bet that most nuisance calls were made even later, fuelled by alcohol or the loneliness of big-city nights. What was the point of a helpline which wasn't staffed at the very time it was needed? She speed-read to the end of the section, vainly hoping to find an out-of-hours number, and discovered instead that the detective had been telling the absolute truth. "Trained counsellors," the section ended oleaginously, "will always take an extra step to assist you further."

So they really did offer counselling, she thought, irritably closing the directory. Not a word about tracing the call, which was the most obvious way of solving the problem, yet surely New York had one of the most up-to-date telephone systems in the world? With computerised switchboards, finding out someone's number must be easy, more or less instantaneous. Loretta picked up the phone, wishing she knew more about technical matters; she had had to ring the operator in Oxford to find out which kind of switchboard she was on, tone or pulse, when she bought a cordless phone and then, after a whole day without incoming calls, discovered that the unit wasn't working because the cat had accidentally pulled the plug out of the wall.

"Hello, I don't know if you can help me," she said when the operator answered, annoyed with herself for immediately sounding apologetic. "The thing is, I've had an obscene—"

"You want the Annoyance Call Bureau. Here, let me give you their number."

"I've already got it, thanks, they're closed till tomorrow. What I need to know is, how long does it take to trace a call? I mean, is it stored in the computer?"

"Sorry, ma'am, the helpline—"

"I *told* you, it's closed." Suddenly Loretta lost her temper. "And what use is it, packing up at four or whatever, what if he rings back at midnight? What am I supposed to do, keep him talking till nine o'clock in the bloody morning? Don't you realise I'm here on my own?" She was panting, incoherent, and the operator said in an offended voice, "Keep it clean, ma'am, there's no call for—"

Loretta slammed the phone down and hugged her chest. She was more disturbed than she wanted to admit and all at once it seemed imperative that she get out of the flat; she hurried to Toni's desk and flicked on the answering-machine, seized the spare keys from the coffee table and dropped them into her clutch bag. Honey was fast asleep, slumped against the front door, and Loretta stirred the dog's flank none too gently with the toe of her shoe. "Come on," she said loudly, "are you going to let me out?"

Honey opened her eyes, thumped her stumpy tail on the floor and heaved herself ponderously out of the way. Loretta had her hand on the latch when she recalled Toni asking her to switch on the radio or TV for the dog whenever she left the flat. She groaned, left the front door ajar and went back into the room.

"I'm, like, a Marxist," a high-pitched male voice said unexpectedly when she pressed the radio's "on" button. He giggled nervously, as though waiting to be cut off, and launched into a rambling denunciation of American foreign policy in Chile in the early 1970s.

Loretta paused by the door. She was in a city where victims of crime were offered therapy—during office hours only—and radio stations gave airtime to youthful revolutionaries who were still fighting twenty-year-old battles. The voice on the radio gathered speed, throwing out names and accusations, Kissinger and Allende and ITT, and Loretta wondered if he was even born when the events he referred to happened in 1973.

"Have a good evening," she said satirically to the dog, and left the apartment without a backward glance.

"Excuse me. May I take a look at your programme?"

"What?" Loretta was abstracted, staring into space, and it was only when she turned and saw her neighbour's outstretched hand that she realised what he was asking. As if he had read her mind he added, "I guess I left mine in the john," and she had no choice but to pass it to him, glancing at her watch as she did so. The interval had another twelve minutes to run before the second half of the play began and she hoped he wasn't about to engage her in conversation. The circle seats were narrow and close together, without much leg room, and she wished she had persuaded Toni to cancel the reservation at Stramiello's, her father's restaurant, instead of telling the maître d' to set a table for one. The theatre was in a street running off Broadway and there were probably dozens of little cafés and restaurants within walking distance, whereas to get to Stramiello's she'd need a cab. Her tiredness had returned and Loretta shifted uncomfortably in her seat, not looking forward to the second half.

The man next to her, who had bought Toni's ticket, seemed to be having similar problems—more so, in fact, since he was a couple of stones overweight. He had fidgeted and perspired throughout the first half of the play in spite of the air-conditioning and now he leaned towards Loretta with a puzzled look on his face.

"Excuse me," he said again, "but there's something here you might be able to help me with." The programme was open at the cast list and he tapped it with his fingers. "Why I come to this play, my sister in Springfield told me be sure and not miss it next time I'm in New York. There's this actress, see, she's supposed to be in it but I don't see her name. What I'm thinking is, do I have the right play?"

"What's her name?"

"Judy."

"Judy what?"

"Wait a minute—you talking about my sister?"

"No," Loretta said patiently, "I meant the actress."

He looked sheepish. "I don't remember exactly. Madeline—Madeline something. I'd know it if I saw it."

"Sorry," said Loretta, trying to keep her face straight, "I don't think I can help."

He sat back in his seat, shaking his head and turning the pages of the programme. After a while he exclaimed: "She *left*. Look"—he waved it in Loretta's face—"she was in it but the cast changed. Judy will be *so* disappointed I missed her."

Loretta smiled politely, so unmoved by the play that she didn't think it would make much difference if the Royal Shakespeare Company arrived *en masse* and took it over. It was meant to be a light comedy, with a trivial plot about three

American sisters enjoying a reunion in a swanky flat in London, but the jokes went over Loretta's head and she couldn't understand why the rest of the audience had been rocking with laughter during the first half. She wondered glumly why Toni had picked it, and thought of all the other things she could have done with forty dollars. A new pair of sunglasses, a couple of hardback books, a pair of earrings from the shop at the Metropolitan Museum . . .

"What happened to your friend?" her neighbour asked conversationally. He held the programme out to her but Loretta waved it away.

"Keep it."

"I can? My daughter'll love that, she always wants to know what Dad's been up to in the big city. He get ill or something."

"Who?"

"Your friend. The guy who's supposed to be in my seat."

She was about to give him a discouraging look when she remembered that he'd insisted on handing over almost the full price of Toni's ticket, and he didn't seem to be enjoying the play any more than she was. "It's a woman, actually," she said reluctantly. "Something came up at the last minute."

"You're British, right? You live in New York City?"

"No."

"Me neither."

She glanced covertly at him, taking in his bright yellow shirt, lurid bow tie and, as her gaze travelled down to his feet, high-top trainers. Thinning sandy hair made it difficult to guess his age but his face and scalp were shiny and pink, as though he had recently been scrubbed. He looked honest, open and not very bright; Loretta felt a little sorry for him, guessing he was lonely and out of his depth, but she still didn't want to be drawn into conversation. She pulled her hair back from her face, cooling her neck, and crossed one leg over the other in a vain attempt to find a more comfortable way of sitting. The movement made the edges of her wraparound skirt fall open and she caught her neighbour looking appraisingly at her knees; embarrassed, she pulled the edges together and his eyes moved up to her face. He grinned.

"OK, let me guess. You from London?"

"No." He waited and politeness forced her to add: "Oxford."

His face lit up. "*No.* You really from Oxford?" He placed the stress on the last syllable, Ox*ford.*

"Well, I wasn't *born* there. I've lived there for the last few years."

"No kidding? This is *some* coincidence—I have to be in Oxford next month." He spoke with childlike enthusiasm, as pleased as Punch to find they had something in common. "I work in automotive parts and I have to meet with some guys at the car factory. Bigtime stuff, huh?"

She wasn't quite sure what he meant but she did her best, saying: "Not as big as it used to be." She had driven round the ring road in the spring, just before she left for San Francisco, and was amazed when she came upon the industrial wasteland where the British Leyland North Works had once been. The site was being redeveloped and her car had got stuck in road works, giving her plenty of time to observe the bulldozers and scarred earth where the car plant had been demolished. The South Works was still making cars, as far as she knew, but she remembered ominous forecasts in the *Oxford Times* of more redundancies to come. "I'm not even sure it's a British company anymore. I think it's owned by Honda."

Her companion shook his head. "Not anymore, the Japs

bailed out. The Krauts are in there now, my company's hoping to do a deal with the new guys . . . You work in Oxford?"

"Yes, at the university."

"You don't say? You teach English?"

"Yes."

He gestured towards the stage. "What d'ya make of it?"

"To be honest, I'm not enjoying it much."

"Me neither. I mean, why's she wasting her time with that guy, the English one? Don't seem to me like he's interested in *girls*."

He nudged her in the ribs, just in case she hadn't got his meaning, and Loretta instinctively drew away.

"I guess maybe the humour . . ." he went on, oblivious to her reaction. "I'm from Ohio and it seems to me like it's very New York. Jewish," he added when she failed to respond.

Loretta wasn't sure from his tone whether he intended the adjective pejoratively and she sat glumly in her seat, wishing he'd shut up.

"You here on vacation?"

She nodded.

"Me too. See the sights, take in a show."

"This isn't exactly a show," Loretta said doubtfully. It crossed her mind that he was the kind of man who probably went to strip clubs but she thought again about the money he'd wasted on Toni's ticket and added: "What about musicals? I noticed there's a new Sondheim—"

"No *way*," he said emphatically, "not after tonight." He spoke as though *The Sisters Rosensweig* had taught him a cruel lesson.

"What sort of things *do* you like?" Loretta asked with mild irritation.

"Well—you know."

"No, I don't," said Loretta. "Films? Museums?"

"You mean—pictures? Old stuff?"

Loretta shook her head. "Not necessarily. I mean, I *love* looking at pictures, I'm going to the Metropolitan Museum tomorrow morning, but it's not just art. For instance, they've got a complete Egyptian temple. Your daughter, is she interested in history? They have a shop which sells things for children, jigsaws and cut-out books." She had relaxed a little now that they were on safe territory and she continued: "You know where it is, on Museum Mile? I'm lucky, it's just across Central Park from where I'm staying. According to the map I should be able to walk it in twenty minutes—half an hour at the most."

"Where did you say you're staying?"

Loretta hadn't but she told him now. "With a friend on Riverside Drive. Riverside and Seventy-third. It's a big block of flats, she's gone away for the weekend so I've got it to myself."

"Riverside Drive? That the East Side?"

"No, the Upper West."

"I'm on West Fifty-second. In a hotel. What else you planning on doing?"

"In New York? I'm really keen to see the Frick. I thought I'd go on Saturday afternoon."

"He was some big industrialist, right?"

"Frick? I think so." She tried to conceal her surprise that he knew, aware that her reaction was patronising. "Wasn't he from Pittsburgh, one of those steel towns? Apparently he put together an amazing collection, everything from Piero della Francesca to Whistler."

"You seem to know a whole lot about art."

"Me? God, no, I'm a complete amateur. I just like pictures."

He wiped his sweating forehead with the back of his hand. "Tell me about Oxford. I have two days."

"Two days?" Loretta's lips turned down. She thought of her favourite places, the Ashmolean Museum and the Pitt-Rivers, Port Meadow on a winter afternoon when the flooded fields reflected a sky as dull as pewter. "Oh, you know, the colleges . . ."

"Some of them are pretty old, right?"

"Yes, and they're mostly in the centre of town so—" To her relief a bell rang, signalling the end of the interval. Loretta moved her legs to one side as people began to return to their seats.

"Ouch," she exclaimed as a middle-aged woman with up-swept frosted hair stumbled and crushed her toes.

"She hurt you?"

"No, really," Loretta said quickly, not wanting a scene. "Honestly, I'm fine."

"You sure?" He regarded her suspiciously as he subsided into his seat.

"Really." At that moment the lights went down, sparing her further conversation, and the cast trooped back onstage. They took the second half of the play at a faster pace, veering towards farce when one of the actresses changed onstage into a Chanel suit. It was the kind of theatrical set-piece Loretta most disliked but the audience around her was convulsed. Even the car salesman—she hurriedly corrected herself, remembering he sold car parts—even he joined in, clapping enthusiastically when the final curtain fell. The three main actresses joined hands and took a bow, obviously expecting several curtain calls, and Loretta seized the opportunity to slip out ahead of the crowds. She was at the door leading to the stairs when she felt a hand on her arm.

"Ma'am? I hope you won't take offence," said her erstwhile neighbour, removing his hand, "but are you free for a drink? Seeing as we're both strangers in town—I'd like to hear some more about *Oxford*—"

He registered her expression and stepped back. "Hey, what's the big deal? It's only a *drink*." He lifted pudgy hands, emphasising the space he had put between them. "I'm a happily married man, just because my wife's back in Ohio—"

"Excuse me," ventured an elderly woman, leaning heavily on a stick and trying to beat the exodus from the dress circle. She was followed by a noisy, good-natured crowd which forced Loretta and the car salesman apart. "I'm sorry," she called, standing on tiptoe, "I really didn't mean—" She stopped, not wanting to tell a lie and remembering how he'd looked at her legs.

"I get the message," he called back, the rest of his words carried away by the departing theatre-goers. An angry flush had risen up from his neck, mottling his face, and as he turned to push his way through the crowd, using his bulk to clear a space, he threw back over his shoulder a sarcastic retort: "*You* have a nice evening now."

His balding head disappeared round a bend in the stairs. Loretta remained where she was, jostled by the crowd and cross with herself for not handling the situation more tactfully. She was pretty certain he had been coming on to her but she could have refused his invitation more politely; she put her over-reaction down to being in a strange city, that and the obscene phone call she'd received just before she left for the theatre. Thinking Michael had a lot to answer for, she followed the stragglers down the stairs, bracing herself to face the muggy night air while she searched for a taxi on Broadway.

3

. . . .

Loretta lay on her back, one arm thrown up above her head and her legs splayed apart. She was unbearably hot, the sheet ridged underneath her and the quilt lying in a tangled heap at the foot of the bed as though someone was hiding in it. Groaning and struggling into an upright position, she rubbed sleep from her eyes and tried to remember where she was. Not her room in Alberto's house, nor her bedroom in Oxford—she let out a yelp, hearing the unmistakable pant-pant of heavy breathing, and grabbed at the quilt. The events of the previous night came back to her, the salivating voice on the phone and the man ogling her legs at the theatre, and for a moment she imagined one of them had got into the shadowy, unfamiliar room where she was sleeping. Then, just in time, full consciousness returned and she realised she was in Toni's flat, and that the source of the panting wasn't even human.

"God, dog," she exclaimed, throwing herself back against the pillows, "you nearly gave me a heart attack." Honey heaved herself up from the floor and placed her front paws on the edge of the bed, her mouth drooping open as though she was about to have a seizure. Loretta pushed her away, kindly but firmly, wondering why it was so airless in the flat and she could not hear the air-conditioning. A memory stirred, a dim recollection of stumbling over to the window during the night and switching it off, unable to bear its clatter a moment longer, but now she swung her legs off the bed, hurried across the room and turned it on at the highest setting. Cold air blasted out and she placed herself directly in front of it for a moment, imagining that it was blowing the night's accumulated sweat from her skin. She reached for the blind cord, remembered she was naked and went into the bathroom to borrow Toni's robe.

"All right, I know you're hungry," she told Honey, who followed her from room to room letting out little whimpers. In the kitchen she spooned dog food from a can, wrinkling her nose in distaste at the smell, and left Honey snorting and gulping over the bowl. She ran the blinds up to discover a hazy day, the sun invisible behind a thick layer of mist, and turned on the TV to discover that the humidity outside had already reached 85 percent. The TV was tuned to NY1, a local news station, and the top story was an overnight shooting in the South Bronx.

"One man died and two were injured in what's believed to be a drug-related attack," a reporter was saying, speaking in the fast, solemn tone which seemed to have been universally adopted by American TV journalists. "The dead man, who's been identified as Wayne Roberts, twenty-six, was caught in a hail of bullets as he returned home from a nightclub in the early hours. Roberts, who was only released from jail Monday, died instantly when an assassin opened fire from a speeding car. Neighbours here in the high-rise where Roberts lived say they're too scared to let their children—"

The phone rang. Loretta turned off the TV and picked it up.

"Ms. Norton?"

"Norton? No, I think you've got the wrong number. Un-less—my name's *Lawson*."

"Sorry, Ms. Lawson, I guess I was given wrong informa-tion. I have a fax here saying you reported a nuisance call last night. Is that correct?"

Astonished, Loretta said eagerly: "Yes, that's right, I rang the . . . I can't remember which precinct it was but they didn't seem the least bit interested. You mean you're a policeman? Thank God for that, I couldn't get any sense out of—" She sat down on the bed, aware she was gabbling. "I mean, thanks *very* much for calling. I was just wondering what to do, the man I spoke to last night was *so* offhand, I had to make him take down my name and number . . ."

"I'm sorry, Ms. Lawson, we are trying to eliminate that kind of response. You have my assurance I'll speak to the offi-cer concerned, his name's on the fax. If I could just introduce myself, I'm Lieutenant Donelly, one N, two Ls, and I head up a task force on obscene and threatening calls. We work closely with the telephone company and—"

"You mean the thing in the phone book? The—" In her excitement she couldn't quite remember its full title. "The ob-scene calls bureau? So you *can* trace his number?"

"Wait a minute, Ms. Lawson, it's not quite as simple as that. First off I need to ask you some questions, find out if we're talking about the same guy."

"How d'you mean, the same guy?"

"In the fax I have in front of me it doesn't say whether he asked about your hair colour. Did he say anything that might—did he express an interest in whether you are blonde?'

"Ye-es. What's this about?"

"OK." The detective was obviously relieved. "Sounds like our guy."

"You mean he's done it before?"

"Ms. Lawson, we've been on his tail five, maybe six weeks. He has an obsession with blondes. If he dials a brunette or a redhead, he hangs up right away."

"You mean he picks numbers at random?"

"Not precisely. There's a high density of apartment blocks on the Upper West Side, a lot of women living alone. He give you a name?"

"Yes. Michael."

"He's used that one before. The way he operates, if the woman who picks up the phone sounds Hispanic, he calls himself Miguel."

"He puts on an accent?"

"That's right. Ms. Lawson, would you be willing to cooperate with us? Our best hope is to trace his number while he's on the line—"

"On the line? But I thought . . . with computerised exchanges and so on . . . isn't his number stored somewhere? Automatically, I mean?"

The detective sighed. "We think that's the other reason he chose this exchange, which suggests he may have inside knowledge. It's one of the last to be modernised, it isn't due to be updated till . . . wait a moment, I have the NYNEX schedule on my desk." She heard the rustling of pages. "December, from memory . . . no, sorry, October, sooner than I thought. In the meantime—"

"You mean it isn't computerised? You actually have to have him on the line to catch him?"

"I don't want to get technical but basically, yes, that's the present situation on this exchange. And no one he's targeted so far . . . unfortunately they haven't felt able to keep him talking long enough for us to trace the number."

Loretta said doubtfully: "How long would it take?"

"We're talking four, maybe five minutes."

Loretta remembered Michael's voice and said nothing.

"Ms. Lawson?"

"I'm here." She massaged the back of her neck with her free hand. "I can't say I'm enthusiastic."

"I understand totally but can I ask you another question? Am I correct in thinking you're a stranger in town? I checked with NYNEX before I called you and they list the subscriber to this number as Antonia Annetta Stramiello."

"You did?" Loretta was impressed that he'd done his home-work so early on a Saturday morning. "Toni's a friend, actually, I've borrowed her flat for the weekend. I go back to England on Sunday."

"I don't want to pressure you, Ms. Lawson, but I'm de-lighted to hear you say that."

"You are? I don't understand."

"First point, if he hasn't called again by Sunday, you're out of it. Second point, say you agree and we get him—he gets bail, you're not even in the country. You don't have to worry."

Little shivers ran down Loretta's spine. "What about Toni? *She'll* be here."

"She had any of these calls?"

"Not as far as I know. I mean, I haven't spoken to her since it happened. I was going to ring her this morning but it says in the phone book you shouldn't tell anyone. Not even a friend."

"That's good advice. Ms. Stramiello needn't know anything about it. *You're* the complainant and you'll be back home in—where did you say you come from?"

"I didn't. Oxford."

"Oxford's a long, long way from New York. Will you help us, Ms. Lawson?"

"I suppose," she said reluctantly. She looked round for her notebook, spotted it on the coffee table and returned to the bed.

"You'd better give me your name and number," she said, pen poised. "Donelly, did you say?"

"That's it. Let me give you my direct line. This is a busy office so you may have to try a few times."

After she put the phone down Loretta thought for a moment, her arms folded and one hand nervously stroking her left elbow. She didn't like the idea of not telling Toni what was going on but presumably Donelly knew what he was talking about; she was about to ring him back, go over the point again, when it occurred to her to speak to Dolores, who was so far away that she couldn't possibly have any connection with Michael or prejudice the inquiry. Loretta rapidly dialled the San Francisco number, remembering the time difference only as Dolores's answering-machine cut in and informed her— luckily, since it was only five-thirty in the morning—that Dolores had gone to Los Angeles for the weekend. Loretta cut the connection, thinking there was no point in leaving a message; she tried Donelly, muttered something when his prediction proved correct and she got the engaged tone, and went into the kitchen. On the fridge door, secured by a magnet, was a list of essential numbers Toni had left behind, starting with the emergency vet. Loretta found Jay's parents' number in Sag Harbor and dialled it, hearing the phone ring only twice before an answering-machine cut in and an unctuous female voice—Jay's mother, Loretta assumed—announced that the minister wasn't able to come to the phone right now.

"You may leave messages and requests for prayers after the tone," it went on. "Please specify the full name of the friend or relative who needs the minister's intervention, and a *brief*"—heavily stressed—"outline of their affliction. Please also leave your own name and telephone number so we can follow up with you. Donations to church funds may be made by credit card. Please remember to give the name of the cardholder, number and expiration date and the amount of your donation. God bless you."

"Blimey," said Loretta. Resisting the temptation to invent an aunt at death's door and trying not to betray her amusement—was Jay's father listed in the Yellow Pages under Dial-a-Prayer, she wondered? Prayers-to-Go?—she spoke quickly into the receiver, asking Toni to ring her back in the next half hour or in the early evening. She put the phone down and went into the bathroom, reflecting that the Christian Right probably took a tough line on obscene phone calls but she preferred to put her faith in more worldly forms of intervention. Loretta turned on the taps, splashed some lily-scented oil into the bath and distractedly prepared to wash.

In the other room, the phone sounded again. Loretta approached it warily, realising she had not asked Lieutenant Donelly how long it would be before the tap was in place.

"Hello," she said, steeling herself to deal with Michael.

"Loretta," cried Toni's voice, sounding a long way off. She

was shouting above background noise, what sounded like the insistent bleeping of a car alarm. "Loretta, can you hear me?"

"You're *very* faint. Where are you?"

"At a payphone. It's on the main street, that's why there's so much—thank God, someone's finally turned off that alarm. How's Honey doing?"

"She's fine." Loretta glanced at the dog, puzzling over why Toni was using a payphone.

"Can you do me a favour?"

"Of course. Actually, I've just left a message for you with Jay's parents. On their answering-machine. What's all this stuff about requests for prayers?"

Toni said impatiently: "He freelances."

"What?"

"He *freelances*," Toni yelled, as though Loretta hadn't heard her the first time. "People call him from all over the States. Loretta, I need most of these quarters to call my gyno—I left my address book behind and I need you to look up her number for me."

"Your what?"

"My *gynaecologist*. It should be in my desk drawer, the second one down. A little red book. Don't be too long or my money'll run out."

"Give me the number you're on and I'll call you back."

"Excuse me? Sorry, Loretta, I don't think this phone takes incoming calls. Can you go get it?"

She found the book easily and returned to the phone.

"What's her name?"

"Rosenstein. Dr. Hester Rosenstein."

Loretta read out the number. "Toni, before you go." She hesitated, not sure what to say, and in the end asked baldly: "Do you know anyone called Michael?"

"Michael? Sure. Why? Did someone leave a message?"

"Ye-es."

"Didn't he give his last name? It's most likely Michael Koganovich, we've been developing a new course together, he said he'd call before he went off to Rome for the summer. Have you read his work on Derrida? He has a very interesting perspective on—shit, I don't have many of these things left and I have to call Dr. Rosenstein."

Loretta realised this was not the time to discuss obscene phone calls. "Ring me later," she said. "I'm going to be out all day but you can get me between five and seven. Toni? *Toni?*"

The line went dead, presumably because Toni had cut the connection in her eagerness to ring Dr. Rosenstein. Loretta wondered idly what it was all about, having got used to the way Americans routinely hooked up with an array of specialists, approaching them direct instead of waiting months for referrals as happened under the NHS. The system was faster than the British one, much more expensive, and Loretta had a suspicion that it resulted in unnecessary medical treatment, particularly operations. The bath was almost full and she turned off the taps, removed Toni's robe and stepped into the water. Perhaps she was having tests, Loretta speculated as she added more cold, trying to recall exactly what Toni had said the previous afternoon—something about how difficult it was to conceive at her age. It would explain why she had sounded so distracted a few moments ago.

The bathroom door, which Loretta hadn't fully closed, swung eerily open as if propelled by an invisible hand. Getting more used to the set-up in the flat, Loretta postponed her panic about intruders and waited for Honey to appear. Sure enough, she was rewarded by a series of peremptory barks; the dog, it seemed, was reluctant to cross the threshold into the bathroom, perhaps because she associated it with doggy shampoo and other unwelcome grooming procedures.

"Five minutes, dog," Loretta sang out, and slid deeper into the perfumed water.

Central Park was hillier than Loretta remembered, and teeming with people. Half of New York seemed to have been lured out by the prospect of brilliant sunshine when the mist cleared, and she was continually overtaken by joggers, roller skaters and even the occasional pony and trap. Loretta turned to watch one of them clip-clop smartly into the distance, surprised by the realisation that at the turn of the century this would have been an everyday form of transport even in New York. Her impression of the city as a twentieth-century creation, with entrepreneurs competing with each other to build higher and better, was so vivid that she hardly connected it with the city she knew from the novels of Edith Wharton and Henry James. Smiling to herself, and wondering if she'd have time over the weekend to visit Washington Square, Loretta resumed her walk across the park. There was a relaxed, almost carnival atmosphere in spite of the heat, and the fact that virtually everyone except Loretta was wearing some variation on sports gear—tubular cycling shorts, track suit bottoms, vests in acid purples and greens—fostered the illusion that she was on the periphery of some major sporting event. It was certainly more pleasant than the narrow, scrubby strip of land sandwiched between Riverside Drive and the fast-moving traffic on Henry Hudson Parkway where she had walked Honey earlier that morning.

The dog had dragged her on a zigzag course, sniffing the ground and setting off on trails which petered out in dusty earth until Loretta decided she had had enough and turned for home. Honey promptly initiated a noisy quarrel with an over-sized poodle which Loretta recognised as a *bichon frise* even as the lead slipped through her fingers and she realised she was contravening at least one and probably several of the city's by-laws. "*Don't* let her off the lead," Toni had warned, relating an incident in which a friend had been fined by the parks police. She hadn't mentioned Honey's hysterical dislike of dogs larger than herself and Loretta lunged forward, panting as she seized Honey's collar and extricated her from the snarling mass of fur.

"Is he always so aggressive?" the poodle's owner inquired in a tone of detached interest when the dogs were eyeing each other from a safe distance. "You thought of taking him to a shrink?"

Loretta didn't waste time explaining Honey was a girl. She apologised curtly, hurried back to the flat and discovered that the dog had spent part of the hot, suffocating night chewing the handles of her weekend case. Thoroughly disgruntled and muttering under her breath, she scooped up all her belongings and put them out of Honey's reach—shoes perched incongru-ously on bookshelves, her passport and spare cash on top of the fridge. So far the dog had shown an interest only in leather but Loretta did not want to risk coming home and finding her air ticket punctured with teethmarks and sodden with canine saliva. Honey reacted as though it was a game, rearing up on her hind legs and barking noisily every time Loretta thought of a new hiding place. Either Toni's neighbours were a tolerant lot or the walls of the flat were thicker than she imagined, for no one banged on the front door to complain about the racket. She eventually escaped from the apartment block a few minutes before eleven, quite a lot later than she intended.

Nodding to the lift attendant, who recognised her from her earlier outing with Honey, she waited for the lift to de-

scend and compared Toni's cramped flat, with its fearsome list
of rules and regulations about everything from having visitors
to stay to separating different types of rubbish for recycling,
with her own house in Oxford. Loretta's study, and her bedroom, were at the back of the house, overlooking the garden
and the canal; on sunny mornings she had breakfast outside
on a small terrace, watching boats go by and smiling as her
grey cat stalked bees and butterflies. He was a companionable
animal and his vocal range was in an altogether more subtle
register than the fusillade of growls and barks which Honey
seemed to let loose on the slightest pretext. Loretta got out of
the lift, reminding herself that the dog was only a puppy, and
probably bewildered by the unexpected absence of her owner.

Before setting off for the Metropolitan Museum Loretta
had left a message for her American agent, Kelly Sibon. She
also recorded a new outgoing message on Toni's answering-
machine, punctuated by strange chomping sounds as Honey
worried a rubber bone, in case Kelly or John Tracey tried to
contact her before she returned. Loretta frowned as she
thought of Tracey, and as she emerged from the park on to
Museum Mile she worried about what he would do if he had
to leave the *Sunday Herald*. He freely admitted he had neither
the desire nor the confidence to go freelance; when Loretta was
offered a part-time lectureship at Oxford, enabling her to give
up a job she hated in London, he had been both admiring and
envious. Their situations were not dissimilar in that Loretta's
unhappiness had been brought about by what her former boss,
the Professor of English at Fitzroy College, insisted on referring to as "new working practices." He enthusiastically welcomed the idea of working more closely with industry, so
much so that Loretta once lost her temper at a staff meeting
and snapped that she didn't want to spend her working life

turning out literate food department managers for Marks & Spencer.

Unlike Loretta, John Tracey usually described himself as apolitical but from the little he'd said in phone calls to San Francisco he seemed to be finding the brash new regime at the *Sunday Herald* hard to take. He was pessimistic about his chances of finding a staff job on another newspaper, even though he had recently won two awards for his reporting of events in Eastern Europe. Just before she left England Loretta had rather diffidently suggested that he should write a book about the conflict in the former Yugoslavia, whereupon he rolled his eyes upwards and said: "You write the books, Loretta. I'm a fifteen-hundred-words man."

The fountains outside the Met were turned off, apparently for maintenance work. Loretta climbed the graceful stone steps, putting Tracey's problems out of her mind as she reached the top and went inside. In the lofty atrium she heard an eager buzz of conversation in several languages—tour guides briefing their charges, sleek women in gold jewellery discussing where to have lunch, tired children complaining and plucking at their mothers' sleeves. She was surprised by how familiar it all seemed, from the graceful pillars fronting the wide staircase to the great urns of fresh flowers whose sweet perfume floated on the artificially cool air. It was a relief just to escape the clammy late-morning heat, which had drawn out a film of sweat on her bare arms, and Loretta stood for a moment, enjoying the change. She put her hands in the pockets of her trousers and lifted her head, expecting to find Rosa Bonheur's flamboyant canvas of a horse fair, but saw in its place a florid picture which looked like a Tiepolo. A glance round the atrium revealed three others in the same style, a special display Loretta assumed, and she wasted no more time on them. She handed over the seven-dollar entrance fee, clipped a metal badge on the collar of her shirt to show she'd paid and went upstairs.

She had allowed herself an hour or so before lunch, knowing from past experience that her senses gradually become exhausted before the visual richness of Ghirlandaio, Bronzino, Giovanni di Paolo. Looking at pictures was like gorging on chocolate, she thought, strolling from room to room, the appetite feeding on itself until quite suddenly it was sated, and nausea threatened. She hadn't quite reached that point when she stopped in front of a Filippo Lippi she hadn't seen before, an unconventional portrait of a couple in profile. The woman's elaborate dress and graceful figure filled most of the frame, literally relegating her husband to the margins, and Loretta wondered whether the unusual composition reflected the woman's superior wealth or rank. There was an unspoken intimacy between the sitters, a hint of a smile on the woman's face which suggested smothered amusement, and Loretta suddenly felt like an intruder on some intensely private moment. She stepped back, uncertain whether the sexual history she had conjectured was really present or had been prompted by her knowledge of the artist's own prodigious carnal appetites. The effect faded with distance, almost as if it cut the painting down to size, and Loretta noticed for the first time that the woman's hands were quite awkwardly depicted. She looked down at her watch, realised she was hungry and decided it was time for lunch.

To get to the ground floor restaurant she had to retrace her steps, a route which took her past a very small Sassetta, *The Journey of the Magi*, which had been almost completely obscured by a party of Japanese tourists when she passed it earlier. This time the room was almost empty and Loretta paused for a moment, entranced by the tiny figures and characteristic

Sienese colours—limpid pinks, purplish blues and drab greens. One of the tiny horses carried a brown monkey, so brilliantly rendered that Loretta thought Sassetta must have painted it from life rather than copying it from a bestiary. Absorbed in the painting, she hardly registered soft footfalls until they stopped behind her, so close she could hear—she could *feel*—someone's breath over her right shoulder. She edged to the left, aware that she had been blocking the approach to the painting and expecting whoever it was to respect the space she had put between them. Instead he moved with her, trapping her between his body and a glass case housing a processional crucifix. She could see his outline reflected in the glass, easily overlapping her own, and for an instant she was paralysed by a claustrophobic sensation of *déjà vu*—the memory of a *frotteur* who had pushed up against her on the London Underground. She had been so shocked by the touch of his body on hers, the pressure of his penis pushing into her back on a crowded train, that she failed to react quickly enough and was left shaking and furious when he got off at the next station.

"Leave me *alone*," she gasped, elbowing the stranger out of her way and hurrying into the next room. Once there she stopped short, flooded by a feeling of inadequacy because she hadn't actually confronted him. Wouldn't he just find another victim, some other woman to menace? She hesitated, gripped by indecision, and an attendant approached.

"Something wrong, miss?"

"Yes, there was a man—" She glanced back the way she had come, putting her hand up to her mouth. "He—I was looking at a picture when he—"

"He touch you, miss? Is that what you're trying to say?"

"He didn't—I don't *think* he touched me. But he was so close."

"Would you recognise him?"

"I—yes, no. I didn't really see . . . Maybe he's still there." She plucked at the sleeve of the attendant's uniform, pulling her back the way she had come.

"There he is," she said in an agitated whisper, and they both stopped just inside the room.

"The same guy?"

Loretta peered through the glass case, not entirely sure. The man was leaning forward, bending towards the painting as though he was short-sighted. His height was about right, she thought, or would be when he straightened, but what about the rest: age, clothes, hair colour? She could summon only the vaguest outline, an impression of someone taller and certainly heavier than herself. There was one way to find out and, pushing aside her doubts, she approached him.

"*Excuse* me."

He turned to look at her, his eyes screwed up as though he had trouble focusing. Loretta stepped back, registering with shock the disfiguring blotches on his face, Kaposi's sarcoma, the way he leaned heavily on a stick.

"This the guy?" The attendant was beside her.

"No. I'm sorry, I've made a mistake." She gestured helplessly towards him, not knowing how to make amends.

In a cultured, slightly foreign accent he asked: "Is there a problem?"

"Did you see—" Loretta stopped, appalled by her tactlessness, certain there was something wrong with his eyes. She knew the disease could do that, in its later stages.

The attendant said: "You wanna make an official complaint?"

"God, no," Loretta said quickly, feeling her cheeks grow red. "I'm sorry," she said again and turned towards the doorway, aware that the museum attendant and the man with the stick were joined together in a tableau of bewilderment. "I'm sorry," she said again, backing towards the exit.

When she got to the stairs she hurried down them, wanting to put as much space as possible between herself and the scene of her embarrassment. She could not imagine how she had come to make such a terrible mistake. It was obvious now that the man's sight was affected and he had only been trying to get a better view of the painting . . . She crossed the lobby and entered the Roman section of the museum, hardly noticing wall paintings in eidetic colours over which, in normal circumstances, she would have lingered and exclaimed. In the restaurant she joined a short queue, was shown downstairs to a table and ordered the lightest dish on the menu, pasta with a simple sauce, her appetite deserting her even though she'd only had a cup of tea for breakfast. She couldn't stop thinking about her narrow escape, what would have happened if she'd actually *accused* him—always assuming, of course, that the thickset figure whose reflection she had seen looming behind her in the glass and the sick man were one and the same. Doubts set in: wouldn't she have noticed the marks on his face, even subliminally? The fact that he needed a stick? Loretta leaned back in her chair, wondering if she'd somehow been fooled . . .

After a moment she leaned down and reached inside her bag, pulling out a paperback, the American edition of her biography of Edith Wharton. She had brought it with her because she was due to meet a journalist from *New York* magazine that afternoon. The woman had been vague on the phone but she seemed to be writing an article on Edith Wharton, Martin Scorsese, *The Age of Innocence*, literary adaptations in general . . . It seemed a bit late in the day to tackle the subject, the film had been out for months, but Loretta opened the book at the introduction and read the first few lines, taking comfort in their familiarity.

Her food arrived and she ate it mechanically, refusing pudding and asking for a cup of hot tea. She rarely ordered it in American restaurants, they were brilliant at coffee but had a tendency to produce a tea bag dunked in a cup of stale hot water from an *espresso* machine instead of a properly warmed pot of Earl Grey or Darjeeling. Today was no exception and she stirred the teabag violently, still preoccupied by what had happened upstairs. Someone, she was sure, had done research into minor sexual offences like flashing and dirty phone calls; the consensus was that they didn't move on to other, more threatening activities like—well, like following their victims or harassing them in public places. Loretta moved uneasily in her chair, thinking there was always an exception to every rule and if Michael actually knew Toni, rather than dialling her number at random, he would also know her address and where Loretta was staying. She wished she'd brought Donelly's number with her. She had passed a couple of payphones on her way into the museum, but she had left her notebook at the flat, not thinking for a moment that she might need it.

She had been turning the pages of the introduction with her left hand, not really seeing them, and now she came to the end and read her own name, followed by the date and place she had been living when she revised it for this edition: "Oxford, 1991." She was still clutching the teaspoon in the fingers of her other hand even though she had long ago given up stirring.

4

The journalist was waiting when Loretta arrived at the Café Noir, rising from a corner by the window and waving to attract her attention. "Dr. Lawson? Over here."

Loretta skirted her way between the circular tables, accidentally hooking her bag over a chair back so she had to stop and disentangle it. She shook the journalist's outstretched hand, thinking she looked quite a lot younger than she sounded on the phone. "Carole Coryat? How did you recognise me?"

The woman picked up a copy of the book Loretta had been looking at in the museum restaurant. "From your cover photo," she said, even though the picture of Loretta was not a particularly good likeness. She smiled shyly. "I can't tell you how pleased I am to meet you. Do you mind sitting alongside me? I usually tape interviews . . . Can I get you a drink?"

Loretta glanced at the menu, taking in little more than the fact that it was handwritten in black ink with the day's date at the top. "Just a Perrier, please."

She settled back in her chair, lifting her head so she could see over the lace curtain which obscured the bottom section of the window. The café was on a cross street between Fifth Avenue and Madison, the traffic not as heavy as on the avenues but still busy enough for short queues to form. A woman was getting out of a taxi which had stopped at an awkward angle, blocking two lanes, and there was an instantaneous angry blaring of horns.

"That's New York for you," Carole Coryat said, smiling ruefully, and Loretta looked at her.

"Sorry?" She gave her head a slight shake, almost as if by doing so she could dislodge her preoccupation with what was going on outside. Carole Coryat's smile faded, giving way to a puzzled expression, and Loretta tried to look reassuring. The journalist was fair and big-boned, with springy hair held back from her wide forehead by a hairband—the kind Hillary Clinton used to wear before she became First Lady, Loretta thought, and just as unflattering. Her face and neck had the reddish tint of someone who habitually worked outdoors, as though she'd stepped off a farm somewhere in the Midwest—not at all Loretta's idea of a sophisticated city journalist.

"How long have you worked for *New York*?" she asked curiously, trying to guess Carole's age. Twenty-one? Certainly not more than a couple of years older than that.

"I'm not exactly on staff," Carole said in a rush, "but they've used two or three of my pieces since I left college last year and they're very interested in this idea . . ." She stopped with obvious relief as a waiter approached, giving her a chance to order an *espresso* for herself and Loretta's mineral water. "How do you like New York?" she asked, changing the subject as soon as he returned to the bar. "Have you been here before?"

"Yes, but not for a long time. I only arrived yesterday afternoon so I haven't really had time to look around." She surveyed the other customers as she spoke, becoming aware that several were speaking French. At a table next to the bar, overlooked by an industrial-sized *espresso* machine, two men had their heads bent over a chess board. An ashtray piled with untipped cigarette butts was testimony to how long they'd been absorbed in the game.

Carole Coryat said: "I live on East Sixty-second Street and I eat lunch here most days . . ." She grinned. "Some days I help out waiting tables—the owner, Yves, he's a friend of mine, it's a shame he isn't in today or I could introduce you. Sure you aren't hungry? I can recommend the *Salade Niçoise*."

"No thanks, I had lunch at the Met." Loretta pushed her hair back from her forehead, feeling a bit sorry for the girl, for her gaucheness and undirected enthusiasm, and guessing there was a very good chance the interview, feature, whatever it was, wouldn't get printed. It was too late to back out now and she said tiredly: "What can I tell you about Edith Wharton?"

Carole reached for a roomy kitbag, all shiny zips and buckles, which she'd dumped on a nearby chair. "Let me get this set up," she said, taking out a Walkman-sized tape recorder and placing it on the table in front of her. She pressed a couple of buttons, picked it up and examined it anxiously. "One two three . . . testing . . . I have a terror of this thing not working, I only just bought it." She fiddled about some more, played back her own voice, set it on the table again. "Are you ready? Um—I don't know how you feel about Scorsese? Did you see the movie?"

"What?" Loretta's attention had wandered to the window

again while Carole was occupied with the tape recorder. She made an effort: "Scorsese . . . yes, I've seen it."

"Phew, that makes it easier. I guess I'd like to start by asking you why you think Scorsese chose *The Age of Innocence*? A lot of people would say he's not . . . I mean, if you think about *Goodfellas*, Edith Wharton isn't the obvious place to go next."

At that moment the waiter returned, interrupting the interview while he emptied a tray of a small bottle of Perrier, a glass with ice and an *espresso*. Loretta poured water into the glass, trying to picture Daniel Day-Lewis and Michelle Pfeiffer in the film.

"The thing about Scorsese," she said slowly, "is that he's always been interested in masculinity, both as a system of power and because of its inherent contradictions. I mean, I haven't written much about film but I'd say right through his work, going back to *Mean Streets* and *Taxi Driver*, he's always adulated masculinity and at the same time wanted to . . . to interrogate it."

Carole Coryat looked apprehensive. "Could you run that past me again? I'm not sure I follow."

Loretta said impatiently: "It's a novel in which men initially seem to have the power, they're the ones who go out to work and have the money and pay for the big houses, but it's the *women* who manage everything. The entire course of Newland Archer's life . . ." She lifted a hand to her head.

"Are you OK?"

"Could you switch that thing off for a moment?"

"Sure. As you like."

Loretta waited until the tiny spools stopped turning and gestured towards Carole's bag. "I don't suppose you've got any what's it called? Tylenol? I'm getting a headache."

"Sorry. I could ask at the bar." She started to get up.

"No, don't bother, it's not that bad." Loretta drank some of the Perrier and refilled her glass.

"If this isn't a good time—"

"I know it sounds ridiculous," Loretta blurted out, "but I think I'm being followed."

"*Followed?* Where? Here?" Carole's startled gaze travelled round the room.

"Not *in* here. I mean on the way. From the Met."

Carole looked nonplussed and she leaned very slightly away. Caught up in what she was saying, Loretta did not notice the movement.

"It started before that," she said, speaking abnormally fast. "First he came up behind me, I think he was playing some sort of game, seeing if he could scare me—and he did, he really did. I was looking at a picture and I didn't hear him, at least I don't think I did, not till he was more or less *touching* me. I mean, closer than you and I are now." This time Carole actually moved her chair, scraping the floor, and the noise made Loretta look at her in surprise. She continued: "When I went back with the attendant he'd gone, there was this other man in the same place and I was confused . . . He had, you know, blotches on his face and I thought I'd made a mistake, you can imagine how embarrassed . . . But later on, a lot later, after lunch I mean, I caught him watching me—spying on me through the legs."

Carole stared at Loretta as though she'd gone mad. "*Legs?* Whose legs?"

"The statue," Loretta said impatiently, "the *diadoumenos*. I was over here"—she moved the empty Perrier bottle with her right hand—"and he was on the other side of the room, about this far." She pushed her glass sideways, towards Carole, accidentally knocking over the little tape recorder. She righted it and went on as though nothing had happened: "Have you ever been in a crowded room and you get the feeling someone's watching you? You might not know who it is, when you turn round there are so many faces, but that's the point, you *do* keep turning round. That's exactly how I felt."

The door to the café opened and a young couple came inside, accompanied by a brief burst of traffic noise. Loretta barely registered it, so anxious was she to persuade Carole—and herself—that she hadn't imagined what she was describing.

"Say I'm here," she went on in what seemed to her a more normal tone, pointing to the Perrier bottle. "In front of a statue of a—an Amazon I think it was. And he was watching me from over here." She touched her glass. "These statues, they're enormous, more than life size, and they're on what's the word? Plinths. He was here, behind the statue, staring at me through the legs." She ended triumphantly: "Why else would he go round the back if he didn't want me to see him? They're not meant to be looked at from *behind.*"

Carole Coryat didn't sound convinced. "So did you . . . I mean, did he *say* anything to you?"

"Oh, by the time I moved across he was gone."

"Did you get a good look at him?"

"Only his back, I mean, I think he had on a—a dark jacket, light trousers . . ."

"You didn't . . . he wasn't anyone you knew?"

"Someone I knew?" The thought had not occurred to her. "I didn't—I only saw him from behind."

"Then what happened?"

Loretta lifted her hands, palms upwards to show they were empty. "Nothing. He was too quick for me, maybe he knows the layout better than I do." This was another possibility that hadn't previously occurred to her and she hesitated, turning it over in her mind. "The next room's full of bronzes, helmets and things. I couldn't see him but there's an exit to another room, a corridor actually, it leads to the—the Rockefeller wing." She shivered, remembering how she had stood alone among the jutting visors with their dark, empty faces. "I went back and walked round the statue, the *diadoumenos*. And I found this." She reached into the pocket of her trousers and held up a small shiny rectangle.

"A matchbook from the TriBeCa Grill? I don't get it."

Loretta frowned. "It proves he was *there*. I didn't imagine it."

The door opened again and a man entered. He glanced round, made his way across the room and sat down a couple of tables away, asking the waiter for a *kir* and opening a copy of the Metro section of the *New York Times*.

Carole said, sounding genuinely perplexed: "You're saying there were two guys? The one who came up behind you and the one behind the what's it called? The big statue?"

"*No*, that's what I'm saying, it must have been him both times. I was just confused by the man with AIDS—"

"Man with AIDS? I don't think I—"

"Oh, *forget* it," said Loretta, angry with herself for confiding in a total stranger. She hadn't told the story well, there was no reason why Carole Coryat should believe her.

"Hey, I didn't mean . . ." Carole touched her arm lightly, sounding embarrassed. "Do you know anyone in New York? Do you have friends here? I read an article in the *Times*, I don't recall the figure they mentioned but it was like—a really big percentage. Eighty percent?"

Loretta stared at her, slightly hostile. "What are you talking about?"

Carole shifted in her chair, obviously a habit of hers when she was uncomfortable. "It was about these guys who, you know—get fixated on a woman. They follow you on the street, hang round your apartment, call you up in the middle of the night, send you flowers. According to what I read, more often than not it turns out to be someone you know. Someone you worked with, an ex-boyfriend, even the guy who fills your car with gasoline. There was a woman in Texas—"

"Hang on, you're saying it's someone I know, someone who recognised me? But I hardly know anyone in New York."

"OK, it was just an idea. Think of O. J."

Loretta grimaced. "My ex-husband's arriving this afternoon. From Washington. But he doesn't—we're on very good terms." If it hadn't been for the ache in her head she would have laughed out loud at the notion that John Tracey intended her harm: *British Academic Stalked by Jealous Ex-Husband*? No, she couldn't see it. "I've said a lot of things about John but he's not a what-do-they-call-it? A stalker."

"Sure?"

"Of *course*." Loretta stared at the journalist as though she had taken leave of her senses. "Anyway," she added, clinching it, "John's too short. The man I'm talking about is—" She hesitated, confused by her attempt to picture the space between the statue's legs. She held her hand up horizontally a few inches above her head. "Taller than me, anyway."

"You know anyone else in New York?"

"My agent, and before you ask she's a woman. So is the friend whose flat I'm staying in, Toni Stramiello."

"Stramiello as in the restaurant? On East—East Twenty-fifth Street?"

"East Twenty-sixth, her father owns it. I had dinner there last night."

"Where does she live? I mean, where're you staying?'

"Riverside Drive."

"Dr. Lawson—"

"Loretta." The correction came automatically but Carole Coryat did not immediately respond to the invitation.

"What I'm thinking," she began again, anxiously, as though she wasn't sure whether to say it, "is maybe you should talk to the cops? It sounds kinda weird, everything you've been saying. I mean, they must deal with this stuff all the time, maybe they could tell you . . ." She saw Loretta's reaction and added quickly: "They're much better than they used to be, really. There was a time when their attitude to any kind of a sex crime, spousal battery—"

"*Spousal battery?* I told you, John and I are on good terms, better than we've been for years. And his plane isn't arriving till this afternoon."

"That's what he told you. It's only an hour from D.C."

"Oh, for God's sake." Loretta looked at the journalist's wide and, as it now appeared to her, somewhat bovine face. "Listen," she said, trying to adopt a conciliatory tone, "I shouldn't have bothered you with this. I haven't been to New York for a long time and . . ." She did not know how to finish the sentence, not wanting to prompt any more crackpot theories; John Tracey lurking behind statues in the Met, the idea was absurd. "My head's getting worse and I'd like to lie down before . . . before I meet someone for dinner. Can we get on with this?" She pointed to the tape recorder.

"If you say so. I mean, I have some free time tomorrow if you'd prefer."

"Let's do it now," Loretta said curtly, meaning—let's get it over with. "How far had we got?"

Carole put out a hand and activated the tape recorder. She said hesitantly: "You were talking about . . . something about the women making all the decisions in the *The Age of Innocence*."

"I remember." Loretta sat back in her chair, her mind reengaging with Carole Coryat's original question. She began to feel calmer, her headache less insistent, and she said: "Scorsese's obviously interested in hierarchies and how you move through them—what happens to people who *challenge* them. Up to now his interest has been the Mafia but if you think about Old New York as it's presented in Wharton's novels, it's hard to imagine a more structured society—"

"Just a moment, Dr. Lawson. You mind if I order another coffee?" Carole sounded depressed.

"Fine, but nothing for me." Loretta waited while Carole signalled to the waiter behind the bar, her eye lighting on a headline in the newspaper which the lone man was reading two tables away: *Pupil Slays Teacher, Injures Classmates, in Shoot-Out.* As she watched he lowered the paper, shook a cigarette from an open packet of Camels and felt in his pocket. His hand emerged empty and he leaned across to Carole, who was nearer to him than Loretta: "Excuse me, do you have a light?"

She picked up the matchbook Loretta had left lying on the table and passed it across.

"Thanks."

"You're welcome," she said, gesturing that he should keep it. Loretta was about to protest when she realised the uselessness of asking for it back. What was she proposing to do, fingerprint it?

Carole prompted: "Dr. Lawson?"

"Sorry," she said, and attempted to pick up her interrupted train of thought. "What *The Age of Innocence* is about," she said distractedly, glancing towards the bar, "is—is the limits of individual action within a hierarchy, a hierarchy composed of families. That's where I'd see the link with the Mafia, since both types of society are essentially tribal . . ."

Her confidence returned and she began to speak more fluently, almost forgetting what had happened at the Met. She answered Carole's questions patiently, even the ones which struck her as silly or off the point, and imperceptibly the journalist slipped back into the role of student which she had given up so recently. Loretta started to enjoy herself, throwing out ideas and challenging assumptions exactly as if she was back in her room at St. Frideswide's, taking the last supervision of the day on a muggy summer afternoon in Oxford.

The TV news was on when Loretta opened the front door of Toni's flat, the dog snoring gently in front of the television with her stubby legs stretched out; she seemed to like the sound of human voices, even though she couldn't understand them or make sense of the accompanying images. Loretta glanced at the screen and saw a sickly boy in a wheelchair, incongruously dressed in a child's version of the New York police uniform and surrounded by real cops. As she put down her shopping, her eyes still on the screen, she heard a female reporter explain that the child, who was dying of AIDS, had been made "cop-for-a-day" by officers from the 7th Precinct who were touched by his predicament. The child's skin was grey and he stared listlessly up at the adults from sunken eye-sockets, a deep weariness evident from the effort it took even to move his head. "The boy was born with the disease," the reporter went on relentlessly, "after his mother contracted the virus when she was raped. Doctors say—"

Loretta stepped over the sleeping dog and snapped off the TV. Honey lumbered to her feet, whined and trotted towards the kitchen.

"In a minute," said Loretta, interpreting this unsubtle signal that the dog wanted to be fed. "Let me put this stuff in the fridge and then I'll give you something."

She picked up the plastic carrier bag which contained mineral water, orange juice, milk and bread from a nearby deli and carried it into the kitchen, smiling to herself as she realised she had begun to talk to Honey as though the animal were human. She fed the dog and returned to the living-room where she took a hanger from the big cupboard and hung up a shirt she'd bought in Bloomingdale's on sale, noticing as she did so that the message light was flashing on the answering-machine. There were four calls, one for Toni and the rest for Loretta: John Tracey had left the address of a restaurant opposite Carnegie Hall where he'd booked a table for dinner that night; Kelly Sibon greeted Loretta enthusiastically, raved about the proposal for her new book and invited her to a small drinks party at her flat the next evening; and Carole Coryat left a vague, anxious message full of silences and hesitations—exactly like a student apologising for the late delivery of an essay.

"I thought you'd be home by now," she finished, unaware that Loretta had felt so much better by the time she escaped from the Café Noir that she'd revived her original plan of doing some shopping. She had headed down Madison Avenue and across to Lexington in search of Bloomingdale's, relieved that on this occasion at least, unlike her earlier walk down Fifth Avenue, she had no impression at all of being followed or under surveillance.

"I just wanted to make sure you have my home number," Carole was saying, "and to say call me anytime. I mean, if you're worried or . . . I never go to bed early so it doesn't matter how late . . ."

Loretta already had Carole's home number in her notebook and as the machine rewound she took down Honey's lead. The dog bounded out of the kitchen, leaving her dinner half-eaten, and Loretta immediately felt guilty for not coming back to walk her sooner; the poor animal must be desperate.

She allowed Honey to drag her up and down Riverside Park for fifteen minutes, opening the front door of the flat when she got back to the sound of the phone ringing.

"Hallo," she said breathlessly, drooping the lead just inside the door as she dived for the receiver.

"Loretta, is that you? This is Michael."

She was quite unprepared, had almost forgotten about him in fact.

"Loretta? Are you there?"

"Yes." She sat down heavily on the edge of the bed.

"Loretta, I'm worried that I may have offended you yesterday. I hope you didn't think—I wouldn't like you to get the wrong idea. Have you talked to Toni?"

"Yes."

"Did you tell her about me? About our little talk last night?"

Loretta hesitated, the advice from the telephone directory inhibiting her: what was she supposed to say? "No, I . . . How well do you know her, Michael?" She relaxed a little, her voice steadier now she'd regained the initiative.

He laughed softly. "Let's say I used to know her *very* well. Lately we drifted apart. You know how it is."

"Do you—" Loretta looked at her watch, wishing she'd noted the time as soon as Michael started talking. How many minutes had the detective said were needed to trace the call? She couldn't remember but anyway they hadn't been talking long, probably not more than half a minute.

"You were about to say, Loretta?"

"Nothing. Is your name really Michael?"

He laughed again. "What do you think?"

"I'm not *that* interested."

"Then why'd you ask? What's wrong, Loretta, you have a bad day?"

"No."

"Where'd you go? You were out a *long* time, I tried your number over and over."

"Why didn't you leave a message?"

"Oh, I guess I get tongue-tied when I hear those machines. Have you been doing the town, Loretta? Seeing the sights?"

"Yes."

"Like what? Where'd you go?"

"Why do you want to know?"

"Like I said, I'm building a picture of you from your voice. You sound like an educated kind of a person, I guess you wouldn't be interested in the usual tourist junk—the Empire State Building, that's not exactly your scene, right? Come on, tell me where you went all day. Some gallery maybe? The Met?"

"The *Met*? Why'd you say that? Have you been *watching* me?"

"Why would I watch you, Loretta? Talking's much more fun." Then, in a businesslike tone, as if the conversation up to now had been an exchange of pleasantries between colleagues: "OK, tell me what you're wearing."

"What?"

"Your clothes. Tell me what you're wearing."

Involuntarily she glanced down. "Trousers."

There was a moment's silence. "I'm disappointed, Loretta. I don't much care for women in trousers. Unless they're tight. Are they tight?"

"No."

"OK, what else?"

"A—a shirt."

"This is not very *interesting* to me, Loretta. How about underneath?"

Loretta said: "A body."

"I know you have a *body*, sweetie, we'll come to that in a moment. You're keen tonight, Loretta, you're getting right ahead of me." He was starting to get excited, she could hear it. "First I want to hear about your bra, your panties. What colour are they?"

For a moment Loretta saw the funny side. "Don't you know what a body is? You're not very up-to-date, are you? I thought everyone knew—"

"Cut the crap, what're you saying? This is some kind of ladies' underwear?"

"It's—it's like a leotard."

"You mean one of those all-in-ones?"

"Yes."

"Cut high on the leg?"

"Yes." He was back on course, recovered from the temporary reverse.

"And a low neck?"

She said nothing.

"Come on, Loretta. I'm waiting. Does it—I want to know about cleavage."

She blurted out: "Why are you *doing* this?"

"Doing what? We're just having a nice little talk."

She said more calmly: "Asking all these questions."

"I'm just being friendly, Loretta. You're a stranger here—"

"How'd you know that?"

"You told me last night. Loretta, you're not getting all antsy again? What's your problem?"

"What's *my* problem? All right, Michael," she said in an altogether different tone of voice, "why don't you tell me something about yourself? Shall we start with what *you're* wearing?"

"This is not playing the game. Do you have a boyfriend, Loretta?"

"No."

"I hoped you might say that. But you do like men, Loretta? You're not one of those . . . *dykes?*"

"My sexual—"

"You better not be because I'd like us to get together and have some fun. Do you like fun?"

"Fun?"

Michael started gabbling: "Do you give head? Do you, Loretta? Uh . . . I'm imagining your head in my lap . . . uh, your hair . . . my dick in your—"

"Fuck off."

She slammed the phone down so hard it bounced and she scrambled to put it back, her breath coming in short, angry gasps as she seized her notebook, rifling the pages in search of Lieutenant Donelly's number. She dialled it, letting out a whimper of dismay when she heard the engaged signal, and fell back on the bed. Honey trotted over, alarmed by this unaccountable behaviour, and Loretta sat up, stroking the animal's head, redialling Donelly's number with her other hand. It was still busy but the moment she put the phone down it rang.

"Ms. Lawson, what happened?" It was Donelly, sounding irritated. "I've been trying to call—"

"Oh, thank *God,*" Loretta interrupted. "Did you get him?"

"Why'd you hang up? Another minute and—"

"You mean you still don't—you let me go through all *that* for nothing?"

"We had an unexpected technical problem," he said shortly. "Obviously there wasn't any way we could let you know without tipping him off as well. And frankly, Ms. Lawson, compared to some things I've heard, so far this guy is only borderline offensive."

"I don't *believe* this," exclaimed Loretta. "I mean, having to

talk to some pervert about . . . about *fellatio* is not my idea
of—It's *obvious* what turns him on, he was practically *salivating*, getting me to answer all those stupid questions—"

"I hear what you're saying, Ms. Lawson," Donelly said
more reasonably, "but please try and see it from my point of
view—from the point of view of this office. You would not believe some of the stuff my officers have had to listen to. When
he calls again—"

"Again? Why should he? I've put the phone down on him
twice."

The detective said patiently: "One of the things we've
learned since the unit was set up is that these guys are unbe-
lievably persistent. If I can give you some advice—"

She started to protest, then changed her mind. "All right.
Go on."

"In our experience, profane language only excites these
guys—coming from a woman, that is. Next time, if you could
stay calm and just answer his questions—"

"Is *damn* all right or will that turn him on as well?" she
asked furiously. "Oh, look, sorry, I'm more upset than I—I
didn't think he'd upset me so much."

"I understand, Ms. Lawson. That's why we have to get
him, so other women don't have to go through this experience
you're having now. Are you willing to continue?"

"I don't have much choice, do I? There isn't any other way
you're going to catch him." A thought occurred to her and she
asked abruptly: "You don't think—has it occurred to you he
might work for the telephone company?"

"That's a line we've been pursuing, yes, but it isn't easy, getting hold of employee records, not without a lot more to go
on. I'll get the tape over to our labs—"

"Tape? What tape?"

"We have engineers who can work on the recording, boost up the background and see if there's any indication what type of a place he's calling from. There was one guy, always made calls around two in the morning, turned out he worked the overnight shift on a hospital switchboard. I can't promise anything but we'll give it our best shot."

"All right," Loretta said tiredly. When the detective hung up she remained where she was, cradling the phone in her lap while Honey leaned against her calves and dribbled on her trousers. It occurred to her that she hadn't said a word about her experience at the Metropolitan Museum and the eerie way in which Michael appeared to have known—guessed, more likely, she reassured herself—her movements. She picked up the receiver and dialled Donelly's number but it was engaged again, perhaps he was already talking to someone at the lab he'd mentioned. What a job, she thought, wondering if it affected his private life: could you spend day after day soothing frightened women, exposed to a bizarre range of male fantasies, *without* being affected? Loretta tried the number again, wondering if there was a female officer on the team, she might feel better if she talked to a woman, but the line was still busy.

She glanced at her watch and saw it was nearly seven, yet Toni still hadn't called back. With an exclamation of impatience Loretta got up, hurried into the kitchen and came back with the Sag Harbor number in her hand. The line connected at once but only to the answering-machine, Jay's mother's voice reciting that ridiculous, prissy message. Loretta waited impatiently for her to finish, tapping her foot when the outgoing message was followed by what seemed like dozens of beeps; half the population of the Hamptons must be undergoing some spiritual crisis, to judge by how many there were. She tagged her own message on the end, another request for Toni to ring her as soon as she could, with a rider to the effect that she was about to go out which made it rather pointless . . . Suddenly Loretta realised she had around seven minutes to wash and change if she wasn't going to be terribly late meeting John Tracey.

From the closet she seized a dress she'd hung up the night before, hopping across the room as she struggled out of the trousers, that wretched body . . . In the bathroom she splashed water on her face and arms, feeling soiled as well as sweaty, not fully realising that what she was doing was at least in part a response to the dirty phone call. She hastily reapplied her make-up, trying not to think about what Michael had said, but her hand was shaking a little when she outlined her lips with lip pencil.

"For God's sake, Honey," she exclaimed, returning to the living-room to find the dog dragging her shoulder bag across the floor by its strap. A frantic chase followed, the dog only releasing its trophy when Loretta finally sat down on the bed and forced herself to feign indifference. She pulled on the blue silk dress, snatched up the bag with no time to investigate the damage and flipped on the radio, stopping in her tracks when she recognised the chorus of a corny Christmas hit from the early 1970s: "So here it is, Merry Christmas, everybody's having fun . . ."

Christmas songs in *July*? Loretta yanked open the front door, thinking angrily that she wasn't having any fun, none at all, and glanced over her shoulder when she heard Honey roll on to her side with a loud sigh. In too much of a hurry to care that she might be abandoning the dog to an evening of glam rock, Loretta stalked out of the flat as the last bars of Slade faded and were replaced by Gary Glitter.

5

John Tracey poured himself a glass of wine, put down the bottle and picked it up when he remembered Loretta. "More?"

"Not this minute," she said, aware that his tolerance of alcohol far outstripped hers. She did not want to wake up with another headache.

"I mean," said Tracey, topping up her glass as though she hadn't spoken, "I was at Oxford with the bloke. How do you think I feel, grubbing around for dirt on a con . . . a contemporary of mine?'

Loretta said, bewildered: "You were at Oxford with Bill Clinton? I didn't know that."

Tracey drank some wine. "I'm not saying I *knew* him but we were there at the same time. Haven't I ever mentioned it?"

"No. Did you meet him?"

"I *think* he went out with a friend of mine. I remember her going out with a Rhodes scholar, big bloke with fair hair who was very into politics. I may have met him at a party at Univ."

Loretta frowned. "I don't quite see what you're saying. You don't want to write about him just because you happened to be at Oxford at the same time? Isn't that a bit . . . tenuous?"

Tracey scowled. "Either you see it or you don't, Loretta. The guy's practically the same age as me—"

"Give or take a year or two."

"When you get to our age—"

"Which I'm not."

Tracey ignored this reminder that he was nearly ten years older than Loretta. He was in good shape for his age, his hair having turned grey so long ago that it didn't seem to have anything to do with advancing years, his face craggy and attractive if not conventionally handsome. He said irritably: "What I'm saying is, even if I don't actually know him, he's one of my generation. The sixties."

"The sixties?" Loretta was startled. She had never heard Tracey make this claim before; on the contrary, perhaps because he was a mature student, going up to Oxford in his early twenties after leaving school to work on a local newspaper, he had always expressed a degree of mild contempt for the sit-ins, demonstrations and revolutionary rhetoric of 1968. His attitude was incomprehensible to Loretta, who had watched enviously from Gillingham Girls' Grammar School as *les évènements* unfolded in Paris and her friends' older siblings went by coach to London to take part in demonstrations against the Vietnam War. She wondered what had prompted this *volte face*; surely not the reflected glory of having been at Oxford at the same time as the president?

"Wait a minute, John," she said, "I'm not being deliberately obtuse, I just don't see why you feel this . . . this personal attachment to Bill Clinton. What about Whitewater? Are you saying there's nothing in it?"

Tracey made a dismissive sound. "Whitewater, smoking bimbos, Vince Foster—what's it actually amount to? What you have to appreciate, Loretta, is that the Right in this country aren't used to being out of office. They'll do *anything* to get back. This is not about some piddling little loan company in Arkansas, it's about the elections in October. It wouldn't surprise me if the Republicans take the Senate and then Clinton's really fucked. Health care, you can forget it."

Loretta waited but he didn't add anything. "So why don't you ring up the foreign desk and tell them that's the story?"

As though she had said something incredibly naïve, Tracey said: "Times have changed, Loretta, this new foreign editor's not interested in what his reporters think. He gives you a story and you're supposed to go out and stand it up. It doesn't matter how you do it as long as you don't invade Princess Di's precious bloody privacy."

"What?"

"The Princess of Wales's private life, it's the one thing nobody on the *Herald's* allowed to touch. It's ludicrous, given what everyone else writes about her, but it's the one absolute no-no, even if I find out she's been bonking Clinton. Which she hasn't, as far as I know. Dirt on Bill's what he wants, and I'm here to get it. Or Hillary, of course—he doesn't care which."

He fell silent after this not altogether lucid speech, picking up his fork and chasing a cold sautéed potato round his plate.

Loretta watched, eyes narrowed, wondering how best to penetrate his mood of volatile introspection. "John," she said finally, "there's something I—"

"What's the line on Hillary, by the way?"

"The line?"

"The sisters. What's the feminist line on Hillary?"

Loretta made a little gesture of annoyance. "I don't know there is a line. If you want my personal opinion, she seems very capable but I'm not comfortable with women who derive their power . . . whose power is contingent on someone else. And it's not as if he gave her Defence, is it? Health's traditionally a women's issue."

She watched him fumble in his jacket pocket for his cigarettes, take one out and light it without going through the usual ritual of asking her if she minded—not that it usually made much difference. He showed no sign of having heard what she'd just said, indeed he had behaved throughout the meal so far as if he was only intermittently aware of her presence.

The evening had got off to an unpromising start, with Loretta arriving at the restaurant a few minutes late to find Tracey hunched lugubriously over a whisky at the bar. She kissed his cheek, apologised for being late and tried to lighten the atmosphere with a remark about the painting behind the bar. It was a pastiche Tuscan landscape with a foreground of noses, each of them allegedly belonging to a celebrity—painters, actors, writers.

"I can never remember what Pascal said about Cleopatra," she observed to a blank look from Tracey, who obviously hadn't the least idea what she was talking about. "You know, about the history of the world being different if her nose had been shorter—or was it longer?"

His response was a rather ungracious demand to know why she hadn't returned his call when she got back to the flat, even though he hadn't asked her to. "I was beginning to think you weren't coming," he said, looking at his watch. "I told you half past seven."

"Oh, for God's sake," Loretta responded, resisting the temptation to blurt out that she was late because she'd had to deal with an obscene caller who wanted to know if she did fellatio. "Let's see if our table's ready."

Since then she had listened sympathetically to a lengthy account—outlasting their starters and main courses—of Tracey's problems at the *Sunday Herald*. She now knew about the clampdown on expenses, the rigid imposition of a five-day week on reporters used to working four (at most), the hard-faced people brought in from the tabloids . . . Making a fresh attempt to divert his attention from himself, Loretta pushed aside her empty plate, folded her hands on the table and said seriously: "I need your advice, John. A man's been phoning the flat, he's done it twice so far—" She stopped, suddenly realising the significance of something Michael had said in his latest call. *You've been out, I tried your number over and over* . . . If he was telling the truth, he couldn't have been watching her or shadowing her at the Metropolitan Museum. Instantly a warm glow of relief suffused her, making her realise how uneasy she'd been.

Tracey was staring at her. "What man? What are you talking about?"

Loretta said, "I'm coming to that," but her internal dialogue had thrown her off course and she found herself unintentionally starting in the middle. "There's an outside chance he's a friend of Toni's, I don't want to ask her outright because of what it says in the phone book. And it doesn't really matter because the police are bugging the phone, they would've traced his number this evening if I hadn't—"

"Bugging the *phone*?" She had his full attention at last, his expression revealing how startled he was by her garbled version of events. "Loretta, you only got here *yesterday*. How come all this—you didn't mention any of this when you rang last night."

"You were rushing off somewhere. I didn't want to worry you."

He rolled his eyes upwards. "Another wild-goose chase. Another man who knows a woman whose sister *might* have been propositioned by Clinton when he was governor of Arkansas."

Loretta said: "John, *please*."

"Sorry. What's he want, this bloke?"

"I suppose he's your common-or-garden obscene caller." Loretta hadn't expected to be embarrassed but she felt her cheeks flush. She picked up her fork, turned it sideways and, in desperation, pretended to read the maker's name.

"Meaning what exactly? What colour knickers are you wearing? That's the standard one, isn't it?"

"Is it? To be honest I didn't realise at first, not the first time he called. His questions weren't . . . I mean, they were weird, all about whether I'm an English rose—"

"An English *rose*? Doesn't sound very obscene to me."

Loretta snapped: "That's what Lieutenant Donelly said. If you must know, I put the phone down tonight when he asked if I did oral sex. Is that obscene enough for you?"

"Sorry, Loretta," he said contritely. When she didn't respond he leaned across the table and touched her arm. "Come on, I've said I'm sorry."

She shrugged his hand away. "It's OK, I can handle it."

"Maybe you can but . . . Here, have another drink." He re-filled both their glasses. "OK, go back a bit. You say this chap may be a friend of *Toni's?*"

Loretta sighed. "I don't know. It says in the phone book you shouldn't tell anyone, not even your best friend, which of course she isn't—she came to supper a few times in Oxford and we went to a couple of exhibitions but we're hardly *close*. I don't think I'd have been so upset," she added unguardedly as a waiter cleared their plates, "if it hadn't been . . ."

Tracey waited. When she didn't complete the sentence, he said encouragingly: "If it hadn't been for what?"

"Well, say it *is* a friend of Toni's, that means he knows her address."

"You mean he knows where you're staying? You're worried he might come round to the flat?"

Loretta lowered her voice. "Not necessarily to the flat."

"I'm not with you, Loretta."

"I just—oh, God, you're not going to believe this. This afternoon, at the Met, I had the feeling I was being—watched." She frowned, realising she had watered the story down. "Followed," she added quickly.

"Followed."

"Yes."

"And you think it's the same bloke?"

"Yes. *No.*" She was confused, remembering what she'd worked out about Michael a couple of moments ago. "How should *I* know?"

Tracey said: "You're not going to like this, Loretta—"

"But?"

He grimaced. "You have got an unusually vivid imagination. OK, obviously the phone calls are real, I'm not denying that. But they've upset you, anyone can see that, and maybe you're . . . not exactly *imagining* things. Jumping to the wrong conclusion. You're an attractive woman—"

"Thanks."

"—and it's hardly surprising if men look at you. Maybe you don't usually notice but this time, because you were feeling jumpy . . . Remember the time we went to Rhodes and you accused the waiter at that taverna—"

"*What?* That was *ten years* ago. More. And he definitely touched my breast." She sat back in her chair, her hands gripping the edge of the table. "I can't believe you're bringing it up *now*." The incident he was referring to had taken place on their last, disastrous holiday together, only a few weeks before they separated, and Loretta hadn't given it a thought for years. "What's wrong with you tonight?" she asked crossly.

To her surprise, Tracey ground his second cigarette out and raised his hand to his forehead. "I don't know. Now you mention it I do feel a bit—I don't know how to describe it. Maybe it's the heat."

Loretta said unsympathetically: "It isn't hot in here and if you've got a headache you shouldn't be drinking red wine."

"It's not a headache—not exactly."

Loretta stared at him. "You've gone very pale. You're not going to be sick?"

"Um—I hope not. Sorry, Loretta, I think I'd better go to the gents. You didn't happen to notice it on the way in?"

She shook her head. "Sorry. I'm sure we can find out." She peered over her shoulder in search of their waiter. When she turned back, Tracey had lowered his head and was mumbling something too low for her to catch.

"What's the matter? Do you feel worse?" She glanced in alarm at the empty wine bottle, thinking he couldn't possibly be drunk on half a bottle of house red and a couple of whiskies at the bar while he was waiting for her. "John, can you hear me?"

He lifted his head, stared at her without focusing for a few seconds and slumped in his chair. Loretta started to get up, caught sight of their waiter and signalled urgently for him to come over.

"Is your friend all right?"

She bit back another sarcastic reply. "I think he's ill but I don't know what . . . Could you get me the bill? Quickly?"

"Sure." He moved away and she reached across the table to grasp Tracey's forearm through his jacket. "John," she said urgently, trying to rouse him. "I've asked for the bill. We're leaving in a minute, maybe some air . . ." She recalled what it was like outside, the sticky heat which had settled on her during the taxi ride to the restaurant, and thought it might actually make him worse. But the only thing she could think of was getting him back to his hotel as soon as possible and asking reception to call a doctor.

Tracey was breathing noisily now, snoring almost, and people at nearby tables were turning to look. Loretta had hardly ever seen him drunk and on those few occasions he had been nothing like this—alcohol made him voluble and argumentative, a bit of a loose cannon at dinner parties, not comatose.

"*Thanks*," she said, throwing her Visa card onto the plate the waiter was holding out without checking the bill. She turned back to Tracey, remembering he had been ill after his last trip to Bosnia in February; he had picked up a kidney infection from infected water in Sarajevo which lasted several weeks but she had no idea whether it was likely to recur, or have such spectacular effects if it did.

The waiter returned and she scrawled her name on a credit

card voucher. "Your hotel, John," she said as she got to her feet and came round the table to help him up. "What's the name of your *hotel*?" She thought back to the message he'd left on Toni's answering-machine, almost certain he hadn't mentioned the hotel by name, only its phone number and the address of the restaurant they were in.

"Shit," she said in a low voice, propelling him towards the street door. The waiter went first, clearing a path, and at least Tracey was docile, leaning on her with his eyes closed and doing exactly what she told him. They passed a phone in the lobby but the time difference meant it was too late to ring the *Sunday Herald* office in London; it occurred to Loretta that, unless she was prepared to prop him against a wall and search his pockets, the only sensible course of action was to take him back to Toni's flat. She got him out into the street, supporting him with both arms while the helpful waiter looked for a cab, and felt sweat break out on her forehead as they were enfolded by the predatory heat.

A taxi stopped and she heaved Tracey inside, squeezing herself after him. "Riverside Drive," she said tiredly, "Riverside and Seventy-third." When the driver hesitated she raised her voice: "What're you waiting for? Can you see he's *ill*?"

Her tone warned him not to argue and he set off, taking an immediate right which threw Tracey even more heavily against her. Loretta struggled to push him upright, agonising over what she should do when she got to Toni's flat. Put him to bed? Call a doctor? Toni had left the vet's emergency number, but no doctor; Loretta recalled the name of Toni's gynaecologist, Hester Rosenstein, but that wasn't much use in the present situation. Tracey's head rolled sideways onto her shoulder and she turned away, repelled by the combination of alcohol fumes and stale cigarette smoke emerging from his slightly open mouth.

"John," she said urgently, trying to shake him awake, but got no reaction other than a burst of coughing which prompted the taxi driver to glance anxiously at the back seat as he waited at a red light. With some difficulty she encircled Tracey with her left arm, propped him upright and tried not to think about the next hurdle—how she was going to drag an almost insensible eleven-stone man along the path to Toni's apartment block, through the foyer and into the lift to the fifteenth floor.

The time on Loretta's watch, when she woke up with a start and turned on the bedside lamp, was four-sixteen on Saturday morning. She had been catapulted into wakefulness by a dream which left only the lightest impression of itself, evaporating so quickly that she could not say what it was about or why her heart was pounding. She blinked, temporarily blinded by the electric light, and came fully awake only when she looked across and saw the huddled form of John Tracey on the sofa. She tiptoed across the room to check on him, reassured by the even rise and fall of his chest, and as she watched, Tracey murmured and heaved himself into a new position under the blanket she had thrown over him. It was slightly chilly in the room, the air-conditioning working too hard now the outside temperature had fallen, and Loretta moved silently to turn it down. Honey, who was lying on the floor near the sofa where she could keep an eye on John Tracey, made a long, whiffling noise through her nose and glanced sleepily at Loretta over her shoulder.

"Shh," she whispered, "go back to sleep." The dog regarded her for a moment, eyes glazing over when she sensed it was too early for breakfast or a walk, and obeyed.

Loretta slipped back into bed, pulling the quilt up over her knees and resting her arms on it. She glanced anxiously at Tracey but he was almost completely hidden by the blanket; in any case, at this distance she probably wouldn't be able to make out the tiny puncture mark she'd found on his bare arm when she pulled his jacket off and helped him onto the sofa. He was wearing a short-sleeved shirt, which surprised her until she thought about the climate in Washington at this time of year, and the mark was on his inside forearm, no more than a pinprick but the surrounding area was slightly pinker than the rest, like a faint halo. She had traced the circle with her finger, feeling the hard dot at the centre where the substance, whatever it was, had gone into the vein. Then, hardly believing what she was doing, she had examined both his arms for needle tracks and found—nothing. Tracey had moaned and tried to shake her off, but he was still too much under the influence of whatever he'd taken to be properly aware of what she was doing.

He occasionally smoked a joint but she did not think he was remotely interested in other drugs, not even speed which, he said, one or two of his colleagues at the *Sunday Herald* used to keep awake when they were working into the early hours on a big story. Not that anyone injected speed, as far as Loretta knew, and what Tracey had taken clearly wasn't a stimulant. She found it impossible to picture him injecting himself yet the puncture mark was much further down his arm than any vaccination she'd ever witnessed; in fact, the spot was almost exactly where the vein would come up if he applied pressure above his elbow. An adverse reaction to a drug would explain his disjointed speech and sudden collapse at the restaurant, yet Loretta still couldn't quite bring herself to countenance it. On the other hand she was reluctant to call a doctor—always assuming there was one listed in Toni's red address book—when

she had absolutely no idea what he'd taken. She was still agonising, crouched by Tracey's head, when there was a barely per-
ceptible change in his breathing. Loretta held herself still,
hoping she wasn't imagining it, and as she listened the rasping
breaths which worried her so much began to give way to a
shallower, more even pattern. In a while, when Tracey and the
dog began to snore gently, unfortunately not quite in sync
with each other, she got up, shook each of her feet in turn to
get rid of the pins and needles which had set in during her
vigil, and undressed for bed.

She had fallen asleep more quickly than she expected and
the anxiety which invaded her dreams and woke her up shortly
after four was only partly to do with Tracey. She needed to
know he was all right, that he hadn't developed any alarming
new symptoms while she slept, and as soon as that had been
established her brain scrolled down to the next worry on her
list. The same unfriendly porter who had been on duty when
she rushed out to meet Tracey was at the desk when they returned, regarding her impassively as she struggled towards the
lift with him. At the last minute, as her hand reached out to
press the button, he called out: "You staying in 15G?"

Loretta looked back over her shoulder. "Yes. It's in the
book," she added irritably, assuming he was questioning her
bona fides.

"Visitors gotta be announced."

"Oh, come *on*," she said, assuming he meant Tracey. "Even
in this state?"

"Not *him*. Other guy."

"What?"

"Tried to sneak into the elevator without me seeing." He
pulled back the cuff of his dark jacket and looked at his watch.
"Hour, maybe two hours ago."

Loretta heaved Tracey round so she could face the porter. "What're you *talking* about?"

"I tell him right out, visitors gotta be announced. He says, 'I'm going up to 15G' and I say, 'No you ain't, buster, not without me calling up first. Far's I know, lady's out for the evening.' "

"15G? You mean he wanted Toni's flat—Ms. Stramiello? Didn't he know she's away?"

He ignored her and said stolidly: "Just so's you know—visitors gotta be announced. S'why I'm here."

Loretta let out an impatient sound. "It's not my—he can't have wanted me. I'm not expecting anyone. I don't *know* anyone." Her muscles ached and she eased Tracey's weight onto her chest to give her arms a break. The porter continued to watch her, making no move to help, and she took a deep breath, preparing to propel Tracey into the lift.

"Hey—I ain't finished."

"*Now* what?"

"This guy. I don't like his attitude." He pronounced it att-i-tood.

"His—how d'you mean?"

"Sneaky. Like he don't wanna be seen."

Loretta said impatiently: "Maybe he didn't know he was supposed to speak to you first."

"He don't wanna tell me his name, no way. Soon's I ask him, he's out the door." He nodded towards the swinging doors Loretta had just come through.

Loretta said: "What did he look like?"

The porter shrugged. "Was a guy."

"Young? Old?" The porter was black and she hesitated before adding: "Was he white?"

He nodded. "White guy. How old? I can't rightly—"

The phone on his desk rang. He picked it up, turning his back on Loretta, who waited just long enough to hear him embark on a lengthy conversation about a faulty air-conditioning unit in one of the apartments. When he took out a ledger and began to record the problem, insisting nothing could be done before Monday, she finally pressed the call button and got Tracey into the lift.

It occurred to her now, several hours later, that the porter must have noticed *something* about the unknown visitor, some detail like hair colour or height which might help to identify him next time she spoke to Toni. She pulled the quilt more tightly round her, frowning and shivering even though she had turned the air-conditioning down. Taken in isolation, the fact that someone had tried to come up to the flat in this slightly clandestine manner meant nothing, other than suggesting that the stranger was unfamiliar with the building security system. It might have been one of Toni's students, someone who was used to seeing her in her office at Columbia; it was not unknown for students to descend uninvited on their lecturers, it had happened to Loretta in Oxford the previous winter when one of her third-years had had an alcohol-fueled panic attack. Yet there was nothing unusual about having to check in with a building superintendent or porter. Loretta thought the system was likely to be the same at most apartment blocks in this part of New York. Perhaps he hadn't liked the look of the admittedly rather surly porter, and thought he could sneak past when his attention was engaged elsewhere. There were sufficient unknowns to worry Loretta and although it was an eccentric time to go downstairs and interrogate the man again—twenty minutes to five when she checked her watch once more—she thought it was worth it to put her mind at rest. Anyway—and this hadn't occurred to her before—if she left it much later he might go off shift at six or eight. She flung off the quilt, swung her legs out of bed and padded over to the chair on which she had discarded her own clothes and Tracey's jacket.

His wallet, she saw as she slithered into her underwear, had fallen out of his jacket and was lying on the floor. She bent to retrieve it and several pieces of paper fluttered out, including his return air ticket to Washington. It was too long to fit in any of the wallet's compartments so she tucked it back between the covers as Tracey must have done, giving the other pieces of paper a cursory examination before doing the same with them. There were several taxi receipts, the printed sort which issued from the meter in yellow cabs if a passenger asked for one, and Loretta looked curiously to see how much he had paid for the journey to his hotel from LaGuardia that afternoon. Three dollars more than it had cost her, she discovered, but it was the times on the print-out which arrested her attention. "St. time 09:18 A.M.," it recorded, "End time 10:01 A.M."

Tracey had arrived in New York hours earlier than expected, early enough to have been in the Metropolitan Museum at lunchtime as the journalist, Carole What's-her-name, had suggested. Loretta turned to look at the recumbent form of her ex-husband on the sofa, only his wavy grey hair visible above the blanket, but it was enough to stir the deep affection she still felt for him. Whatever Tracey had been doing in New York that morning, Loretta was 99 percent certain that he hadn't been spying on her. As though they might contain the answer, she hastily looked through the other taxi receipts, discovering only that Tracey seemed to have spent the day making short journeys up and down the city. She shrugged, telling herself there was bound to be a simple explanation, and turned over a blue air-mail envelope which had also fallen from the wallet. It had been posted four days ago by Swiftair, the express letter service, and Loretta was immediately curious to know who was sending Tracey urgent letters from Hampshire.

Neither the sender's name, M. Stephenson, nor the address—a house called The Warren, in a village near Basingstoke—meant anything to Loretta. She held the envelope between her finger and thumb, studying the writing for clues. There were longish spaces between the words and the letters were crammed together with tall perpendicular strokes, but it didn't tell her whether the writer was a man or a woman. Loretta perched on the edge of the chair, careful not to crush the clothes she'd taken off earlier, and slid the thin pages from the envelope. Suddenly aware that she was sitting there in her knickers, she picked up a shirt and slid it over her head, distracting herself from the moral problem of what she was doing reading Tracey's private correspondence.

A single word leapt out at her from the first page, "Darlingest," and the moral problem evaporated. She was hooked.

"Darlingest," she read again, deliberately keeping her face averted from the slumbering figure on the sofa, "*another* whole day without a letter or phone call. Perhaps you've written and the letter's gone astray or you've been travelling and haven't had a chance to pop it in the postbox—I *know* you said you might have to go to Arkansas, darling. I'm sure Pete, you remember Pete the postman, I'm sure he thinks I've taken leave of my senses, waiting at the door every morning and *snatching* the letters from his hand! Pretending, of course, that I just *happen* to be taking in the milk—but who cares what he thinks? I'm not ashamed, it's been *a whole week* since you phoned—yes, darling, I *am* counting the days and no letter either! You would—"

Loretta reached the bottom of the first page. On the sofa John Tracey stirred, muttered, and threw an arm free of the blanket. The pink halo was still there on his forearm, a little more faded now, and Loretta averted her eyes, not wanting to think about it. She turned the page.

—tell me if something was wrong, if you were having doubts? I understand, I truly *understand* what a big step it must seem, getting married again, especially after such a *rotten* experience first time round—

"What?" Loretta's hand flew to her mouth and she looked fearfully at Tracey. He did not seem to have heard her exclamation and she turned back a page, reading the sentence again from the beginning, wondering just what exactly Tracey had told this M. Stephenson person about their marriage. It hadn't been *that* bad.

—first time round, but remember, darling, we're in this *together*! We're both older, and wiser (*you* are, at any rate, I can't speak for me!) and I just *know* we wouldn't make the same mistakes. Trust me! I was too young when I married Tim and then the children came so fast (Susie sends her love, by the way, and keeps asking when Uncle John's coming home—yes, *home*, isn't that sweet of her? And a bit of self-interest, of course, she's *longing* to be a bridesmaid! I suppose it was a blessing in a way, you and Loretta not having children, but I know how *miserable* it must have been for you. A man *needs* a son, that's what I've always thought, and I'm not too old! Look at that woman in Italy, twins at fifty-nine and I'm *years* younger than her!

A bracket seemed to be missing somewhere in the paragraph, emphasising M. Stephenson's agitation. Loretta read on, the handwriting becoming steadily more difficult to decipher although she was able to make out a sentence about *career women* and their *selfishness*. From here the letter digressed abruptly into local news, recorded in a much more legible hand: Rufus had decided to give up German next year, he'd struggled with it for so long and they were just going to have to face the fact that he wasn't a linguist. Susie was looking forward to the school holidays because she'd been invited to go to France for a week with Tamara, which meant that if John could get a week off, they'd only have Rufus to think about. Finally the letter returned to Tracey's failure to phone or write:

Darling John, I know I'm not exactly Cinderella but you really have come into my life like Prince Charming and I just *can't* bear the thought—I *won't* bear it! I know I'm an old silly, doubting you like this, but you've no idea how *lonely* it is without you! When I come back from taking Susie to school in the morning, I'd go absolutely mad if I didn't have the rabbits to see to, never mind all the orders for the shop. I know—

Tracey's new friend kept rabbits? Loretta remembered that her house was called The Warren and pulled a face, scenting whimsy. He had had a series of unsuitable girlfriends in recent years, including a married gym teacher he had met in a launderette in Brixton and a Greek student half his age, but the fevered tone of M. Stephenson's letter made Loretta wonder if she knew him as well as she thought she did. The phrase "male menopause" came into her head and she read on:

—we haven't known each other for long, it seems like so much more than five months. I keep thinking about the day I sat down and wrote you a letter, *never* thinking—not in a million years did I imagine you'd write back. I thought someone as famous and important as you was bound to have a secretary and I was so *touched* when I saw the envelope with the *Sunday Herald* postmark and your writing—I didn't recognise it then of course, I'd only ever seen the photo at the top of your columns. I don't know if I ever told you but it was the photo that made me write. Your articles are so brilliant, I used to cry when I read about the poor children in Sarajevo—

Sorry, darling, I'm rambling! That's the effect you have on me you see. Lord, I was so nervous that day, I could hardly dial the number you'd put in your letter. And then you very sweetly invited me to lunch and on the tube from Waterloo I had the feeling my life was about to change. And I couldn't bear—no, I *won't* bear the thought of—I can't even write it.

Loretta stopped reading, hastily collated the pages and shoved them back into the envelope. She put the letter on the coffee table and nibbled at a fingernail she'd broken on the journey back from the restaurant, wondering distractedly if Toni had an emery board. No wonder John Tracey was hanging round Washington, she thought, but how had he got in so deep in such a short time? She was about to put the flimsy blue envelope back in his wallet when she realised she had no idea what the initial M stood for. Mary, Marilyn, Maureen, Martha? Reluctantly Loretta reached for the envelope, drew out the letter and went straight to the last page.

"Yours forever and always, darling—Mo," she read, and slid the folded sheets back inside. Mo for Maureen? She thrust the envelope into Tracey's wallet, along with the air ticket and all his other paraphernalia, and slid it into the inside pocket of his jacket. Going down to interrogate the porter no longer seemed so urgent but she was less sleepy than ever; slightly shamefaced, Loretta pulled her jeans from her weekend case, slipped into them and stood up to fasten the button fly. She crossed the room to switch off the bedside lamp and gazed for a long moment at the grey dawn light which had begun to leak through the slats of the Venetian blinds. Then she picked up Toni's spare keys and, without looking at Tracey, let herself quietly out of the flat.

6

Growling, snarling, shouting: Loretta awoke to mayhem. "What's going on?" she heard herself say, almost before she was out of bed, but the racket was too great for either of the combatants to hear. John Tracey was standing on the sofa, rearing back out of the dog's reach, his hands tangled in the blanket which he was using as a flimsy shield. "Get away," she heard him bellow, "get *away*," but the dog merely barked more ferociously, her front paws on the sofa, angrier than Loretta had ever seen her.

"*Stop it,*" Loretta bellowed, unsure whether she was addressing the man or the dog. "Stop it *at once*. Honey!" she added menacingly, advancing on her from behind. The dog was so intent on hauling her stubby back legs onto the sofa and finding a tender part of Tracey's anatomy to bite that she failed to hear Loretta's approach. Loretta seized her by the collar, pulled with all her strength and fell back against the coffee table, taking the dog with her.

"*Christ,*" exclaimed Tracey, crumpled and furious, "where'd it come from? Where am I? What the fuck's going on? Loretta?"

"Shut up," she said, struggling into a sitting position and hanging on to the dog. "Honey, stop it. Don't you *dare* bite me. *Sit,* I said." She was mildly astonished and very relieved when the dog obeyed.

Tracey climbed down off the sofa, adjusting the open neck of his shirt and looking highly disgruntled. "Loretta, would you please tell me what's going on?"

"What did you do to her? She's not normally aggressive." Except with other dogs, Loretta thought, but she didn't mention that. "I mean, just look at her. She's terribly upset."

The dog was panting and shaking, her cavernous jaw hanging open and her thick pink tongue fully extended. Loretta hugged her, crooning—to her own surprise—"There, there, it's all right. He won't hurt you."

"She's upset? What about me? I wake up God knows where, in a totally strange flat, with this hound from hell slobbering all over my face. How'd you think I feel?" Tracey sat on the sofa and put his head in his hands.

"I'll put her in the kitchen," Loretta said diplomatically. "It's time she was fed. Honey, this way." She used her foot to herd the dog through the doorway and spooned food from a can onto a plate, enough to pacify her for the next few minutes, switched on the electric kettle and returned to the living room. "Tea or coffee?"

Tracey said grumpily: "What I'd like is a civil explanation of what I'm doing here. And why's it so bloody hot? Doesn't this place have air-conditioning? Where are we?"

"Toni's flat," Loretta said shortly, going to the window and pulling up the blinds. She turned various knobs on the control panel of the air-conditioning unit and cold air began to blow. "I can't seem to get this thing right, I woke up in the night and it was actually quite chilly so I turned it off." She turned back to Tracey. "After you passed out last night—"

"Is that what happened?" Tracey looked puzzled. "I don't remember anything after—I mean, I remember a bar. And noses. Why do I remember noses?"

"There was a mural in the restaurant. Or a picture, I can't remember which. Famous people's noses."

Tracey scowled. "No wonder I feel peculiar."

"You were sitting at the bar when I got to the restaurant. You didn't *seem* drunk but you were in a bad mood right from the start, you complained about our table and you wanted to send the wine back. You drank it, though."

"It's beginning to come back. You say I passed out?" Tracey rubbed the back of his neck, methodically massaging the muscles.

Loretta nodded. "We'd just finished the main course when you went very pale. Next thing I knew, you'd more or less keeled over." She pulled the chair closer to the coffee table and sat down, leaning towards him, and said earnestly: "John, are you *on* anything?"

He stopped rubbing and looking at her, completely blank. "On what? What d'you mean?"

She rolled her eyes upwards, cross that he was making her spell it out. "You know. Drugs. You can *trust* me," she added, a bitter note entering her voice. The remarks about her, and career women in general, in Mo Stephenson's letter were fresh in her memory.

"I haven't got the faintest idea what you're talking about." He leaned back and stretched out his arms. "God, I'm stiff. Why on earth did you bring me back here?" Suddenly he looked embarrassed. "You weren't—we didn't—"

"What?"

"*You* know." It was her turn to look blank and relief flickered in his eyes. "Obviously we didn't. Look, I'm sorry about last night—"

"*John*, you haven't answered my question."

"I told you, I've no idea what you're talking about."

"*That,*" she said, leaning forward and jabbing his forearm. "What was it?" She hesitated and added tentatively: "Heroin?"

"Heroin?" Tracey looked down at the puncture mark and began to laugh.

Loretta sat back in her chair. "What's so funny?"

"You are. Honestly, Loretta, do you have to be so melodramatic? You really want to know what this is?" He touched the pink dot with his finger and winced. "Christ, it's still sore."

She said nothing.

"A wasp sting," he said, grinning in anticipation of her reaction. "I was taking my jacket off before I got into the taxi and the little bugger got me. At the airport, this is. LaGuardia."

"You were stung by a wasp?"

"Well done, Loretta, full marks for comprehension. You know I'm allergic? I mean, I haven't been stung since I was a kid but you can't take risks. Some people go into what's-it-called, anaphylactic shock. Soon as I got to the hotel I asked the receptionist and she gave me the address of a doctor, some bloke they have an arrangement with. He gave me some

tablets, he said not to mix them with alcohol but I forgot."
Tracey saw Loretta's expression and added: "All right, that's not
strictly true, I thought he was being over-cautious. Obviously
he wasn't." He leaned forward and touched her bare knee.
"Sorry, love, did I give you a fright?"

She said stiffly: "Only insofar as I didn't have the faintest
idea what was wrong with you. And I had to get you out of the
restaurant, into a taxi and all the way up here."

"What floor are we on?"

"The fifteenth."

He grimaced. "If it's any consolation, I feel terrible. Like a
bad hangover or flu. Did you say something about coffee?"

"Mmm." She got up. "Black?"

"Please. I suppose I ought to take another one of those
tablets." He felt in his trouser pocket and brought out a foil-
covered strip.

Loretta said: "Should you? I mean, you've survived the
night."

Tracey shrugged and put them away. "You're probably
right. By the way—why didn't you put me in a taxi and send
me back to my hotel?"

"I didn't . . . I don't know where you're staying."

"The Gramercy Park. Right at the bottom of Lexington."

"Oh. Anyway, that's miles away."

"Is it? Where are we?"

"Riverside Drive." She moved towards the kitchen, tugging
at the bottom of her shirt, which she had gone back to bed in
and which suddenly seemed very short. The dog heard her approach and barked imperatively on the other side of the door.

"Don't let that animal in here!"

Loretta said over her shoulder: "She does live here. What's
the time? I'll have to take her for a walk soon."

"Twenty past nine."

"God, she must be desperate. Down, Honey, there's a good girl."

"Honey?" John Tracey called from the living room. "Sure it's not Fang? Or Saliva?"

Loretta closed the kitchen door while she made coffee for Tracey and tea for herself.

"What is this muck?" he asked when she returned with two mugs.

"It's instant." She yawned. "I didn't get much sleep last night, one way and another, and I couldn't be bothered to dig out the cafetière."

He tasted it. "It's not as bad as it looks. I have to go, Loretta, I have a piece to finish for tomorrow's paper and with the time difference."

"Whitewater?" she asked, thinking about their conversation in the restaurant.

"Mmm? No, something and nothing about some actress. I got a message on Thursday night, could I hold the stuff on Clinton and doorstep this actress instead. She's pregnant and won't say who's the father, not that I care but they wanted me to meet a photographer outside her flat yesterday morning."

Loretta looked up from her mug. "Yesterday morning?"

Tracey got up, groaning. "Christ, this sofa's uncomfortable." He grinned at Loretta, his good spirits apparently returning. "I notice you didn't let me have the bed."

"The bed?" She glanced over her shoulder.

"Only joking. As I was saying, I had to get up at the crack of dawn yesterday for the shuttle and as soon as I arrived in New York that bloody wasp got me. By the time I got to her flat she'd gone out, the photographer was thoroughly jacked off and I wasted the whole day chasing round New York in taxis. It'll have to be a cuttings job *and* they'll probably query my expenses. Where's the loo?"

"In there."

A moment later he emerged, still talking. "Can you imagine, Loretta, six months ago I was in Bosnia and now it's come to this, cobbling stuff together from the *National Enquirer*." He drank more coffee, put the half-empty mug on the table and planted a kiss on her cheek. "Thanks, love, I owe you one." He pulled on his jacket, checked that his wallet was in the inside pocket and went to the door. He turned, his hand on the latch. "You didn't really think I'd become a druggie, did you?"

Loretta flushed.

"It's all right," he said good-humouredly, "we'll talk about my dependent personality some other time." He waved and was gone.

In the kitchen Honey began to whine. Loretta ignored her and went into the bathroom, where she bundled the plastic shower curtain out of the way and turned on the bath taps. The phone rang and she went to answer it, still thinking about the wasp sting.

"Ms. Stramiello?" A woman's voice, clearly thrown by hearing Loretta.

"No, sorry, she's away for the weekend. Would you like to leave a message?"

"This is Dr. Rosenstein's secretary, her gynaecologist. Ms. Stramiello left an out-of-town number where she could be reached but it seems to be busy this morning. Do you have another number for her?"

"Sorry, no. Do you want to leave a message in case she rings me?"

"Please. Dr. Rosenstein needs to speak to her fairly

urgently. If I could leave a couple of numbers since it's Saturday . . ."

Instead of returning to the bathroom, Loretta thought for a moment and dialled the Sag Harbor number herself. There was a silence, then the engaged tone. "Damn," she said softly, looking down at her bare feet and wiggling her toes. She wondered what was taking so long, perhaps Jay's father was offering spiritual advice to a member of his flock?

Loretta remembered she had left the bath taps running. On her way to test the temperature of the water, the phone rang again.

"Shit," said Loretta, going back.

There was a pause. "Ms. Lawson? Donelly."

"He hasn't phoned again," she said rapidly, remembering the detective's homily about "profane" language. Then: "Oh— I suppose you'd know." She pushed her hair back from her forehead.

"That isn't why I'm calling, Ms. Lawson. There's been a development—"

"What? What d'you mean, a development?"

"I have a fax here from the lab. They've subjected your tape—"

"It's not *my* tape."

Another pause. "They've subjected the tape to a new system called anemone, the results are—"

"Anemone? You mean the flower?"

She heard the faint rustle of paper. "Ambient . . . Hold on a minute while I find the page. OK, this is it. ANEMONE— Ambient Noise Enhancement and Monitoring System. State-of-the-art stuff. By running your tape through ANEMONE, they've been able to detect a very faint noise in the background which they've tentatively identified as bells."

"*Bells?*"

"That's what it says here. Church bells."

Loretta breathed out. "What good's *that*? I don't see—"

Lieutenant Donelly said reprovingly: "I have an officer coming in to work on it right now, Ms. Lawson. Records are about to fax me a list of churches in Manhattan, with telephone numbers—"

"Churches in Manhattan?" She thought of St. Patrick's Cathedral on Fifth Avenue, and St. Ignatius Loyola on Park Avenue where Jackie Kennedy's funeral service had been held earlier in the year. "There must be . . . dozens. Hundreds. And what if he's calling from somewhere else? Kansas or . . . I don't know, California."

"We have no evidence to suggest he's calling long-distance. This may just give us a location—"

"Wait a minute. There's something I wanted to ask you, about whether the people who make obscene phone calls ever . . . whether there's any evidence of them going on to . . . other types of crimes?" She stood with her head bowed, clutching the receiver close to her ear. "I mean, is there any evidence that this man, Michael or whatever his real name is . . . Have any of his other victims reported being followed?"

"Excuse me?"

"Did any of the other women . . . Have any of them ever had the impression that someone was following them? Spying on them?"

"Ms. Lawson, are you suggesting this guy—that he's trying to make physical contact with you?" He sounded incredulous.

"Physical contact? That's an odd way of putting it but I suppose—yes."

"Ms. Lawson, you don't think you're over-reacting to what happened last night? I know these calls are highly disturbing to a woman on her own but we have no evidence that—what I'm saying, it's not his *style*."

"So far. You mean I *imagined* it?"

"Imagined . . . what precisely?"

She let out a sound which eloquently conveyed her exasperation. "Someone following me, at the Met and down Fifth Avenue. I'm—I'm an English lecturer, I'm *not* the sort of person who imagines things and I *know* he was there. I just *know* it."

"Take it easy, Ms. Lawson, I'm very grateful for your co-operation so far and I certainly don't want to jeopardise our—"

"Well, you have. I'm not sure I want to go on with this. I mean, whether he's following me or not, you're no nearer catching him than you were yesterday. All you've come up with is this nonsense about *bells*—"

"Hey, hey. Ms. Lawson." His voice was soothing, as though he was talking to a distressed child.

"There's no need to speak to me like that."

"I'm sorry, I guess this was just—unexpected. I'll file a report at once if you'd like to give me the details, where and when the incident happened. Let me find a—OK, fire away, I have a pen."

"Shit," exclaimed Loretta, remembering the bath taps. She threw down the receiver and rushed into the bathroom, where the water in the small tub was just beginning to lap over the side. She wrenched the taps off, slipping on the damp floor as she pulled out the plug, and hurried back to the phone.

"I've flooded the bathroom, can I ring you back in ten minutes?"

"Ten minutes? I have a meeting, maybe I could call you?"

"How long's the meeting going to go on?"

"An hour, then I have to go over to the lab. I could call at—would twelve suit you?"

"No, I'll be out all day."

"All day? What about tonight?"

Loretta remembered Kelly's message inviting her to a drinks party. "I'm coming back to change between, I don't know, five and six."

"Sure?" He sounded anxious, worried that he'd offended her. "I'd like to get these details down."

"Yes, I have to be somewhere at half past six."

"OK, I'll call between five and six." He rang off.

Still imprisoned in the kitchen, Honey began to howl—a high, despairing note Loretta hadn't heard before. "Oh God," she said, foreseeing another domestic emergency, and reached for the jeans she had put on when she went downstairs in search of the porter during the night.

"All right, I'm coming," she called to the dog, pulling her hair back from her face and securing it with a band from her jeans pocket. Honey hurled herself at the kitchen door as Loretta opened it, shooting past her into the living-room and performing a frenzied dance below the hook where Toni kept her lead. The dog was so obviously desperate that Loretta had time only to glance into the bathroom as she passed, reassuring herself that the water had almost drained away, before allowing Honey to drag her through the front door and round the corner to the lift.

It was around eleven when Loretta finally left the flat, her plans for the morning upset by a prolonged heavy shower which had only just eased off. Steam rose from the pavement as she headed towards the junction of Amsterdam Avenue and Broadway, the air a damp caress on her bare arms and the triangle of her neck and throat not covered by her cotton dress. Almost every parked car she passed had a handwritten notice taped to a window or lying on the dashboard: "no radio," "no valuables," and from one particularly despairing owner, "no nothing." Loretta's own car radio had been stolen twice in six months in Oxford but it had never occurred to her to plead with potential thieves in this way. A resigned acceptance to crime seemed to be woven into the fabric of everyday life in New York, so much so that even the TV weather forecast she had watched before leaving Toni's flat was squeezed between live news reports from a siege somewhere in the East Village. Loretta had sat down to watch, fascinated and horrified, as a reporter on the spot described how three men with masks and guns had burst into a sports shop earlier that morning, giving the manager just enough time as they entered to press a panic button. Now he, his assistant, the raiders and an unknown number of customers were holed up inside the shop, the street cleared of people and traffic except for police marksmen, the inevitable TV crews and a negotiator trained to deal with hostage situations.

That was how the reporter had characterised it in her terse, rapid-fire commentary: "a fast-developing hostage situation." Loretta wondered whether the people in the shop would get out alive; the camera had zoomed in briefly on one of the window displays, trainers and steel-framed tennis racquets and Speedo swimming costumes, and she thought how awful it would be to die for a pair of Nikes. The live coverage of the siege was interspersed with cheery updates on the weekend weather, colourful maps of New York and Long Island with dark clouds like a child's first attempt at drawing scudding across the shoreline. Loretta had pulled a light summer dress over her head and fastened the buttons, thinking that the outfit had not yet been invented which could withstand the volatile climatic conditions of New York. Immediately she felt guilty for worrying about such trivialities when lives were at stake only a few miles across the city, not that there was any way that she could affect the outcome. She had turned the sound down on the TV while she tried Jay's parents again, her eyes fixed on the small screen, and was annoyed but not surprised to get the answering-machine. Hardly bothering to disguise her irritation, she relayed Dr. Rosenstein's message and left another one of her own, pointing out that she was still waiting for Toni to ring her back.

Loretta turned south on to Broadway, occasionally skipping sideways to avoid being splashed by thoughtless drivers. The heat was sticky and intense, the brief interval of freshness after the storm ending almost as soon as the rain clouds passed over. Loretta could not understand how anyone managed to live in New York all year round, especially people like Toni whose only access to green space was in scruffy urban parks like Riverside. It occurred to her that Toni must be planning to move to a larger apartment, perhaps with Jay, if the calls to and from Dr. Rosenstein's office meant what she thought they did. She stopped to watch two women carry buckets of flowers out of a shop and set them up on the pavement, most of the blooms taller and much more striking than anything Loretta had seen for sale in England. The birds of paradise were especially exotic, their orange and purple heads shaped like beaks, and the vibrant red of amaryllis contrasted with the slender whiteness of lilies. Loretta was admiring frilly white heads of dill when one of the assistants emerged with a container of green roses—dyed, of course, but no less alluring for that—and she was sorely tempted to buy the lot. She would only be able to enjoy them for a day but Toni would be back on Monday and they'd probably last well beyond that. Common sense restrained her, she could hardly continue her walk down Broadway with her arms full of flowers, so she memorised the location of the florist instead. She'd almost certainly pass it later on her way back to the flat.

Three or four minutes later dark clouds rolled over and translucent pearls of rain dropped out of the sky, dissolving in warm pools as they made contact with her skin. Loretta had never experienced hot rain before; the sensation was disconcerting but not unpleasant until the drops began to multiply. Within minutes the wide skirt of her cotton dress clung damply to her legs, her toes were gritty in her open-toed sandals and her hair hung about her face in damp tendrils. A bus swept past and Loretta broke into a trot, catching up with it at a bus stop a few yards down the road. She waited as the woman ahead of her in the queue methodically shook and furled a large umbrella, ascending the steps with maddening slowness while Loretta fretted behind her. She took the last window seat, sliding gratefully across and running her hands through her wet hair. According to her map, which she unfolded as soon as she'd finished trying to repair her appearance, they would soon be in the Theater District, passing right through the middle of Times Square.

By now the rain was hurling itself against the glass, obscuring her view of shopfronts and people sheltering from the rain. Loretta studied the map, turning it sideways to read the names of the few churches it marked. Plenty of other landmarks were shown, places she'd heard about in films or books without knowing their location: Radio City on Sixth Avenue, the United Nations headquarters on First, Bellevue Hospital a few blocks down from the U.N., but the map was clearly not intended for the more devout tourist. Loretta assumed that one of Donelly's subordinates was even now working his or her way down a list of ecclesiastical telephone numbers, questioning puzzled clerics as to whether they were in the habit of holding services on Friday nights. Evensong? Loretta was so ignorant about the liturgy that she had no idea whether bells were rung before an evening service and it occurred to her that the faint sound on the tape might just as easily be bell practice. The exercise seemed a waste of time and resources, such a long shot as hardly to justify the cost of making the calls, but she supposed Donelly's unit had to do something to justify its existence. She tugged at her skirt, which was bunched uncomfortably under her, and went back to the map, this time trying to remember the name of John Tracey's hotel. He'd said it was at the far end of Lexington and she traced the avenue with her finger until she came to what she was looking for: it ended at East Twenty-first Street, at a small green blob marked on the map as Gramercy Park, which she recognised as the name of his hotel. He should have finished his story by now and faxed it over although he might still be dealing with subs and lawyers in London. Loretta thought she'd give him a bit more time before calling to ask if he had time to meet her for a drink before she left New York the following evening.

She yawned, thinking how fond she was of Tracey. They had been getting on very well in the last few months, better than at any time since their divorce, and he was her closest male friend in spite of their surface incompatibilities. Knowing him as well as she did, she could not imagine him settling down in some backwater in Hampshire; his natural habitat, if not actually a war zone, was somewhere with a population of several million and plenty of late-opening bars. He had an exhaustive knowledge of London by night, once taking her to an all-night café in Brick Lane where a burly man with a glass eye acknowledged him with the slightest of nods. Tracey refused to reveal the man's identity, even to Loretta, but said they had "helped each other out" on numerous occasions. Loretta suspected he was a retired mercenary, if such a species existed.

Tracey occasionally sent her maudlin letters from war-ravaged East European cities, talking longingly of having someone to come home to, but they were usually written late at night and, Loretta guessed, under the influence of several whiskies. In a recent telephone call to San Francisco he had even spoken regretfully of the fact that they hadn't had children, prompting an acerbic reply from Loretta; she was fairly sure that Tracey liked to indulge in wistful regret about not being a father while having someone else to blame for a situation that suited him very well. She had noticed that he soon tired of his boisterous twin nephews on the rare occasions he paid a visit to his brother and sister-in-law's house in Ealing.

The bus stopped and an overweight woman in tight red trousers lumbered down the aisle and fell into the seat next to Loretta. She exuded an odour Loretta couldn't quite identify, stale food and old perfume, and she turned her head to the window, wrinkling her nose to shut it out. She yawned again and did not at first notice that the rain had very nearly stopped, skimming down in diagonal lines so fine as to be almost invisible. A weak sun was struggling to come out, as yet only a luminous disc in an opaque white sky, but Loretta guessed that the weather was about to make another of its abrupt changes. The fat woman reached into her bag and drew out a Hershey bar, peeled off the wrapper and broke it in halves; the smell of the chocolate reminded Loretta she was hungry. She had skipped breakfast for the second day running and her last uninterrupted meal, in the restaurant at the Met, was almost twenty-four hours ago. Shaking off the trancelike mood of passivity which had settled on her since she got on the bus, she stood up and asked her neighbour rather brusquely to allow her to pass.

"You getting off, honey?" The fat woman turned on her a smile of such transparent benevolence that Loretta felt ashamed of herself. She nodded, retrieved the remains of the Hershey bar as it slipped to the floor and received another radiant smile when she returned it. Standing passengers blocked her way to the doors and she eased herself through, reaching the exit just as the bus stopped. On the pavement she blinked in the bright sunshine and felt in her bag for her sunglasses, discovering when she put them on that she was much further down Broadway than she thought. She had somehow managed to miss the Flatiron building, one of her favourite New York landmarks, and a glance at the map told her she was almost at Union Square. She walked a couple of blocks, hot and damp but confident that the heat would soon dry her clothes, and spotted an *espresso* bar on the other side of the road. She crossed, dodging through stationary traffic, and studied an inviting window display of *patisserie*: Danish pastries, *pains au chocolat*, and *croissants* studded with apricots as round and glutinously yellow as egg yolks. Her mouth began to water and she went inside, took a table near the window and ordered a double *espresso*, an apricot *croissant* and, feeling only slightly greedy, a warmed-up *pain au chocolat*.

7

Loretta was examining a secondhand copy of her most recent book, looking inside the cover to see if the person who had sold it to the huge bookshop on Broadway had left any trace. There was nothing, no name or dedication, only the price in pencil, and she was miffed to find it disposed of so quickly. The American edition had not been out long, no more than six months, and she was mildly affronted by the speed with which it had found its way onto a table displaying unsorted volumes which fell vaguely under the heading of language and literary criticism: dusty hardbacks which had long ago lost their jackets, scruffy paperbacks, books by and about Barthes and Foucault back to back with F. R. Leavis. Loretta's book stood out in its shiny jacket, the bright red lettering of the title, *Milton's Cook: Fiction's Invisible Woman*, super-imposed on a reproduction of Eve being expelled from Paradise from the Brancacci chapel in Florence. On the back cover was the quotation from *Shirley* which had suggested the title, the heroine's complaint that Milton was unable to visualise Eve when he was writing *Paradise Lost* and had mixed her up with his cook.

Loretta held the book so it fell open, turning her head sideways to examine the picture of herself on the back flap. It had been taken in London by a friend of John Tracey, an occasional contributor to the *Sunday Herald* magazine who patiently experimented with studio lamps until the light was just right—highlighting her cheekbones and creating a soft glow around her hair. Staring at the black-and-white image now, aware of the ratty curls on her forehead and her dress sticking to her body after another torrential rainstorm, Loretta couldn't quite connect it with herself. Nor, it seemed, could John Tracey; when she showed him the contact prints, he had paid her the dubious compliment of exclaiming "God, Loretta, you look quite sexy!"—a remark she had brooded over all the way back to Oxford.

Someone came and stood beside her, picking up books and discarding them with startling rapidity. She moved sideways, furtively sliding her own volume back onto the table, and the young man, who looked like a student, pounced on it and began to read the blurb. Loretta inched round the table until they were on opposite sides, her eyes flicking up every few seconds to gauge his reaction. He had a narrow, pale face under thick dark hair and although she could not see his eyes, she was not at all surprised when he flipped the book shut and slid it back on the table. She sighed, the air rushing out of her lungs like a deflating balloon even though she hadn't known she was holding her breath.

Struggling not to take the rejection personally, Loretta lowered her head and immediately a name leapt up at her from a book jacket. Her hand shot out, colliding with the bony fingers of the pale young man who had also spotted it. "Sorry," she said, gripping the book firmly as he said, "Excuse me," and tried to take it from her. They glared at each other and Loretta said, without much justification: "I think I got there first."

The student shrugged and let go with a bad grace. Loretta put down her purse, which she had taken the precaution of removing from her bag before handing it in at the front desk, and examined the plain blue volume. It was not a proof, as she first thought, but a finished copy in the style of some austere French publishing house, Gallimard say, rather than the small university press whose imprint it bore. *Form, Fiction, Phallacy: Re-Reading the Victorians* by Hugh Puddephat, she read in small black type, trying to ignore the scowling presence of the student on the far side of the table.

"The late Hugh Puddephat," the biographical details began, and Loretta's eyes widened in surprise. She hadn't known of a posthumous edition of Puddephat's work, she couldn't recall seeing a review in the *TLS* but it was an American edition and expensive—almost an exercise in vanity publishing, she thought, given the quality of Puddephat's earlier books. An explanatory note revealed that he had all but completed a collection of essays at the time of his death, and that they had been brought together in this volume by his "friend, colleague and admirer," an obscure American academic called Irving Ashby. Loretta read:

The late Hugh Puddephat was one of the most brilliant minds of his generation. He was known to colleagues in France and the United States as an incisive interpreter of Foucault, Althusser, Derrida—those iconoclasts grouped loosely round the École Normale Supérieure in Paris. Dr. Puddephat's project was to import their methods into the profoundlyinsular climate of English academe, of which hisown college, St. Mark's, Oxford, was unfortunately representative.

Undeterred by the intemperate and frequently personal attacks of his critics, he was unflinching in his determination to apply structuralist theory to the icons of the English literary canon.

Loretta let out a "hmmph," indicating her sceptical attitude to this hagiography of the dead don. She had never actually spoken to him, their connection had come too late for that, but as far as she knew he had got into Althusser and Paul de Man just as everyone else was getting out. A joke in thoroughly bad taste came into her head, something about the death of the author, and she was shocked by her own callousness: after all, the man had been killed when he was in his early forties. Apparently the habit was catching, for a moment later she came to a bit about Puddephat having been "cut down in his prime"—a singularly unfortunate phrase to apply to someone who had fallen victim to a savage and still unsolved knife attack in a dingy flat in Paris. There was no mention of it in the biographical notes, just Puddephat's dates and the information that he had died suddenly in France. Loretta chewed her bottom lip as she glanced through essays on Dickens, Wilkie Collins, the Brontës, and George Eliot, uncomfortable with the memories the book had stirred up. It was all a long time ago, she told herself, and found a welcome distraction in being able to identify the exact point in the essays at which Puddephat had discovered Jacques Lacan and Hélène Cixous.

"Who can be said to 'possess the phallus' in *Wuthering Heights*?" Puddephat asked pompously. "The most obvious candidate, Heathcliff, runs away precisely at that moment when he is forced, by overhearing Cathy's denunciation of him to Nelly Dean, into an admission of its ontological lack: his failure, in Lacanian terms, to act as the whip/phallus for which Cathy, in furious recognition of her own castration, begs her father at the book's outset."

A rumour had reached Oxford, via the French police, that Puddephat was an early victim of a serial killer who had never been caught—the Gay Ripper, as the British tabloids inevitably called him when the story got into the press. A senior detective in Paris had been quoted in the *Guardian* to the effect that the same man was believed to be responsible for the deaths of five gay men and a female transvestite in and around the Rue Monge, the area Puddephat had been staying in when he died. The bizarre detail about the transvestite caused a flurry of excitement at North Oxford dinner parties where former colleagues of the dead don affected always to have known he was gay, in spite of his very public marriage to a peer's daughter. On one occasion Loretta had even heard it whispered, as the port was being passed, that Hugh Puddephat was wearing a blonde wig, low-cut red dress and stiletto heels when he was attacked. Not only did this make no sense—the murdered transvestite was a woman dressed as a man, not the other way round—but Loretta found herself sitting miserably between her host and a Classics don from St. Mark's, Puddephat's college, as they vied with each other to produce yet more scurrilous details. As soon as she could do it without drawing attention to herself, she made an excuse about an early lecture the following morning and left.

She closed Hugh Puddephat's book with a snap. The pale young man had moved away and she put it on the table as far from *Milton's Cook* as was physically possible. It was stiflingly hot, a foetid combination of airlessness and perspiration which seemed to be untouched by the plug-in electric fans whirring at intervals throughout the shop, and Loretta would have left at once if she hadn't promised to look for an out-of-print book on Samuel Richardson for her friend Bridget Bennett. She picked up the cookery book she had found earlier and turned her head towards the tall bookcases at the rear, dismayed by the sheer number of books crammed into them. Doubting whether she would even be able to find the right section, she walked reluctantly towards the back of the shop, thinking that with every breath she took she was inhaling the effluvium of dead knowledge. This morbid mood was doubtless something to do with encountering Hugh Puddephat's book and Loretta tried to shake it off, holding herself very straight and approaching the shelves in a deliberately businesslike fashion. She was standing on tiptoe, reaching upwards in the dark, narrow space between two high bookcases when a quiet voice inquired: "Excuse me?"

She turned. "Sorry, am I in your way?"

The woman who had spoken shook her head. She was shorter than Loretta, dark and fine-featured, probably in her late forties though her immaculate make-up made it hard to tell, wearing a short black skirt, uncreased white blouse and half-a-dozen gold chains. In one hand she held a recent novel, most likely an unwanted review copy, and in the other Loretta's purse.

"You left this. Back there." She indicated with her head.

"Did I?" Loretta felt a belated spurt of alarm. "God, how stupid of me. It's got everything in it, all my credit cards and . . . well, everything."

"You're English, right?" She peered up at Loretta, holding her head at an angle that was almost birdlike. "Is this your first time in New York? You should take more care, it's lucky I got there first."

"First?"

"There was a guy." She half-turned, surveying the shop, still talking in a low, curiously unemphatic voice. "I don't see him now but I thought he knew you."

"Oh," said Loretta, much relieved. "Young, with short dark hair? We were both after the same book, that's all."

The woman shook her head. "Guy I'm talking about was older, thirty-five, forty? It's hard to tell with these guys who lose their hair. It happened with my first husband, he was twenty-eight when I divorced him and people regularly took him for forty." She patted her matte black bob, which looked dyed to Loretta. "I used to say, he got the knives and forks, I got the hair."

"What?"

"Joke," she explained laconically. "Guy I'm talking about, he's five nine, five ten, kind of flushed because he's carrying too much weight—a hundred eighty, maybe a hundred ninety pounds?" She added in explanation: "I'm a nutritionist, I see guys off and on the scales all the time. You're how much, one twenty?"

Loretta said distractedly: "I don't know, not in pounds. You say he . . . you think he was after my purse?"

"That's how it looked. I see him watching from across the way"—again she gestured towards the front of the shop—"and at first he has a look on his face, kind of puzzled, like he's trying to work out where he saw you before. So I'm saying to my-self OK, most likely the guy knows her, no call to get spooked. But all the time I'm thinking about my friend Miriam, she's in a store on Thirty-fourth Street three, maybe four weeks ago. Guy pushes up against her, she says what-the-hell and he's full of apologies, I'm so sorry, my wife's sick, on his way to the hos-pital and so on. And you know what?"

Loretta shook her head.

"She gets home and takes off her jacket and there's"—she lowered her voice—"*stuff* on it."

"Stuff?"

"You know. He jerked off on her."

Loretta stared.

"So when I see this guy watching you, I'm thinking—uh-oh. And it's as well I did, because soon's you walk away I see he's got his eye on your wallet."

"Five feet ten? And bald?" There was a hollow feeling in Loretta's throat.

"Bald, no. He had some hair left here," she patted her own head, more or less on the crown. "I guess it was kind of brown. Mean anything to you?"

"I'm not sure." She tried to think, disturbed by some-thing the woman had said without being able to pin down what it was. "You're absolutely certain it was me he was look-ing at?"

"Sure I'm sure." She turned her wrist and read the time on a gold watch, small and elegant like herself. "I have to pay for my book. You want this or not?"

Loretta took her purse. "Sorry, I was just . . . I mean, it's not a nice thought, someone watching me."

The woman touched her lightly on the arm. "This is New York, hon. You take care now."

"Yes," said Loretta, watching her walk away. "Yes, I will. And thank you."

"You're welcome. Have a nice day."

Loretta remained where she was, the book she was supposed to be looking for quite forgotten. The woman's watch had said twenty past two, there was no point in going straight back to Toni's flat because the bad-tempered porter wouldn't be back on duty until four o'clock that afternoon. She had discovered this from his replacement when she went downstairs at five o'clock in the morning; they worked eight-hour shifts and the black porter had ended his stint the previous night at ten, while she was still worrying about whether to call a doctor for Tracey. Although he had volunteered almost nothing about the man who tried to sneak upstairs to Toni's flat, Loretta thought the result might be different if she asked specific questions: if she were to put to him, that is, the description she had just been given by the nutritionist. She leaned back against the dusty shelves, tiredness and anxiety catching up with her again. After her stupid mistake over the wasp sting she had been willing to concede John Tracey might be right, that her imagination had been working overtime since she stepped off the plane at LaGuardia, especially when she also had Donelly's scepticism to contend with. But this was different, this time she had corroboration from someone else that she was being watched, a description even, and the woman hadn't seemed like a crank. She had made a rather cruel joke about her ex-husband but that hardly made her a nutter—

Loretta hugged the cookery book to her chest. She had intended to get a taxi from the bookshop to the Frick on East Seventieth and Fifth but now she wavered, tempted to go back to Toni's flat and wait for the porter to come on duty so she could interrogate him at once. Then she asked herself what she would do in the meantime, other than sit miserably in Toni's flat with only the bulldog for company. If someone *was* following her, she was probably safer in a public place, with other people around, than alone in a fifteenth-floor flat where the neighbours might not even hear, or do anything, if she called for help. She levered herself forward from the bookshelves, ran a hand through her damp hair and moved back into the main section of the shop, glancing right and left as she headed for the tills. There was no queue and she handed the cookery book to an assistant, a puzzled look passing across her face as she watched it being wrapped and tried to remember why it had seemed so important half an hour ago to buy a collection of authentic Cajun recipes. She handed over twenty dollars, put away her change and collected her shoulder bag from the counter next to the door. Outside the pavement glistened with moisture under a bright blue sky but Loretta was too preoccupied to notice, struggling to fit the book into her bag while the vague outline of the man the nutritionist had described continued to trouble her. Something in the woman's description had started a train of thought, some detail Loretta couldn't quite pin down, and she hardly registered a distant, retreating rumble of thunder, the tail end of a storm she hadn't even noticed in the gloomy recesses of the bookshop. Glancing up and down the street in a nervous, disjointed way, she finally recalled what she was supposed to be doing and stepped off the curb with her hand upraised.

"Taxi," she called, uncertain whether the scruffy yellow vehicle with the buckled fender was about to stop, and jumped back as it squealed to a halt and threw up a plume of dirty water which only just missed her ankles.

The eyes were heavy-lidded, languorous, as though their owner was on the verge of sleep; the nose flared gently, in perfect harmony with the smooth contours of the cheeks. Loretta stepped back, as though the slightest noise from her might break into the unknown woman's reverie, and then laughed at herself. The marble woman had been in the same position for around five hundred years, she was not even particularly life-like when Loretta came to study her properly, mainly because the sculptor had left the eyes blank. Loretta took out her floor plan and studied it, discovering she was not yet half-way round the collection, and wished she had brought someone with her, even John Tracey; Bridget Bennett had once unfairly accused him of not knowing the difference between Canaletto and cannelloni but he did at least have a sense of humour. Loretta was surprised by the reverential posture of the other people going round the gallery, their awkward, mincing gait as they walked across priceless carpets, their acquiescent admiration of works of art which did not move her at all.

She was increasingly out of sympathy with the late Mr. Frick, who appeared to have written out cheques indiscriminately, his taste not so much eclectic as random. To be fair, she was hardly in the mood to appreciate dozens of old masters, most of them unfamiliar to her or in styles she disliked; each time she moved from picture to picture, or stopped to look at a piece of furniture, she could not examine it properly until she had first thrown a nervous glance over her shoulder to see if anyone was showing undue interest in her. It was actually a rather pointless exercise as she had only someone else's vague description to go on; she spotted several balding, overweight men but none of them was alone, as far as she could tell, or absorbed in anything other than the Goyas and Gainsboroughs. She was left with a restless sensation of anxiety and an unusually clear idea of the kind of people, their ages and class and nationalities, who visited the Frick. She had arrived at the East

Seventieth Street entrance at the same time as a small group of Swedes, mother, father and two teenage children, who were progressing through the gallery at roughly the same pace, their four blonde heads always immediately behind or just ahead. She had passed two American women so often that they had begun to nod like distant friends although their taste was radically different from hers. They were slender, wearing almost identical sleeveless dresses, one with a pastel cashmere cardigan draped over her shoulders—it was at least cool in the Frick, presumably more out of consideration for the pictures than the visitors—and while their ages were hard to judge, their restrained gestures spoke eloquently of inherited wealth.

They were talking in hushed tones when she arrived in the Boucher room, murmuring their admiration in voices so low that Loretta could catch only an occasional word: peerless, ravishing, incomparable. Loretta had turned from the brunette's upturned face—which bore, she realised, a slight resemblance to Jackie Kennedy—to the first of the four canvases, a dainty female with a rosebud mouth representing Spring. Boucher had painted her on a mossy river bank, her youthful swain plaiting flowers in her hair, and she appeared to be quite unconcerned by the damp rising up through her gold satin frock and knickers—if she was wearing any, which the three fleshy nymphs in the next canvas, Summer, conspicuously were not. Loretta moved towards it and found herself performing an awkward little dance with the New Yorkers as they tried to share out the confined space. Two of the Summer nymphs were naked, sprawling on their discarded petticoats in a way which drew attention to the middle female's generously proportioned and flamboyantly unclothed posterior; the third was *en déshabillé* in yards of white gauze whose lack of resemblance to any standard item of female dress made Loretta raise her eyebrows, like Flora Poste quizzically observing some benign but inexplicable bucolic rite in *Cold Comfort Farm*.

Next door, in the Fragonard room, Loretta had been confronted by an even less restrained exhibition of posturing youths, simpering girls and snogging *putti*. The Jackie Kennedy lookalike and her friend caught up, immediately exclaiming over the delicacy of flesh tones, the *exquisite* rendering of the foliage. Loretta idly looked up the history of the paintings in her guide book, learning that they had been commissioned by Mme Du Barry, mistress of Louis XV, for her house near Versailles. Three years later—inexplicably, according to the guide, although Loretta thought the charitable explanation was a belated attack of good taste—Mme Du Barry had sent them back; speculating that they had perhaps distracted Madame from her functions as a royal mistress, minimal as Loretta conjectured those to be, she decided she would rather live with anything, including late 1980s Laura Ashley, than all these garlands, ribbons, parasols, doves, urns and waterfalls. There was even something that looked like—Loretta stood on tiptoe, trying and failing to make out what it really was—a discarded Thermos flask, abandoned by one of the frisky *putti*.

She had left the New Yorkers in silent rapture in the Fragonard room but now they had caught up, stationing themselves in front of the Italian marble bust which had attracted Loretta's attention. It took her a moment to realise, from their rapid hand movements and facial expressions, that they were disagreeing—*sotto voce* of course, but she only had to move a couple of steps closer to hear what they were saying. The dispute seemed to be about style, whether the bust was "Classical" or "Archaic," but it was sufficiently heated to have brought two bright spots of colour to the blonde's powdery cheeks. Loretta wondered what they were really arguing about, what deep and unacknowledged rift in their friendship had been displaced on to this trivial subject, and was fascinated by the speed with which the dispute died down. It was the brunette who gave way, lifting her hand and flaring the fingers as if by doing so she was literally dropping the subject, and a moment later they walked away. Loretta followed at a safe distance, overtaking the Swedes again and noting that they seemed to have fallen into conversation with a French couple. In the west gallery, which turned out to be by far the largest room in the house, Loretta paused just inside the door, overwhelmed by its size and the sheer number of paintings. It reminded her of the National Gallery in London and she puzzled over Mr. and Mrs. Frick's decision to build and live in a house which so closely resembled a public institution. She drifted towards the small enamel room at the far end, unable to imagine anyone holding a normal domestic conversation about holidays or what to have for dinner in the presence of all these Constables and Turners.

Ten minutes later she decided she had had enough and went through the oval room into the central courtyard she had glimpsed through the long windows in the living hall. There was a pond with a fountain surrounded by small shrubs, a formal arrangement which made her think of Italy, and for the first time she was able to imagine the house as it might have been in 1910 or 1920. Presumably Mrs. Frick had been a socialite, using it as a setting for smart parties: women in dresses by Worth and Callot Soeurs, the men with slick-backed hair, darkly elegant in tail coats and patent leather shoes. Loretta walked the length of the courtyard, politely stepping to one side to allow some Germans to pass, looked back over her shoulder to see if there was room for a small orchestra, a string quartet perhaps or a jazz band . . .

She froze. He was in the far corner, in a doorway, not the one she had come through, his receding hair covered by a baseball cap. A map was open in his beefy hands and Loretta pirouetted silently on the spot, as though he might hear her even at this distance. At first she wasn't absolutely sure, the body shape was right but his face was hidden; in any case, it had been dark in the theatre and his voice was the thing she remembered most. She took a couple of steps towards him and he lifted his head, recognised her and flushed a dull red. The colour rose from his neck just as it had when she turned down his invitation to go for a drink after the play, and the next thing she knew he was trying to fold the map, giving up almost immediately and stuffing it in his jacket pocket. He turned on his heel and she plunged after him, elbowing her way through a voluble group of Italian teenagers, "Excuse me, *excuse* me," recalling with horror how much she had told him about herself, where she lived in England, what she did, even where she was staying in New York. She had had a bad feeling about him right from the start, when he was telling her about his intended visit to Oxford, but he had bought Toni's ticket and she had wanted to be polite—

She came to an abrupt halt in an unfamiliar room and in the few seconds it took her eyes to adjust to the low light saw that she had caught up with him. Furious, she advanced.

"What d'you think you're *doing*, following me like this? How *dare* you? I'm going to—"

His face worked, he was almost as agitated as she was, and he began to bluster.

"Lady, you got the wrong guy. I never saw you in my life."

"*What?* It was you, yesterday at the Met, I told you I was going, I *knew* someone—" She stopped, panting for breath, with no idea what to do next. "The theatre, you had the seat

next to me, I sold you the ticket . . ." A pleading note entered
her voice, the room was filling up and she just wanted him to
admit it. "This morning, in the bookshop, you followed me
there as well but someone saw you, she scared you off—"

She faltered and he took advantage of her confusion,
spreading his arms wide and appealing to the crowd: "Like I
said, I never saw her before."

"He's lying! He's been following me everywhere—"

"*Following* you?" He pointed to his head, sensing that the
onlookers had not made up their mind whose side to take,
and made a twisting motion. "I mean, this is loony-tunes
time." Someone behind Loretta giggled and she saw him relax
a fraction. "You hear about the crazies in New York but you
don't expect . . . This's something to tell the folks back in
Ohio."

"Ohio?" Loretta pounced on the detail. "That's what you
said on Friday, in the interval, *The Sisters Rosensweig*, you come
from Ohio and you're married and you have a daughter . . ."

He flushed again and his eyes glittered. "This really is Fantasy Island. I wasn't in no theatre last night, I went to see *True
Lies*. You seen it?" he asked someone in the crowd, spotting a
sympathetic face. "You oughta go, it's a great movie."

Loretta put her hand up to her head. "I meant *Thursday*."

"First she says Friday, then she says Thursday. I mean, all
I'm doing is standing here waiting for my girlfriend, she went
to find the ladies' room—"

"Your *girlfriend*?"

"What's so weird about that, guy having a girlfriend?" Suddenly his expression changed, fear and cunning playing tag
across his face as he focused on something or someone behind
Loretta. "Here she is now. You find the bathroom, hon?"

"Sure, Eric." A blonde in a mini-skirt pushed past, lifting

her pinched face interrogatively when she reached his side. "What's going on? Who're all these people?"

"What's going on is, the lady here"—he indicated Loretta—"made a mistake, she thought I was some guy she knew, some guy who stood her up—"

Loretta exclaimed: "What?"

"Like I said, it's OK, no need for you to worry. I never saw her before."

People were beginning to drift away, sensing that the scene was over. Loretta swallowed, knowing she'd been outmanoeuvred. She started at a light touch on her left arm, turning to see the woman who looked like Jackie Kennedy, the one who had admired the Fragonards. She said quietly: "Are you all right? Can I help?"

Loretta shook her head, embarrassed and upset. She let out a long shuddering breath. "I made a . . . I thought I recognised . . ." She stopped, certain she hadn't been mistaken but with no idea what was really going on. "I thought I knew him," she said, flapping her hand listlessly in the direction of the man in the baseball cap.

"Let's go," she heard him say to the girl. "You wanna visit the shop?"

Loretta watched their retreating backs, puzzling over the blonde's identity; she could give him twenty years, and if she really was his girlfriend, why would he bother following a woman he'd met briefly at the theatre?

"You want to sit down?"

The dark-haired woman was still regarding her with concern. Loretta shook her head, just wanting to leave: "Thanks, no, I'll be all right."

The woman rejoined her friend. A thought occurred to Loretta, a faint hope of throwing some light on the mystery:

the black porter would soon be back on duty at Toni's apartment block, if she described the man in the baseball cap—Eric, he seemed to be called—the porter might at least be able to tell her whether he remotely resembled the would-be intruder at the flats. Some of her energy came back at the prospect of having something practical to do and she hurried to the cloakroom where she'd left her bag.

She had been in the air-conditioned gallery long enough to have forgotten the heat and as she pushed open the swing doors she experienced a disconcerting illusion of reversal, as though she was entering a ludicrously overheated building rather than stepping outside. The late afternoon air was an overpowering mixture of humidity and car fumes, so tangibly dirty that Loretta was reluctant to inhale it. Trying to limit herself to short, shallow breaths, she hurried down the path to East Seventieth Street, hoping she had left the air-conditioning turned on in Toni's flat.

8

"So what do I say, congratulations I guess. I mean, I was kind of surprised when Don brought up the mail this morning and said you wrote me a letter but . . . not as *surprised* as when I opened it." The woman hesitated, so absorbed in what she was saying that she seemed to have forgotten she was speaking into an answering-machine. "You know, I really hadn't an *idea* you were planning this, it must have been all set up when I saw you last week and you didn't say a word . . . Hon, are you sure you—hell, I didn't mean to say . . . When are you back in town? *Call* me, OK? It doesn't matter what time."

The message ended without the caller giving her name and Loretta added "woman with friend/lover called Don, wants you to call her" below the two messages she'd already taken off the machine. They were both from Toni's friends, one male, one female, and putting the three together it was clear they'd all received notes from Toni in that morning's post announcing she was getting married. Not at some unspecified time in the future, either, but *today*, Saturday. The next caller identified herself as Alice and gushed into the answering-machine, *thrilled* by the news, and Loretta stroked Honey's head absently as she waited for the arch exclamations of surprise and pleasure to end. She was feeling uncomfortable, remembering how Toni had held up the white Bloomingdale's dress and inquired anxiously if it was too short, unable to recall whether this had come before or after her own reckless denunciation of marriage and live-in relationships. She lifted her head and stared unseeingly across the room at the silent, flickering TV screen, and it occurred to her for the first time that Jay's father had probably officiated at the ceremony. She pulled a face at the prospect of evangelistic excess raised by this thought; they had probably been in church all morning, singing and swaying and clapping, and it was hardly surprising Toni had been too busy to return her calls.

The tape beeped and she was relieved to hear Tracey's voice, even though it was distracted and irritable.

"Loretta? Are you there? If you are can you pick up the phone? Damn, I've missed you. What are all those beeps, I thought you didn't know anyone in New York? Listen, I got your message, I was going to ring you back but the lawyer phoned. Can you believe it? After all that coming and going yesterday they *pulled* the bloody thing. They've got these trainees who come in on Saturdays, kids with law degrees, it's cheaper than having a proper libel lawyer on staff, and this guy knows as much about libel as my—he doesn't know his arse from his elbow. Anyway." He sighed, and abruptly cheered up. "Are you doing anything tonight? There's this restaurant I've heard about, down in TriBeCa, it's a bit of a hike but we can get a taxi. How about you coming here around half seven for a drink? I'll meet you in the bar downstairs, turn right as you come through the front door. If I don't hear from you I'll assume that's OK." He spluttered for a moment, a classic smoker's cough. "Sorry about that. I was just going to say I . . . um, I owe you one for last night."

Loretta frowned. Kelly Sibon's drinks party was that evening, at her apartment on the Upper East Side, and she couldn't possibly leave in time to get to the Gramercy Park Hotel by half past seven. On the other hand, Kelly hadn't said anything about dinner afterwards and Loretta was keen to see John Tracey again before she went home. Assuming she could get hold of him, or leave another message at his hotel, she should be able to meet him later at the restaurant he had mentioned, wherever it was . . . The tape rewound and she sagged on the bed, lifting her hands and covering her face, a gesture which prompted the dog to throw back her head and howl.

"What's the matter?" Loretta demanded, leaning forward and putting her hand under the dog's chin. Honey returned her gaze, pleading for reassurance. Loretta said: "Do you have to be so *sensitive?*" and the dog let out a loud sneeze, showering her with droplets of saliva. Loretta wiped her hands on the skirt of her dress, glad she had something to change into for Kelly's party. Across the room, on TV, a succession of adverts flashed past, commercials for breakfast cereal, Toyota cars, Preparation H and a compilation CD of the world's greatest love songs—a nice juxtaposition, Loretta thought, watching the singers mouthing soundlessly, haemorrhoid cream and romance. She stroked the dog's head, wondering how Honey would cope with Toni's pregnancy, which had also been confirmed by the messages on the answering-machine. The calls to and from the gynaecologist's office suggested it wasn't going smoothly, and Loretta felt a little sorry for Toni.

A news programme had just begun on TV and she turned up the sound, recognising a familiar backdrop. "So, Pete," a black reporter with upswept hair was saying, addressing an anchorman back in the studio, "as you can see behind me, a police forensics team is now scouring the sports store where two men were held hostage earlier today." She half turned, gesturing through the open front door of the shop where a dark figure could be seen moving among the weights machines, placing minute samples into a plastic bag. A diagonal black band appeared in the corner of the screen, superimposed in red with the single word "SIEGE!"

In the studio, the grey-haired anchorman said: "What's the latest, Shari?"

She nodded, not missing a beat. "Questions are being asked about the *exact* role in today's dramatic events of store manager Arnie Lorenzo. Earlier today Lorenzo was being hailed as the hero of the hour when he offered himself as a hostage on condition that his assistant was freed. Nineteen-year-old Stavros Jones"—a blurred snapshot appeared briefly on the screen—"was hit in the hand and shoulder when the raiders burst into the store armed with hand guns and semi-automatic weapons shortly after nine o'clock this morning. The hostage deal was brokered by Elder Roberto Rush of the nearby Resurrection Day Chapel after talks between a police negotiator and the raiders reached deadlock."

"Shari, if I can stop you there. You're on the spot; are the cops now suggesting that Arnie Lorenzo is *not* the hero we all thought? That maybe he was in on this from the start?"

"Well, Pete, it's certainly looking that way. Lorenzo's wife Suzanne was escorted home to Queens by the cops and found that items including a suitcase, clothing and securities were missing. There's also no sign of yesterday's takings, which Lorenzo should have banked on his way home last night."

"Any indication how much is missing?"

"It's early days—"

"In ball-park terms."

"OK. Definitely thousands. All this week the store has been running a special promotion, neighbours say it's been unusually busy—"

"Any word from the medics on Stavie Jones?"

"Well, Pete, this is an interesting point. This morning the cops were saying *Lorenzo* hit the alarm button as the raiders stormed in but now it looks like it was Stavie, and that's when he got shot."

"So Stavie's the *real* hero of the hour?" The lop-sided photo appeared again, just long enough for Loretta to make out a youth with glasses.

"Looks like it, Pete."

"And what about Elder Rush? I guess he's feeling kind of embarrassed at this outcome? Did he have any *idea* that Lorenzo was in on the deal?"

The reporter shook her head. "Elder Rush was called in because the mother of one of the alleged raiders worships at the nearby Resurrection Day Chapel—"

"We're talking local boys?"

"From the neighbourhood, yes."

"Thanks, Shari. I'll come back to you later in the hour so you can keep us right up-to-date on developments." Adopting a sonorous tone, he looked directly at Loretta and announced: "Now, Bosnia."

Loretta turned off the TV. She stood by the set for a moment, then returned to the phone and dialled the Gramercy Park Hotel. Tracey answered, still sounding cheerful, and told her he was in the middle of shaving.

She twisted her wrist. "At five to five?"

"Five o'clock actually, your watch must be slow. I had a busy morning, if you remember. We on for tonight?"

Loretta explained about Kelly's party.

"You must be doing better than I thought if your agent can afford a place on East Eighty-first Street. Maybe I should think again about this book business."

"She has other clients, you know. One of them is the woman who wrote that book about reincarnation—*Death: Only the Beginning*, it's been on the *New York Times* bestseller list all year."

"Which one, fiction?"

Loretta said impatiently: "She took me on because she likes Edith Wharton, she's hardly going to make a fortune out of me. Can I meet you at the restaurant?"

"All right. But don't be late, I've booked a table for half eight."

"Without asking me?"

"Come on, Loretta, this is New York. You don't wait till Saturday evening and start thinking about where to eat."

"So what's it called?"

"The restaurant? I said on the machine, the TriBeCa Grill."

"What?" She remembered the matchbook, the one she'd found behind the *diadoumenos*, picturing it quite clearly. "No, you didn't, I would have remembered, you only said a restaurant in TriBeCa."

"So?" He was starting to sound peeved. "I thought you were keen on De Niro."

She said blankly: "What's he got to do with it?"

"Oh, *Loretta*. I thought everyone knew—look, I'll tell you later, I've got shaving foam all over my face. See you at half eight."

"Wait. Have you been there before?"

"Why? What is this?"

"*Have* you?"

"No. If you remember, I only got in to New York yesterday morning and I was with you last night."

"I meant—before."

"Bloody hell. I have never been to the TriBeCa Grill in my life, this one or any other previous incarnation. That satisfy you?"

"All right. Sorry. See you later."

Biting her lip, she went to the hook on the back of the front door where Honey's lead was kept and lifted it down. The dog stretched out her front paws with her bottom in the air, growling and yelping excitedly. Loretta was struggling to attach the lead to her collar when the phone rang. "Stay there," she said sternly to the dog, and went to answer it.

Her hand was actually on the receiver when she remembered Michael. Her fingers opened uncertainly, hovering over the phone as its familiar tone took on the guise of a threat. In quick succession she recalled the phone pest's gasps of pleasure as he masturbated the previous night, the triumphant expression on the car salesman's face when he humiliated her in front of all those people at the Frick—

She rushed across the room and activated the answering-machine, holding her breath while she waited to hear Michael's distinctive, insinuating voice speaking on to the tape. Instead there was a longish silence and then the sound of the line being disconnected. Loretta stood very still and almost at once it rang again, unnaturally loud over the rattle of the air-conditioning. Again she let the machine take the call, telling herself that Toni or any other legitimate caller would undoubtedly leave a message. The silence this time was shorter, but once again there was a click and the unknown caller disconnected without speaking. Loretta shivered, a response which prompted her, illogically since she wasn't really cold, to cross the room and turn down the air-conditioning. It took her a moment to remember that she'd been on her way out and she had got as far as the front door, the poop-a-scoop and a clean plastic bag in her free hand, when the phone rang a third time. A male voice spoke into the room, one she thought she recognised as Lieutenant Donelly until she picked up a faint, foreign inflection.

"This is Detective . . . Detective Destri, Ms. Lawson. Are you at home?"

She pushed the door wide, trying to hook Honey's lead over the handle so the dog couldn't wander off on her own. It slipped off and Honey pranced into the corridor as though they were playing a game, growling at Loretta when she followed. She made an unsuccessful grab at the lead and gave up, hoping the dog would not roam too far while she spoke to Donelly's subordinate.

Inside the flat the detective, sounding anxious and uncertain, was explaining that Lieutenant Donelly had had to go out. "He wanted you to know that we . . . we have a location on your nuisance caller, we've traced the, um, the bells to a church down on First Avenue. He said this is your last night in

New York so it's vital . . . really important you're there when he calls, maybe our last chance . . ."

First Avenue? Loretta listened intently, staring at the phone, making no move to pick it up.

"The lieutenant thought you'd be home right now, what I'm thinking is maybe you've put the machine on while you're in the tub? I guess I better not stay on the line but if you get this message we'd be grateful if you'd pick up soon as you get another call. As long as you know we're . . . we're right on his *ass*."

There was a click and Loretta remained where she was, rooted to the spot. Donelly, Destri, there was no doubt the voices were very similar . . . From the beginning something hadn't seemed quite right, the likelihood that there were still old-fashioned exchanges in New York where numbers couldn't be traced automatically. Yet Donelly had sounded so convincing, and it wasn't as if anybody else she'd gone to for help—the operator, the precinct she had called on Thursday evening— had shown any interest at all. Loretta put her hand up to her head, silently going through the sequence of events, until a loud bark reminded her that Honey was loose in the corridor. She turned to see the bulldog regarding her pugnaciously through the open front door, growling and whining and paw- ing the edge of the carpet.

"All right," she said distractedly, and began collecting her things for the third time—keys, plastic bag, poop-a-scoop. In the lift she leaned back, closing her eyes as it rode down to the ground floor, too wrapped up in her thoughts to notice that the attendant was looking at her oddly. Nor did she react when someone tried to attract her attention as she crossed the lobby.

"Hey, *lady*."

This time she did stop, realising that the porter was speaking to her.

"You wanna see me about somethin'?"

Loretta stared at him, vaguely aware that she'd left a message for him but unable to remember why. She dragged the dog with her to the desk, winding the lead round her hand and ignoring Honey's protests. "I thought—weren't you supposed to come on duty at four?"

He regarded her stonily, obviously thinking his lateness was none of her business. She shrugged to show it didn't matter and an idea occurred to her. "You didn't ring me about ten minutes ago?" she asked hopefully. "When the answering-machine was on?"

"Nope. Couple times I tried, line was busy."

Her shoulders sagged. "Oh, well, never mind." It came back to her, what she had wanted to see him about, and she added in a different tone of voice: "The man you told me about last night, the one who tried to sneak upstairs. Remember?"

"Sure."

"Was he bald? I mean," she amended, mentally picturing the car salesman, "was he losing his hair?"

He grinned. "No way."

"He wasn't?" She stared at him. "Are you sure?"

"Sure I'm sure."

"What colour hair *did* he have?"

The porter considered. "Long," he said finally, as if this was an answer to her question.

Loretta was barely able to contain her exasperation. "He had *long* hair?"

"Sure."

"How long? Like mine?"

He lifted both hands to the back of his head and made a pulling motion, which Loretta could not immediately interpret.

"You mean a pony tail?" she hazarded. She was disappointed and relieved at the same time, thinking the description suggested one of Toni's students. It certainly didn't fit the car salesman. "I mean—it definitely was a man?"

He lifted his eyebrows contemptuously.

"I just thought I'd ask, since you seem to have noticed nothing about him. Oh, well, thanks," she added ungraciously. "Come on, dog."

Honey was lumbering to her feet when she heard the porter say: "Guy was here again."

Loretta turned. "Who was?"

"Same guy." He tapped the book lying open on the desk in front of him, the one in which she'd seen him write down the complaint about the air-conditioning system the night before. Turning it round so she could read it, he pointed to an entry in black biro half-way down the left-hand page. "See?"

The handwriting was cramped and indistinct but years of deciphering students' scripts meant that Loretta was able to read almost anything—including Tracey's new girlfriend's handwriting, she recalled, shoving the thought away. The note was from the porter on the earlier shift, the one who had still been on duty when she came back, covering for his late colleague. She felt a spurt of annoyance that he hadn't mentioned the incident when she inquired about the absence of the black porter, though to be fair she hadn't said why she wanted to speak to him.

This time the man, described as "young guy with long hair," had apparently made some attempt to impersonate a courier, holding up an envelope and saying he had to deliver it in person to 15G. When he was challenged, he flatly refused to leave it at the desk and couldn't produce any evidence of his identity or the company he said he worked for. Loretta made a mental note of the time, 2:10 that afternoon, although it told her nothing.

"I don't understand," she said, straightening up. "If he's really got something for Toni, an essay's the most likely thing, why didn't he just put it in her post box?" She gestured with the poop-a-scoop, pointing towards the rows of wooden boxes on a side wall. The key to the box was on a ring in her skirt pocket with Toni's spare front door key.

"I mean," she went on, thinking aloud, "I know students occasionally get worked up about their essays but—Honey, *stop* that." The bulldog was pulling on her lead, trying to sniff the bottom of a black poodle whose owner was crossing the lobby.

"It's OK. Honey and Lulu are friends, aren't you girls?" said the poodle's owner, clearly a more tolerant woman than Loretta.

Barely acknowledging her, Loretta rolled her eyes upwards and made another attempt to leave the building. Honey went with her reluctantly, casting longing glances over her shoulder until the poodle disappeared into the lift. Then, still a trifle sulky, she allowed Loretta to lead her through the swinging doors into the street.

"So I'm standing in front of this picture and I'm feeling like—" Katha Curran rolled her eyes upwards in a gesture apparently intended to re-create the astonished recognition she had experienced in the art gallery. Loretta looked down at her feet, wondering how soon she could decently sidle away and find someone else to talk to. She was finding the party hard going, all strangers except Kelly and her husband, Alan Larner, whom she did not know well.

"Like?" someone said encouragingly, an older woman who had already told Katha twice that she absolutely *loved* her book.

"Like I've seen her before," Katha said bathetically. "Not *seen* her, because till then I never even heard of her. But I'm getting this feeling, I'm staring right at her and she's looking back at me and I just *know* what she's trying to tell me. She has this little dog, real cute little fella, and it comes into my head that she lost him and some guy brought him home and she's *so* grateful. You can tell from the way she's holding on to him, like she don't want to be parted from him again *ever*."

Across the room, Kelly Sibon caught sight of Loretta's pained expression and grinned sheepishly. She lifted her hands, palms upwards, dissociating herself from what Katha Curran was saying.

"You really never heard her name before?" another of Kelly's clients asked sceptically. She was a cookery writer, and had been telling Loretta about her eccentric recipe for *zabaglione*—apparently she added currants and chopped almonds—when Katha arrived late and took the floor.

"There was a film," said Loretta, trying to turn the conversation away from Katha's book. "With Glenda Jackson as Lady Hamilton. In—oh, 1972 or thereabouts."

A tall man who hadn't been introduced said: "You're talking about the movie based on the Rattigan play, right? Did you ever see *That Hamilton Woman*?"

Loretta smiled. "No, but it sounds terrible."

"Alexander Korda, 1941, if memory serves. With Vivien Leigh and Olivier." He grinned. "It's supposed to have been Churchill's favourite movie."

"I never saw no movie," Katha interrupted. "I never even *heard* of her till my niece takes me to this museum. Lady Hamilton, it says on the frame, and it don't mean nothing to me. Couple days later, I'm at my friend Eileen's house and her library books are on the table. First one I pick up, there she is again, same picture. And *then*—" She stopped.

Loretta said, trying not to sound as bored as she felt: "And then you read it?"

"I did *not*. I wait till my friend comes back with the coffee cups all laid out on a tray and I say to her—Eileen, did you read this? Sure, she says, and I say—you wanna ask me some questions? Go right ahead."

The small group waited.

Katha said: "I got every one. Every single one. That's when I *knew*. That I was her, this Lady Hamilton, in another life."

Loretta frowned. "What I don't understand is, in your book you say you've been able to recall what, five previous lives?"

"Six."

"OK. Who else do you . . ." She hesitated, caught the eye of the man who seemed to know a lot about films, and thought she was going to laugh. "I mean, who else have you . . . been?"

Katha Curran flicked her hennaed hair back from her sallow face, making her earrings tinkle. They were complicated designs in multicoloured beads and silver, the kind of jewellery Loretta had seen in New Age shops in Cow Hollow. She suspected that if she asked, Katha would say they were traditional Native American designs, dream-catchers or some such thing.

"You want them in order?" she heard Katha say. "Like—chronological?"

"All right."

"This is not how I remembered them, right? I mean, when I began hypnosis, I had to really *trust* my therapist before I was able to go all the way back. Imhemet, the Egyptian slave, I only remembered her at the end. She was killed by a rival—"

Loretta said: "Imhemet?"

"—a rival because the king liked her singing better, he was so upset when she died he gave her a state funeral." She held out her hands, half closing her eyes. "They laid her body on a boat and took her down the Nile—"

The man next to Loretta said: "Was this before or after she'd been embalmed?"

"After. I can recall every detail of the process, if you're interested in making a study of it, it's all in my book. Next is Sarah, she was a girl from a rich Roman family, senators and stuff, who heard St. Paul preaching and converted to Christianity."

"What happened to her?" Katha's fan asked breathlessly.

"You never heard what they did to Christians in those days? She was thrown to the lions—absolutely *torn apart*. In my book I have the transcript of the hypnosis where I hear the lions roaring and I describe the place where she died in total detail, *total* detail."

"The Colosseum?" ventured Loretta, trying to remember whether gladiatorial combat had taken place there or in the Circus Maximus. "You do know that Sarah isn't—it's not a Roman name."

"I told you, she converted."

The man said: "Seems like you've had bad luck, murdered twice and four more lives to go."

"I've always wondered," said Loretta, "why people who believe in reincarnation always have these glamorous other lives, Egyptian princesses and so on. I mean, in a hundred years' time I expect people will start claiming they were Mrs. Thatcher."

Katha said ominously: "I just *love* Margaret Thatcher. I don't understand why you Brits got rid of her."

"For much the same reason you got rid of George Bush. What I mean is, why does no one ever remember a previous life where nothing happened? Where they died in bed at the age of eighty-two surrounded by their grandchildren?"

"So what do *you* think happens when we die?"

Loretta shrugged. "Nothing."

"*Nothing?* You mean all this"—Katha made a circling motion with her right hand, encompassing Kelly's living-room as though it was a microcosm of everything she valued—"all this is for nothing?"

Loretta glanced towards the sliding door on to a wide balcony where more of Kelly's clients had gathered, including a man she thought she recognised as a Syrian academic who had written a controversial book attacking America's role in the Gulf War. "In the sense you mean, yes," she said reluctantly.

Katha narrowed her eyes. "*Millions* of Americans disagree with you. Do you have any *idea* how many people already bought my book?"

Loretta realised that her part of the room had gone quiet. Calmly she said: "Several hundred thousand, I should think. There's obviously a market for—for consolatory fictions."

Katha stared at her, open-mouthed. Loretta was bracing

herself for a full-scale row when Alan Larner, Kelly's husband, intervened.

"Loretta. Your glass is empty." He signalled to a waiter in a white jacket who hurried over and filled it with Chardonnay. "Katha, I'm sorry to drag you away but there's someone I'd like you to meet. He's a *big* fan."

Avoiding Loretta's eye, he slipped a hand under Katha's elbow and steered her away, past the big white sofas which faced each other in the middle of the room. On the far side, a man in a collarless shirt was talking earnestly to Kelly, and Loretta wondered whether he had written a book, and if so what it was about. Behind him, a life-size portrait of Kelly gazed radiantly from the wall, posed on the balcony, her arms flung wide as she leaned back against the rail in a strapless white dress. She looked, Loretta thought for the first time, a little like Ivana Trump.

Loretta turned back and saw that the small group of people who had gathered around Katha had drifted away. Only the tall man was left and she immediately felt terrible, as though she had broken every unwritten rule about behaviour at parties. "Oh, dear," she said, "I seem to have upset one of Kelly's most important authors."

"Bestselling," he corrected.

Loretta conceded the point. "You seem very knowledgeable about films. Is that what you write about?"

"Part of the time. It's my day job, if you like." He held out his hand. "Dale Martineau."

"*Oh.*" She had been aware that he looked familiar without being able to place him. "Loretta Lawson. Your book's had terrific reviews." She hesitated, then added: "Since I seem to be putting my foot in it tonight, I might as well admit I haven't read it."

"It didn't occur to me you had. There are around two hundred million people in the States and it's sold five thousand, six hundred and forty copies. On the other hand, I don't have to pay a ghost writer."

Loretta glanced across the room at Katha, who was now lecturing the man in the collarless shirt and a woman in green trousers. "*Did* she?"

"You mean she struck you as literate?"

She heard the bitterness in his voice and said hastily, remembering what his novel was about: "I suppose you can only sell books about old age and dying if you can think of a positive angle. Like Betty Friedan. Or Katha. I don't suppose you remember any previous lives?"

"I have enough problems with this one."

"Me too." She was silent for a moment.

He said lightly: "This is getting very serious."

Loretta lifted her head and their eyes met, his so dark that it was almost impossible to make out the line between the iris and the pupil. A sudden, unexpected sensation of sexual arousal rippled through her and she felt her cheeks grow red.

He smiled. "You were about to say?"

"Nothing. Did you—are you working on another book?"

He started telling her about his new novel and she tried to visualise a profile of him she had read in the *San Francisco Chronicle* when the first one came out. It was mostly anodyne stuff about his job teaching film studies in New York, how he had started to write, what his students made of the book, but one startling detail came back to her: his father had been a policeman, one of the few high-ranking black cops in the NYPD in the 1950s, and he'd been shot dead in an undercover operation when Dale was only eight or nine.

He finished speaking, gave her an amused look and said: "What're you doing after this?"

Loretta felt a rush of disappointment. "Oh, God," she said, not disguising it, "I'm having dinner with someone."

"Tomorrow night?"

"I'm going back to Oxford."

Unspoken signals flew between them. Loretta undid the catch of her bag and felt inside for her purse. "I'll give you my card. In case you're ever in England." She found a pen and scribbled her home telephone number next to her direct line at St. Frideswide's.

He studied it. "I'm in London in September, when my novel comes out over there. That's not too far from Oxford?"

"An hour by train. Will you ring me?"

"You bet."

"Who's your publisher?"

"Bloomsbury." He pronounced it in the American way, three discrete syllables: Blooms-bu-ry.

"Loretta?" She felt Kelly's hand on her arm. "Sorry Dale, but I can't let you monopolise her."

She led Loretta across the room towards the balcony, saying in a low voice, "I hope you don't mind, I just noticed Cary Walker all on her own." Loretta saw a small, lost-looking woman in a pink pantsuit staring out across the city and then Kelly was stepping through the open door, touching her on the arm: "Cary, I'd like you to meet Loretta Lawson. Loretta's an academic, she's written a wonderful book on female characters in fiction but she knows all about journalism as well. Her husband's a reporter."

"Ex-husband," Loretta said quickly but Kelly was already going back inside, arms spread wide to greet a latecomer.

"Are you an author?" she asked, turning back to Cary Walker and trying to look interested. She glanced covertly at her watch.

"I write true crime," Cary Walker said in a gravelly voice. "Like, the real story behind the headlines? I used to be on the crime beat for the *New York Post* but since Kelly took me on I write full time."

Loretta manoeuvred herself into a position which gave her a view of the room she'd just left and saw Dale watching her. He grinned and she pulled a face.

". . . current project is writing the life of the Brooklyn Beast," she heard Cary say. "You hearda Ted Bundy?"

Loretta nodded.

"This guy's not as big as Bundy, not yet, but the cops are going back through files this high." She held her hand in the air, indicating a point above Loretta's head. "This guy *predates computers.*"

"Doesn't it upset you?" asked Loretta, who had avoided reading about the case as far as was practically possible with such a sensational story. The preliminary court hearings, and the prosecution's so-far-unsubstantiated hints about cannibalism, had pushed O. J. Simpson off the front pages of the tabloids for two or three days.

"Upset me?"

"I just meant," said Loretta, "that you're a woman and all his victims are women."

Cary said abruptly, changing the subject: "You read her book?"

"Who?" Loretta peered into the room to see who Cary was looking at. "Katha Curran? No."

"It's about how she's supposed to remember all these previous lives."

"I know."

"Crap. The Beast's my fifth book, you know what they call me?"

Loretta shook her head.

"The True Queen of Crime. Neat, huh? Like Agatha Christie, except what I write about is all true." She leaned towards Loretta and said confidentially: "You know what never came out about him, the Beast?"

Loretta stepped sideways, grasping the rail of the balcony. The light had begun to fail and twelve floors below she could see the tail-lights of cars on a cross-street between Park and Madison, the roar of the traffic muted now; the sun had only just gone down, flushing the sky on the west side of the city a cloudy pink which reflected off the gilded pediment of a nearby skyscraper. Even the heat was bearable, had it not been for Cary Walker's voice describing in minute detail what the Beast had done to his victims in a residential area of Brooklyn.

"Sorry," exclaimed Loretta, interrupting Cary, "but I have to meet someone. Good luck with the book."

She hurried inside, looking for Kelly.

"Thanks," she said, kissing her on both cheeks. "It's been—lovely."

Kelly threw back her head, hardly disturbing her flossy blonde hair, and laughed. "She has this theory, you know, Katha. She thinks anyone who isn't nice to her had a bad time in their last incarnation. I expect she has you down as a roach." They walked towards the front door and she added: "I love your outline. There's someone I'd like to show it to next week, I know Branch Books did a nice job on *Milton's Cook* but I'm not sure this is for them. Is that OK with you?"

"Whatever you think," Loretta said distractedly, aware that Dale Martineau was following them.

He caught up with them at the front door. "You leaving, Loretta? I'll walk you down."

They crossed the landing to the lift, which was waiting on Kelly's floor, and travelled down in tense silence. In the lobby, as the porter held the door open for them, Dale said: "Sure you won't change your mind?"

Loretta pulled a face. "I can't."

"OK. Where're you going?"

"TriBeCa."

"It'll be easier to pick up a cab on Park." They walked the short distance and he waved one down, turning to Loretta with a regretful expression on his rather sensual face. Without thinking she stood on tiptoe and kissed him, not in the usual exploratory way of strangers but sliding her tongue into his mouth, startling him for a few seconds. Then he responded, pulling her close so their bodies pressed together, releasing her only when the taxi driver leaned across and asked bad-temperedly how much longer he was supposed to wait.

Dale opened the door for her and she slid onto the back seat, gasping: "Greenwich Street. Greenwich and Franklin." The taxi pulled away and she turned, watching the dwindling figure of Dale Martineau until she could no longer distinguish him in the gathering dusk.

9

John Tracey pushed back his chair and stood up, beaming at Loretta as she approached his table. He was more smartly dressed than the previous evening, wearing what looked like a new suit, and his hair had recently been washed. He slid his arm around her waist, murmuring, "You look fabulous," and went to kiss her on the mouth.

"Thanks," she said, turning her face so his lips brushed her cheek. Stepping back, she rested her hand lightly on the only other chair and said: "Shall I sit here?"

Tracey gave her a searching look. "That's the general idea. Unless you want to move to another table. The only problem with this one is they want it back by quarter past ten."

"Fine," she said, sitting down. "How's your day been?"

He leaned forward. "Are you all right?"

"Yes. Why?"

"You seem . . . preoccupied. Not all here. And your cheeks are flushed."

Loretta turned to look out of the window, feigning interest in a slender Asian woman who was getting out of a taxi. Otherwise the wide, dimly lit street outside the restaurant was empty and she said: "It's this area. I've never been here before and it's a bit strange. All those warehouses."

Tracey shrugged. "It's quite safe as far as I know. As safe as anywhere in New York, that is. I wouldn't recommend walking round TriBeCa on your own at night but as long as you get a taxi . . . Here, have a look at the menu, I don't want to rush you but I did say half eight."

Loretta picked it up, ignoring the implied rebuke, and ran her eye distractedly down the list. "I'll have the lamb."

"No starter?" Tracey was watching her closely, almost as if he knew—had guessed, somehow—about Dale Martineau.

"I'm not very hungry."

"Something to drink?"

"Anything. White wine." She had had two or three glasses at Kelly's party, it wasn't easy to keep count when the waiter kept topping it up. "Oh, and some mineral water. Sparkling."

"So how was the party? Did you meet the New York literati?"

"I don't know about that." She looked down at the menu again, as though she might want to change her mind, then said as casually as she could: "Katha Curran was there, the reincarnation woman. And Anwar Saady, who wrote that book about the Gulf War. At least, I think it was him. We didn't actually speak."

"You talk to anyone I might have heard of?"

"Carla Griccioli, the cookery writer. And a novelist called Dale

Martineau." His name came out unnaturally, the verbal equiva-
lent of being up in lights, but Tracey appeared not to notice.

"Means nothing to me," he said, and started reading out
their order to a waiter.

When they were on their own again Loretta said: "I don't
know if you remember, last night, in the restaurant, I told you
I'd had a couple of obscene phone calls?"

"Did you?" Tracey sounded genuinely surprised. "Sorry,
Loretta, last night's a total blank." He began to look interested.
"How d'you mean, obscene?"

Not wanting a rerun of the previous evening's conversation, Loretta didn't answer directly. "It doesn't matter," she
said, "what I wanted to ask you is, how do I go about finding
out who a telephone number belongs to?"

"Why? You don't mean this bloke gave you his number?"

"Of *course* not. Well, not exactly. The thing is—" She hesitated, reluctant to say it out loud. "The thing is I think I've
been set up. I mean, I thought I was talking to the police and
all the time . . ."

Tracey held up his hands. "I'm not with you."

She told him the story again, from the initial call from
Michael on Thursday night to Lieutenant Donelly's little lecture that morning about ambient noise and church bells. At
this point, Tracey interrupted.

"Bloody *hell*, Loretta, you don't really think the cops
would go to all that trouble over a couple of obscene phone
calls? Do you realise how many murders there are a day in
New York? They've got serial killers, gang fights, drug wars—"

"You didn't talk to him," she said crossly. "He was very
plausible, and he didn't sound anything like . . . like Michael."

"The other point is, with the technology they've got these
days, they can trace a number in seconds. Haven't you heard

about these phones that display the number of the person who's ringing you? You'll be able to get one in Oxford by the end of this year."

"No, I haven't, I've been out of the country for three months, remember. Anyway, that's exactly what I thought to begin with, I'm not *completely* stupid." She began ticking off all the avenues she'd tried, finger by finger. "I rang the police first, they couldn't have been less interested, then I tried the phone book and all it offers is counselling. No, really, I'm not kidding, have a look when you get back to your hotel. There's this number you can ring, some kind of helpline, but only in office hours. I even tried the operator and she referred me back to it, I was going round in circles. By the time Don—by the time this pretend policeman called I was just incredibly relieved that anyone seemed to be taking it seriously. And he did say something about Toni's exchange being one of the last to be computerised." Contradicting the conclusion she'd come to earlier, she added: "It's not implausible, given how many exchanges there must be in New York City."

Tracey rolled his eyes upwards. "All right, when *did* you get suspicious?"

The waiter was hovering, waiting to pour the wine Tracey had chosen. "I'll taste it," said Loretta, thankful for the distraction. She held her glass under her nose for a few seconds, took a sip and nodded in approval. "Are you sure it's all right for you to drink?" she asked Tracey, a little maliciously, when the waiter went to fill his glass. "After last night?"

"He only said to stay off alcohol while I was taking the tablets and I haven't had any today. Come on, when did it dawn on you something was wrong?"

"Well, I suppose I was always a bit . . . uneasy. And then tonight, when this . . . supposedly this other detective phoned.

He sounded just like the first one, Donelly, except he had a bit of a foreign accent. He said they'd traced the area he, Michael that is, was ringing from and when he mentioned First Avenue, *down* on First Avenue, that's when it hit me."

"What hit you? What's special about First Avenue?"

Loretta said: "I was looking at the map this morning, trying to remember the name of your hotel if you must know, and I thought—oh, I never knew that's where it was."

Tracey was getting irritated. "*What?* What are you talking about?"

"*Bellevue,*" she said. "Bellevue is on First Avenue."

Tracey started to laugh, incredulous. "You mean—the mental hospital?"

"Exactly."

He saw her expression. "I suppose it is pretty sick. Let's get this straight, you think all these people, Michael, Donelly, whatever the other cop's called—they're all the same bloke?"

She nodded. "I said this morning I was going to be out all day except between five and six. And when did I get all these calls? Just after five, as soon as I finished talking to you."

"This number he gave you," Tracey said thoughtfully, "you say it's always engaged?"

"Every time I've tried it. That's why I wondered if—well, you know more about these things than I do."

"Got it with you?"

"Of course." Loretta reached into her bag, took out her notebook and found the right page. She copied the number on to a clean sheet, tore it out and handed it to Tracey.

He glanced at it and put it away. "The obvious possibilities are—one, it's his own and he leaves it off the hook when he thinks you might call, which seems a bit unlikely unless for some reason he's got two numbers. Two, it belongs to someone else and he knows it's out of order. Maybe he works for the phone company, have you thought of that?"

"I've thought of all sorts of things," said Loretta, "including that he might be a friend of Toni's, but she—I haven't been able to get hold of her."

"Some friend," said Tracey. "Go back a minute. Say you're right, how did this bloke Michael know you'd reported him to the cops in the first place?"

Loretta frowned. "I'm trying to remember what he said, Lieutenant Donelly, the first time he rang. I *think* he just asked if I'd reported an obscene call the night before and it all came pouring out. As I said, I was so *grateful*." Looking over Tracey's shoulder she added: "I think this is our food."

They ate in near-silence, Tracey wolfing down his fish as though he hadn't eaten all day and not leaving a single pod of mange-tout on his side-plate. "That was good," he said, finishing before Loretta. "How's the lamb?"

"Great," she said, swallowing a mouthful of vegetables. She was tired, not wanting to think any more about Michael and his probable aliases, and she asked: "How much longer are you going to be in Washington?"

Tracey looked evasive. "The Whitewater hearings are about to start so it could be a while. Three, maybe four weeks." He turned the wine bottle round and studied the label, even though Loretta knew he didn't understand Italian. "Actually, they've asked me if I'm interested in the job. Making it permanent."

"What job?"

"Washington correspondent. Chris Calder's gone back to London to be political editor, he's an old mate of Tony Blair so they're keen to have him at Westminster. I'm not sure he realises yet how right-wing this new regime is, but that's his problem."

Startled and dismayed, Loretta said: "I thought—last night

you were saying how much you disliked it, having to write stories about Bill Clinton."

"Was I? I'd have to cover the '96 election of course but it's not just domestic politics. The Middle East peace talks, Ireland, I was thinking about it before you arrived and there are some advantages. Not being in the office for a start, you know what it's been like since that bloody woman bought the paper."

"It seems a bit . . . sudden. I had an idea you wanted to spend more time in London, especially since you got back from Sarajevo."

"I did," Tracey said gloomily. Loretta watched him while the waiter cleared their plates and left dessert menus; aware of her scrutiny, he lifted a hand and made a brushing motion in the air. "Sorry, Loretta, I didn't mean to bother you with my problems. I got a phone call as I was leaving the hotel and it's been on my mind ever since."

"From the office?" She remembered the time difference and added: "Of course not, silly question."

"From a . . . friend. From Hampshire to be exact. Actually, Loretta, I've got myself into a bit of a situation." He had started to look embarrassed, fiddling with things on the table and avoiding her eye.

"You know how it is," he went on, "you go out with someone a few times, concerts and the occasional dinner, and the next thing you know . . . I didn't think she had my number in New York but apparently she got on to the newsdesk and said it was urgent so they gave it to her. I mean, *Christ*, by the time she phoned it must've been one o'clock in the morning in Basingstoke."

Feeling acutely uncomfortable, Loretta repeated: "Basingstoke?"

"Yeah, she—Mo, Maureen—lives in a village on the road

from Basingstoke to Reading. I met her just after I got back from Sarajevo, remember I had that kidney infection? I was a bit low, I may have phoned her more often than I should, a shoulder to cry on and all that." With a flash of anger he added: "But how was I to know she'd be so bloody *persistent*?"

Loretta picked up the empty water bottle. "Shall we get another one of these?"

"If you like." There was a moment's silence and then Tracey said unexpectedly: "She offered to make you a jumper. She wanted to know your bust size and what colours you like."

"A *jumper*?"

"Yeah, she has her own shop, Mohair, it's called. Get it? Mohair. She breeds rabbits and makes these fluffy jumpers—"

"I'm allergic," Loretta said quickly. "And mohair comes from goats."

"Whatever. You having a pudding?"

The waiter was back and Loretta hadn't even looked at the menu. "No," she said distractedly, picking it up. "I mean, yes." She ordered a confection of bananas with dark and white choco-late sauce and Tracey asked for coffee and more mineral water. Sounding more cheerful after the interruption, he said: "Never mind all that, I don't know how we got on to it. How's Bridget?"

Loretta blinked, knowing he wasn't fond of her best friend. "Much better, thanks. Her mother takes Elizabeth to see her every month, they don't allow children in prison after eighteen months. She's been given a date for her appeal and her barris-ter thinks she's got a very good chance of getting off, especially now we've got this new evidence."

"Which is what?"

Loretta explained that she'd hired a private detective to look into the events three years before which had led to Brid-get Bennett's conviction for manslaughter.

"That must've cost a bit," Tracey observed.

Loretta rolled her eyes upwards. The detective, she went on as though Tracey hadn't spoken, had cast doubt on the alibi produced by Bridget's husband, Sam Becker. The only other plausible suspect—he admitted having had a brief affair with the dead woman—Becker claimed during Bridget's trial at Oxford Crown Court that he'd been in his office on the afternoon she was killed, discussing a complex computer problem with a female colleague. But the private detective had established that the witness, Brenda Perfect, was actually at her dentist's surgery during the crucial period.

"It's a stupid thing," said Loretta, "but we were all so convinced Bridget would get off we didn't actually check Brenda Perfect's story. The dentist was Anthea's idea, she's the detective, and as soon as she spoke to his nurse . . . The surgery's in Bicester *and* Brenda was having a crown fitted, so she must've been out of the office for at least two hours."

"Was she lying? At the trial?"

"Who knows? Anthea, that's the detective, she thinks Brenda had a crush on Sam, she certainly hasn't been very cooperative. But we've got an affidavit from the dentist, so it doesn't really matter."

Tracey said: "When's the appeal?"

Loretta's pudding arrived along with Tracey's *espresso doppio* and she waited a moment before replying. "October. Term won't have started so I'll be able to go every day. In fact I was hoping you'd be in London." Her brow clouded. "You're not really going to stay in Washington?"

"I haven't had time to think." He looked straight at her. "Why, would you miss me?"

Loretta recognised the glint in his eye and sat back in her chair. "Of course," she said lightly, her mind jumping treacherously to Dale Martineau. "Who else would I go to concerts with? You know how ignorant I am about classical music."

"That isn't what I meant."

"John—"

"I've been thinking about yesterday, spending the whole night with you and nothing happened. I mean, we're miles from Riverside Drive, you could come back to my hotel, they've given me a double room." Guessing what she was about to say, he added: "You *know*, I don't mean anything heavy. Just for old times' sake."

Loretta looked at him coolly, thinking nostalgia was one of the worst reasons she'd ever heard for going to bed with someone. Whatever she had felt for Tracey was too far in the past to be revived now, especially when she'd just had an unexpected reminder of the electrifying effect of sudden sexual attraction. Faking a yawn, she said: "It's been a nice evening but I'm tired and I want an early night."

"What d'you mean, *nice?*" he said, and promptly changed tack. "At least you'd be safe with me. You seem to have spent most of your time in New York fending off sex maniacs."

"One obscene caller? You were just saying how many murders and rapes there are in New York. There was a woman on the news who got AIDS when she was *raped*."

"OK, forget it." He grasped the edge of the table and pushed his chair back, glancing down at the floor as though he'd dropped something. Apparently he'd lost his napkin, which he retrieved and smoothed over his knees even though he'd finished eating. He looked up, saw she was still watching him and said gruffly: "Sorry."

Loretta shrugged and picked up her spoon, looking down at the mélange of bananas and chocolate on her plate. It resembled an illustration from an upmarket cookery book, lightly dusted with icing sugar and with a single sliced strawberry reclining in the chocolate sauce.

"Look, we can—er—share a taxi," Tracey said, obviously feeling bad about his ill-judged remark. "I mean, I can get it on expenses, just about."

Loretta smiled rather wanly.

"Eat up," she heard Tracey say, "they're going to want the table in ten minutes. I ought to get the bill."

Loretta slid her spoon across the plate from the edge to the centre, scooping up sauce and bananas, releasing a rich, chocolatey perfume which made her mouth water. She lifted the first spoonful to her lips, lingering over it and allowing the pulpy sweetness to melt on her tongue. It tasted even better than its description on the menu had promised and she began to eat more quickly, hardly aware of John Tracey talking irritably to the waiter, waving his hands and querying something on the bill.

She was in the small bathroom of Toni's flat, removing her make-up, when Tracey rang. She picked up the phone as soon as she heard his voice on the answering-machine, breaking into his surprised monologue, "It's OK, I'm here."

"*Christ*, you gave me a fright. I didn't like the look of that taxi driver, you should have let me drop you off first."

"It's miles out of your way. Anyway, he never said a word, not even when I told him where to stop. I forgot about your change and by the time I remembered he was driving off. Are you sure you can put it on expenses? I mean, I didn't get a receipt." Tracey had insisted on giving the driver twenty dollars when he got out at the Gramercy Park Hotel, more than enough to cover the fare.

He said vaguely: "Don't worry about it. Why didn't you answer the phone?"

Loretta exhaled noisily. "He left another message while I

was out, Donelly, Michael, whatever his name is. I thought it might be him." She lifted her hand to her face, wiping away a smear of cleansing lotion below her left eye.

Tracey began to talk fast, exuding a febrile excitement as though he was in pursuit of a hot story. "I know it's late, I nearly didn't ring you but I thought you'd want to know, I mean, is this bloke *sick* or what?" Belatedly realising what Loretta had said, he stopped and added: "You say he's phoned again? While you were out?"

"Yes, and there were a couple of hang-ups—you know, when someone doesn't put the phone down straight after the tone. What is it? What have you found out?"

Tracey hesitated. "That number," he said, prolonging the suspense, "the one you gave me in the restaurant?"

"*Yes.* What about it?" She glanced at her wrist, forgetting she'd taken her watch off in the bathroom. He had worked fast, it could only be half an hour, forty minutes at the most, since she'd dropped him off at his hotel.

"You're not going to believe this."

Doing her best to be patient, Loretta said: "Try me."

"Not only is there no Lieutenant Donelly, it's nothing to do with the cops."

"It isn't?" She sat down on the bed, unsurprised by this confirmation but not liking it. "John, please. Tell me."

Tracey said triumphantly: "He's only picked one of *the* most popular numbers in the city, you have to hand it to him—"

"*What?*"

"It's a helpline," he said soberly, "a number for women who've been raped or sexually abused."

She gasped.

"Loretta? Are you all right? I told you it was sick."

She leapt to her feet and began to pace up and down, dragging the base of the telephone across the floor behind her. Honey, who had been asleep on the floor, looked up in alarm and tried to crawl under the television.

"Rape?" she spluttered, almost incoherent. "What kind of pervert . . . Oh, *shit*. John, don't hang up." She knelt and fumbled with the telephone cord, which had somehow wound itself round her left ankle. "Hello, are you there?"

He was and she said: "How did you find out so quickly? I mean, I wouldn't even know where to start. God, your contacts are amazing."

"Oh, it was nothing. Hang on while I light a fag." She heard the hiss of a cigarette lighter, followed by a long intake of air as he inhaled.

"Go on," she said eagerly, "how did you do it? The phone company? Or was it the police?"

"Actually," he said, sounding mildly embarrassed, "I just kept dialling the number. It took twenty-two attempts, I counted, and when I finally got through this woman said"— he tried, with a spectacular lack of success, to sound like an American—"Candice speaking. I must say she wasn't exactly helpful at first, I don't know why. Men get raped as well as women, not so often I know but they do. Anyway, when she finally shut up long enough for me to explain she said it's always hard to get through, they only have two numbers and they're trying to raise the cash for another one. I said I'd send her a donation—I thought you'd be proud of me."

Loretta chewed absently at a flaky piece of skin on her index finger, not really listening to him. "It's the *planning*, that's what I can't get over," she said. "Choosing a number that's likely to be engaged, pretending to be a policeman—*two* policemen. All that stuff about ANEMONE, I wonder if it really exists . . ."

It was Tracey's turn to sound blank. "What're you talking about?"

"Oh, never mind. Thanks, John," she added, not wanting to sound ungrateful, "I mean, there's not much I can do but at least I know I was right. What a—a bastard."

"You could report it to the cops. The real cops, I mean."

She shuddered. "I'm not going through all that again. And it's not as if I know his number, his real number."

"You mean you're going to let him get away with it? This isn't like you, Loretta."

She said tiredly: "It's midnight, I'm in a strange city, I'll be on a plane in less than twenty-four hours. I haven't exactly got a lot of options open to me, have I? Of course I'll tell Toni, don't worry about that."

"When's your flight?"

"Nine. Well, just after. I have to be at the airport at six."

"Ring me when you get home."

"All right. Will you be in Washington?"

"Yeah, I'm going back tomorrow."

"John—"

"What?"

"Nothing. Just—don't rush into anything, OK?"

"I'm not going to join a cult, if that's what you're worried about."

"I didn't mean—"

"I know. Listen, it's late, and you wanted an early night. You won't get much sleep on the plane."

"OK. Bye then."

"Bye."

Loretta gazed round the room, unable to recall what she was doing when Tracey rang. The dog, sensing that the threatened crisis had been averted, crept out from her hiding place, flopped onto her side and breathed windily through her nose.

"Make-up," Loretta said aloud, and returned to the bathroom.

She was cleaning her teeth when the thought came back to her: what if Michael, instead of calling numbers at random, really was one of Toni's friends? Had some connection with her, at least? The red address book she had asked Loretta to consult, when she wanted her gynaecologist's office number, contained dozens of names which, judging by the variety of inks and styles in which they were written, looked as if they had been accumulated over a period of years. The only Michael Toni had admitted to knowing was a colleague at Columbia but she had been distracted when Loretta put the question and there might well be others. Rapidly overcoming her qualms about intruding into Toni's private life, she turned off the cold tap, returned her toothbrush to her toilet bag and went to get the red book. Opening it at the As, she checked the page and a half of entries, finding five male names and one which could have belonged to a man or a woman, but not a single Michael. Disappointed, she moved on to the Bs and almost immediately spotted Mike Bompiani. He had two telephone numbers, home and work, but her excitement ebbed away when she saw that the three-figure code was unfamiliar, and the address below it was in Aspen, Colorado. Convinced that the Michael who had planned the elaborate hoax was local, Loretta realised that she needed to be more systematic, dividing the names she found into more and less likely candidates. Seizing her notebook, she divided a clean page into two columns, the first headed by the initials "N.Y." and the second by the single word "other." She wrote Mike Bompiani's name and home number in the second column and moved on to the

Cs, where she drew a blank, although she couldn't help being struck by the extent of Toni's acquaintance. She seemed to know people all over the States, some of them in towns so small Loretta had never heard of them.

A few minutes later she closed the little red book. There were four possibles in New York City although one of these was the colleague Toni had mentioned, Michael Koganovitch. Loretta had an obscure notion, which she knew she would be hard put to justify, that a man who had published a scholarly study of Derrida was unlikely to get his kicks from telephone sex. That left three. Loretta hesitated, inhibited equally by the lateness of the hour and by the fact that she had no idea what she would do if someone answered. Then, telling herself not to be a wimp, she could always hang up without speaking, she pulled the phone towards her and tried the first number. She held her breath as it connected, trying to think of something to say if Michael Day picked up the phone—or his wife, or his boyfriend, or his mother; the possibilities were endless. Listening to the ringing tone, she gradually relaxed as it became clear that, whoever he was, neither Michael Day nor any other member of his household was at home. Returning to her notebook, she read the next number aloud as she dialled, as if by doing so she could give herself confidence.

It rang twice, she heard a click and suddenly her ears were blasted by music so loud that she automatically moved the receiver away from her ear. It faded and a recording began: "Hi, this is Michael Lindsay. If you're calling to offer me the lead role in an exciting new Broadway production, leave a message and I'll call you right back. Or you can try my agent, Frank Sussman, at Actors Unlimited." Loretta gripped the receiver, her knuckles white, as the familiar, confident voice rapped out the agency's telephone number. "Otherwise, if your call is social, leave your name and number." There was another burst of music, this time something lush and romantic which might have come from a film score, and a single long tone; apparently no one else had left a message that evening, which suggested that Michael Lindsay had not been out for long.

Loretta returned the receiver to its cradle, stunned by her discovery that Michael wasn't just a friend of Toni's—she had found his name a couple of lines above her own in the Ls—but an *actor*. Immediately she felt better about being taken in, he was clearly used to changing his voice and accent, and it occurred to her that he might even have acted the part of a detective in a play. Still not quite able to believe it, Loretta picked up the receiver and dialled the number again. This time, taking the precaution of holding the phone a little way from her ear, she was able to make out the words of the song, a woman's voice complaining tonelessly, almost hypnotically, "I feel small when I am next to you, I feel big when I forget you, I feel small when I am next to you, I feel big when I forget you." It seemed nastily appropriate after the lengths Michael Lindsay had gone to in tormenting her and she stabbed her finger onto the rest, cutting the connection as soon as she heard his voice.

The elation prompted by her success began to fade as she thought about what to do next. Her first impulse was to ring John Tracey at the Gramercy Park Hotel but she drew her hand back, uncomfortable with the notion of once again seeking his help. In any case, what could he do that she couldn't? Ring the answering-machine and tell Michael Lindsay he'd been rumbled, threaten to report him to the police or the telephone company; other than going round to his flat to confront him, that seemed to cover all the options. Loretta stretched her legs out in front of her in a wide V, staring discontentedly at a point on the carpet between her bare feet.

Although she wasn't seriously considering going round there, she was curious about where Michael Lindsay lived. She picked up Toni's address book, turning the pages rapidly until she came to the Ls, and ran a finger down the list until she came to his entry. The significance of what she read took a few seconds to strike her, and when it did she started up from the bed in alarm. Michael Lindsay's address was West Eighty-second Street, within easy walking distance, and she wondered what he looked like: youngish, with a pony tail, like the man who'd tried twice to sneak upstairs to the flat? His voice had suggested someone older, in his thirties, but now she knew he was an actor that didn't mean a lot. Perhaps he was middle-aged and balding, like the man in the bookshop? Incidents came back to her in such rapid succession that she felt dizzy, pacing up and down and disturbing the dog again without re-alising what she was doing. There was a spy hole in the front door and she rushed to it, peering into the dimly lit corridor as though she expected to find Michael Lindsay lurking there. The corridor was entirely empty, the front door of the flat op-posite weirdly distorted by the tiny lens, and as she stared she thought she could hear the distant *whoosh* of the lift.

Otherwise, there was silence. Loretta turned and leaned against the door, reassuring herself with its solidity, its failure to give under pressure. On the other hand she was a woman, and a slender one at that; for all she knew Michael Lindsay was six foot four and as powerfully built as Magic Johnson. Even so, he would have to get past the porters, who had proved their reliability in challenging strangers. But what would she do if—

Loretta pushed herself away from the door, trying to stem the influx of gory images. She had seen too many slasher movies, too many films in which single women were stalked by maniacs with knives. Nuisance callers and flashers tended to be timid men, she reminded herself without knowing the exact source of this piece of wisdom, and there was no point in allowing herself to dwell on notorious murder scenes from movies with quasi-domestic settings: Angie Dickinson slashed to death in a lift in *Dressed to Kill,* Janet Leigh in the shower in *Psycho,* the actress whose name she had forgotten at the beginning of *Jagged Edge.* And of course her conversation with that ghastly woman, Cary something, the one who had wanted to confide in her about the Brooklyn Beast, that didn't exactly help.

"Honey," she said, sitting on the edge of the bed and encouraging the dog to come forward. Honey regarded her suspiciously for a moment, then lumbered to her feet, dipping her head so that Loretta could stroke her. She pulled the duvet round her shoulders and was for once relieved when the dog slumped against her bare legs, drawing comfort from her warm bulk. Not wanting to disturb the animal, she raised her head and peered at the books on the shelf above Toni's bed, wondering if there was something among them to take her mind off dismemberment and gore. Honey growled when she made an experimental move towards the shelf and Loretta froze, stretching her right arm as far as it would go until her fingers closed on the only book within her reach. As she lifted it down, a folded press release fluttered to the floor and she saw it was a review copy. Toni occasionally reviewed fiction for the *New York Review of Books* but when Loretta turned the book right way up she was confronted with an amateurish photo of hooded figures cavorting round a bonfire. *Sympathy for the Devil,* she read, and in smaller letters: "a shocking exposé of the *true facts* about Satanic abuse in the United States." She groaned, tossed the heavy book onto the bed and pulled the duvet more snugly around her.

10

Toni gave an embarrassed laugh. "I was going to tell you on Thursday but the conversation kind of—"

"Took an awkward turn," finished Loretta. "I know. It seems a bit silly, saying congratulations, but—well, you know what I mean. I hope you'll be very happy."

"Thanks. Was Mom cross?"

Loretta was glad they were talking on the phone and Toni couldn't see her expression. "More upset than cross," she said guardedly. "Why on earth didn't you tell her?" She had been woken up by a phone call from Mrs. Stramiello, who'd come back from visiting relatives in Jersey City and found a letter from Toni telling her about the wedding. She was so angry and hurt she could hardly speak, and Loretta had spent an uncomfortable few minutes listening to her before she pulled herself together and rang off.

"I guess you gave her this number?"

"I had to. She said she'd ring you when she got back from Mass."

Toni made a little sound. "That's the problem, Dad's not so bad but Mom's so devout. She'd have made such a *fuss* about us not getting married in a Catholic church."

"But Jay's parents, aren't they just as . . ." Loretta trailed off, realising the phrase she had been going to use—just as *bad*—was hardly polite.

Toni appeared not to notice. "Oh, sure, but that's different. Jay's dad is a minister, it's his *job*. There were only eight of us in church and it was over real fast. Mom would have insisted on a nuptial Mass *and* we'd have had to promise to bring the kid up Catholic, which I'm absolutely not going to do, not after . . . well, I wouldn't exactly say I had a happy childhood."

Loretta said: "When's the baby due?"

"January." She made an odd sound, not quite a laugh. "I've hardly told anyone, I'm not superstitious but . . . We'd almost given up hope but then someone told Jay about Dr. Rosenstein. She does . . . her big thing's IVF."

"IVF," Loretta repeated, startled. A vision of laboratories and test tubes floated into her mind. "Did you speak to her, by the way? She left a message."

"Yes, thanks, I did." Toni changed the subject. "Listen, Loretta, I can't talk for long. How's it going, you having a good time?"

"Ye-es."

"Honey's OK?"

Loretta glanced across the room at the dog. "She's fine. You know I asked you about someone called Michael, Michael Lindsay?"

"Michael *Lindsay*? I thought you said Michael Koganovich. Michael *Lindsay* called? How did he get my number?'

Loretta said, puzzled: "I thought he was a friend of yours. It's a bit complicated but basically he . . ." She felt her cheeks redden as she thought again about how she'd been fooled. "Basically he's been making obscene phone calls."

"He what? Are you *serious*? Hold on, I'm taking the phone into the hall so I can hear if anyone comes." Loretta heard footsteps, a door closing, then Toni came back on the line. "Obscene, how?"

Loretta remembered the honeyed yet imperative voice and shuddered. "Do I have to? I mean, I'm sure you can imagine." When Toni didn't respond she added reluctantly: "Fellatio, that seems to be his thing."

"*What?* I knew the guy was weird but he never . . ." Suddenly she changed tack. "You didn't tell him anything? About Jay and me? That we got married?"

Loretta frowned. "I hardly got the chance. I told him you'd gone away for the weekend and he—that's when he started asking all these questions."

"I can't think how he got my number," Toni said worriedly, as though she wasn't really listening. "I changed it after we broke up, I thought everyone knew not to—"

"You mean he was your *boyfriend*?"

Now Toni sounded embarrassed. "A friend introduced us, I'd seen him in a play off Broadway, at first he seemed so charming. It wasn't till . . . gradually I got to think something wasn't quite . . ." She sounded exactly as Loretta had a moment before when she didn't want to spell out the whole story of the obscene phone calls, and Loretta wondered what humiliations Michael Lindsay had inflicted on her.

"I couldn't always tell what was acting and what was for real," Toni burst out and, apparently acknowledging the circumlocution, tried to explain. "One time it was my birthday and he fixed up a surprise, he said to dress up and he'd call for me at ten. I thought it was a little late to eat and when we got out of the cab it was some kind of a club in the East Village. You go down the steps and it's so dark you can't see, then you're in a room with crucifixes on the walls and the waiters dressed up as choirboys. The menu's all religious stuff, Bloody Marys and Holy Joes, and the main course, it was some kind of a paste sandwich but on the menu they called it Loaves and Fishes. Not that I'm still Catholic or anything but—well, I didn't see it was funny and we had a row.

"After I broke it off," she added, "he started calling at peculiar times, two or three in the morning. I used to pick up the phone and I could hear him breathing, he didn't say a word, ever, but I knew who it was. In the end I called the phone company and they changed the number. Loretta, what I don't understand, did he tell you his name? Before he . . . before he did a number on you?"

"He said he was called Michael. I—I'm afraid I went through your address book. I'm sorry."

"You did what?"

"There were only two or three Michaels with New York numbers and I recognised his voice on his answering-machine."

"You mean you called them *all*? What did you say?"

"They were out."

"Thank God for that." Toni thought for a moment, then

added: "You know, it's just like *Vox*. I mean—I wonder if he read it?"

"Is it? I tried ringing the police on Thursday but they just said I should—"

"You called the *cops*?"

"Yes, why not? I was—well, not exactly scared." She hesitated, remembering how frightened she'd felt the night before, alone in the dark flat, when she realised Michael Lindsay knew Toni's address. It was not in her nature to dissemble but Toni's reaction had wrong-footed her.

"The guy's a fantasist," Toni said, "he needs *help*. I guess it doesn't totally surprise me, say he really does have these psychosexual problems. But I don't see it's going to advance the situation, involving the cops."

"So what do you suggest? Who's to say he won't do it again?"

"I hear what you're saying, Loretta. I need time to think about this." Abruptly her tone changed, becoming bright and superficial. "We're leaving now? What's the hurry, hon?" She came back on the line. "Sorry, Loretta, apparently we have to go call on Jay's grandmother. Families, you know how it is. We'll talk later, OK? Your flight's not till tonight. And don't— I know you're pissed but let me handle it. Please?"

"I suppose," Loretta began reluctantly, and then remembered something. "Toni, wait, you haven't told me"—the line went dead and she finished the sentence to herself, flatly— "what he looks like."

She put the phone down, thinking it was all very well for Toni, miles away in Long Island, to take the view that Michael Lindsay needed help—which was probably a euphemism for counselling, Loretta speculated. At the first dinner party she went to in San Francisco, a history professor had told her, when she expressed surprise at the number of people she had met whose lives seemed to revolve around appointments with their analysts, that in America poor people went to jail and the rich had therapy; she didn't know if Michael Lindsay was rich, but judging by his voice he was certainly middle-class. Gazing abstractedly round the room, unable to remember what she had been doing when she answered the phone, it occurred to her that she was perhaps being a little hard on Toni. She actually knew Michael Lindsay, was better placed than Loretta to decide whether he was a threat to women or merely playing some bizarre practical joke; always assuming, of course, that there was a clear distinction between the two. Toni's attitude might be based on no more than her natural reluctance to turn in someone she used to sleep with, and presumably had once liked a lot.

Loretta sighed and ran her hands through her hair. It was a morning of hazy brightness, with no sign of the rolling storm clouds which had made the weather so changeable on Saturday. Half an hour before, when she pulled up the blinds and looked out on to West End Avenue, the nondescript modern buildings stretching away from Toni's apartment had their outlines softened by mist until they were no more than ethereal shapes in a pale, mysterious vista. There was an occasional shimmer of light from a distant high wall of glass, or where the sun reflected weakly from the bronzed peak of a skyscraper, but for the most part the city was softly shrouded, reminding her unexpectedly of Venice. They were the only cities she could think of which sustained the illusion, regardless of weather conditions, of having effortlessly incorporated light and air into the most grandiose of architectural schemes. Now she drifted to the window, peering out and sensing that the mist was starting to dissolve. The sun was a bright disc behind the hazy layers and she could make out windows and other details on apartment blocks which had earlier presented blank façades. Behind her Honey barked, a reminder that she hadn't yet had her morning walk, and Loretta called over her shoulder: "In a minute. I'm not even dressed."

Her weekend case was on the bed, surrounded by clothes and shoes. Rummaging through the piles, Loretta found that most of the things she had brought with her were too crumpled to wear again, or too tight for a seven-hour plane journey. Deciding on thin black trousers and the white shirt she'd bought at Bloomingdale's, she rolled her underwear into a bundle, stowed it at the bottom of the bag and laid the more delicate items of her wardrobe on top. She showered, dressed in the clothes she'd picked out and went to Toni's desk to consult the phone book, in search of a bookshop within walking distance of the flat where she could buy Dale Martineau's novel. She had had a mildly erotic dream about him when she finally fell asleep in the early hours, so pleasant and full of promise that she had actually thought about ringing him to see if he was busy at lunchtime. That was when she realised he hadn't given her his home number in return for hers, probably an oversight but one which was compounded by her discovery that he was ex-directory. There were several Martineaus in the phone book, none of them with the initial D, and she could hardly ring them all in the hope of finding a relative. The next best thing, the only way of feeling connected to him, was to buy his novel; she was about to dial a bookshop on Broadway to find out if it was open on Sunday morning when the phone rang again.

"Hello," she said eagerly, hoping it might be him until she remembered he didn't know where in New York she was staying.

"Hi, Loretta. This is Michael."

It was quite unexpected, he had always called in the evening. Then she realised she was wrong: he had spoken to her in the morning a couple of times, but only when he was pretending to be Lieutenant Donelly.

Her silence made him anxious. "Loretta, you're not going to hang up on me? I missed our little chat yesterday, it wasn't very nice of you, staying out all day when you knew I was waiting to talk with you. You did know, didn't you? I waited all afternoon, first your machine was on and then the line was busy. You're gonna have to be specially nice to me today to make up. I've been thinking about you a lot, whether you work out and stuff . . . I hope you work out, I like hard bodies, not those soft, fleshy types of women." He hesitated, and his voice began to wheedle. "Come on, Loretta, say something, you *know* what I like. Tell me about your body."

She said impatiently: "It's too late, I know all about you— who you are, where you live. I rang last night, you were out and I got your answering-machine."

He laughed, a little uncertain. "Nice try, Loretta, but most folks in New York have machines. Listen, I realised last night I never asked your measurements, I hope you don't have big breasts? I'd be very sorry if you—"

"God," she said, thoroughly annoyed, "you don't give up easily, do you? Wait, I'm going to move to the other phone." She went back into the living-room, picked up the other handset and carried it to the coffee table where she had left her notebook. "OK, here we are. Your name's Michael Lindsay and you live on—"

At the other end of the line there was a muffled sound, somewhere between a gasp and an exclamation. She ignored it, continuing to read his address and phone number into the stunned silence.

"You're an actor, I gather. Are you a good one? Or is this the best you can manage, pestering women over the phone?" She mimicked his tone of voice: "I don't think you're very good, Michael. When did you last work? In panto was it, or don't you have them over here? I'm trying to remember the name of that place, the one in the saying. Will it play in Peoria, that's it, I expect that's about your level, isn't it, Michael, panto in Peoria." To her astonishment, she was beginning to enjoy herself. "What about Lieutenant Donelly, is he there too?"

There was a long pause, then he said lightly: "You really have done your homework. But you have to admit, you were taken in for the longest time. How did you find out, did you talk to Toni?"

"No, actually. I worked it out for myself."

"Clever girl."

Not liking his tone, Loretta said sharply: "Look, it's over, whatever game you think you're playing at. And before I leave New York I'm going to give your name and address to the police." She said it without much conviction, wanting to scare him, thinking he was taking his exposure much too lightly.

"I don't think so."

"You don't?"

"You really think they'll believe you?" He put on a high, womanish voice, a fake English accent: "I've been getting these calls, Lieutenant, this *horrid* man wanted to know all about me, I mean *everything*. Oh, no, I couldn't possibly repeat it, he *made* me talk dirty to him. No, of *course* I didn't put the phone down, I thought I was helping the police." His voice changed back. "You think they're gonna buy that?"

"Why wouldn't they?"

"Fine, I can't stop you. Waste your last day in New York—what time *is* your flight, by the way?"

"It's none of your business." She was losing control and a memory came back to her, an incident in Paris when she'd caught a man slipping his hand into her bag outside the Pompidou Centre. She had shouted, in English unfortunately, and the would-be thief took a couple of steps back and looked her boldly in the eye. She did not know what to do and a moment later he ran off, disappearing into a noisy crowd which had gathered to watch a fire-eater. She felt the same sense of disjunction now, unable to think of a way of ending the conversation without giving Michael Lindsay the last word.

Into the silence he said matter-of-factly: "It was a game, Loretta. Like you said."

"I didn't mean—not literally."

"What I'm saying is, I'm an *actor*."

"I know." She wasn't sure where this was leading.

"I was rehearsing, you were helping. You've heard of the Method, I have to get into a part, really live it. Like De Niro."

She gave a shout of astonished laughter.

"What's so funny? You're a friend of Toni's and you offered to help. Now you've changed your mind. Maybe you got into it, enjoyed it too much, now you're crying rape—"

"*What?* You think anyone's going to fall for that?"

He mocked her: "Why wouldn't they? I'm a respectable guy, I have an agent, I'm up for a part in Tarantino's next movie. You have—what? Twelve hours before your flight? Say you're right and you manage to persuade those guys I'm some kind of a pervert. That makes you a witness, maybe they won't let you fly out, did you think of that?"

"That's ridiculous. They wouldn't keep me here."

"You wanna risk it?"

She was still thinking when he began to speak in a completely different, caressing voice. "Come on, Loretta, we both enjoyed it but it's over. Let's not fight." If a stranger had overheard him, it would have sounded regretful, a lover's farewell.

"God," she said in a rush, "you really like manipulating people, don't you? This isn't about sex, it's about power."

"Wow. A *feminist*."

"And what are you? *Nothing*, just a collection of parts. What do you do when you wake up in the morning, toss a coin? Who's it going to be today, Hamlet or a child molester?"

"Now wait—"

"Or some stupid little pervert who's so scared of women he has to get his kicks over the phone. You weren't acting on Friday night, that's the only way you can—"

"Baby," he crooned reproachfully, "and I was going to invite you to *lunch*."

"What?"

"Loretta, we could have been so *good* together, I would've taken you to Orso's, maybe we'd have ended up in bed together. But you had to go and spoil it. Sorry, babe, but I just don't think I want to talk to you anymore."

There was a soft click as he put the phone down. Loretta stared at the receiver, lost for words. She had heard of people with multiple personality disorder, had read a case history in a magazine, but she had always assumed that in real life the transitions were gradual, nothing like so rapid as she'd just encountered. Unless, of course, Michael Lindsay had been acting all the time, from the first phone call on Thursday to this final flourish . . . Astounded, she handed the phone down onto the floor and sat on the edge of the bed, replaying the bizarre conversation in her mind.

"Honey," she said after a while.

The dog was asleep in her usual place, stubby legs stretched out front and back, next to the television. She opened her eyes and regarded Loretta distrustfully, as if to say she'd been fooled too many times by the promise of a walk which then failed to materialise. Loretta got up and went to the front door, calling the dog repeatedly over her shoulder, and lifted the lead from its hook. Still suspicious, Honey dragged herself to her feet, slouched towards the door and allowed Loretta to slip the hook onto the ring of her collar.

Riverside Park was marginally less noisy than usual, the volume of traffic on the expressway not quite as relentless as on a weekday morning. Loretta recognised a couple of other dog-walkers in the distance, people she'd seen on previous visits to the park, but most of the joggers seemed to have decided to stay indoors until the mist lifted. The drifting, translucent haze in which the city seemed to float when viewed from the fifteenth floor, and through glass, translated at ground level into sticky fumes which Loretta could feel clogging her nasal passages. Honey was as impervious to the weather as ever, sniffing sparse hummocks of grass and squatting every few yards to rid herself of a depressingly diminutive quantity of pee. While the poop-a-scoop and its associated operations still filled Loretta with disgust, she was becoming less self-conscious with every outing about the horrid little plastic bags she had to dispose of on her way out of the park; eager to get the whole business over, she did her best to be patient, aware that the dog didn't really get enough exercise for an animal of her size.

Honey trotted ahead, following invisible trails with the enthusiasm of a truffle hound on the track of some sumptuous underground tuber. So far that morning they had survived a challenge from a yappy, bad-tempered Yorkshire terrier, a familiar nuisance whose sorties Honey magisterially brushed aside, and a more perplexing encounter with a short, squat, black pig. Honey had stopped and growled as soon as she spotted the animal, observing it with growing alarm as it waddled towards her with its owner, a slender woman in skin-tight cycling shorts. To Loretta's astonishment, as the odd couple got nearer, the bulldog backed away as far as the lead allowed and flattened herself on the scrubby ground next to the path, as though forty pounds of muscle and bone could simply merge into the scenery at will. Loretta crouched beside the terrified dog, speaking to her encouragingly, but Honey refused to be comforted, flicking her eyes this way and that until the threat was safely past.

"You useless lump," Loretta finished affectionately, getting to her feet, and they resumed their serene progress through the park. Hearing the pounding footsteps of a jogger gaining on them from behind, the first one that morning, Loretta moved to the side of the path to allow the runner to overtake without breaking his or her stride. "Honey," she said warningly, shortening the lead in case the dog took it into her head to snap at the jogger's heels.

The next moment the jogger barged into her, inflicting a painful blow on Loretta's left shoulder. She staggered, the breath knocked out of her, and let go of the lead. Recovering enough to spin round, already remonstrating with the runner, it took her a split second to realise he wasn't a jogger at all, that she was being mugged. He came at her again, shouting unintelligibly above the furious barking of the dog, his hands seizing her arms, and she felt his superior strength as she twisted and struggled to break free. Gasping that she had nothing to steal, nothing at all, her mind threw up only useless advice—don't make eye contact, don't speak, keep your jewellery hidden. Sheer desperation jerked her knee up into the soft vulnerable flesh of his groin, the only manoeuvre she remembered from an old self-defence manual, and she was unprepared for its spectacular success. He let go instantly, doubled over in pain, his hands between his legs, and the unexpected physical release sent Loretta tottering backwards. The dog, beside herself with rage, saw her opportunity at last and hurled herself at the mugger's legs, bowling him over.

Loretta watched in horror as the scene unfolded: the attacker sprawling on his back, the dog's powerful jaws closing on his leg, her teeth ripping through denim, her noisy grunts as she resisted his frantic attempts to shake her off. Dazed by the speed with which her assailant had been disabled, Loretta did not move until he screamed, a high, inhuman sound which snapped her out of her state of shocked inaction. Throwing herself forward, shouting the dog's name until she was hoarse, she managed to get a hold on the thick leather collar, first with one hand and then with both, and pulled so hard that the animal rounded angrily on her, knocking her off balance. Gravel tore at her hands as she skidded backwards on the path, throwing up her arms to defend her face as the dog turned on her—

"I got him," someone shouted, and the dog reared on her hind legs, jerked backwards by the lead. Loretta scrambled out of reach, still afraid, but the stranger held tight.

"You all right?" she heard him say, unsure whether he meant herself or the injured mugger a couple of yards farther up the path. She struggled into a sitting position, tears streaming unnoticed down her cheeks, peering at the man who had tried to rob her. Not a man, a youth—

"What happened? You know this guy?"

She did not answer, transfixed by the bloody stains on her attacker's jeans. "Get a doctor," she gasped, unable to look away from the ragged, oozing mess. "Get an *ambulance*."

The jogger persisted. "Do you know this guy?"

"No." She lifted her head, wondering why he couldn't just do what she asked. He was middle-aged, dressed in running gear, and an odd detail lodged in her mind, the only thing she could recall about him afterwards: he was wearing wire-rimmed glasses, held on by an elastic band which passed round the back of his head.

A crowd was gathering, converging on the two prone figures, and the runner took charge. "Does anyone here have medical experience?"

"I'm a nurse." A plump older woman pushed to the front.

"Can you take a look at him?"

The mugger lay groaning, in obvious pain, and the nurse knelt beside him, asking him questions in a low voice. When she put her hand out, tentatively, towards the wound in his leg, someone in the crowd called out: "Hey, don't touch, he might have—"

The word AIDS hung unspoken in the air and the woman drew back her hand. Loretta wiped her eyes with her knuckles and watched the boy—he was perhaps eighteen, she now saw—wincing as he attempted to sit up. She could hear his teeth chattering in spite of the damp heat, an effect of shock perhaps, but no one moved, apparently paralysed by the spectre of infection. She panicked, thinking the kid needed help even if he had tried to rob her, and began edging towards him, still too shaken to get up. He lifted his head, met her gaze with dark, anguished eyes, and she noticed for the first time that his long fair hair was tied back in a pony tail.

"Her dog do that?" someone was demanding in a loud voice. "Dogs like that, they oughta be tied up. They oughta be shot."

"No way it's the dog's fault. Guy tried to mug her."

Momentarily distracted, Loretta looked up. "Honey, where is she?"

"I got her," a woman called from the back of the crowd, apparently having taken over the responsibility from the man with glasses.

The boy was protesting, speaking disjointedly: "I'm *not*—I didn't—I couldn't stop. I only wanted to speak with her." A spasm of pain contorted his face and he pushed away the nurse, who was ineptly trying to straighten his wounded leg. "Shit, no, please, it *hurts*." Still addressing her, but looking at Loretta, he said pleadingly: "You don't understand, she's my *mom*."

There was an excited buzz from the crowd as it recognised a new and exciting development in the drama.

"She's your ma, how come she don't seem to recognise you?"

"You know the kid?"

"I thought he tried to mug her?"

"What'd he say? I didn't hear what he said."

Loretta gasped: "His mother? I don't know what he's talking about, I was taking the dog for a walk—"

"You're *British*?"

She nodded, uncomprehending.

He buried his face in his hands and said over and over again: "Oh, shit. Oh, shit. Oh, shit."

An idea, outlandish but just within the realms of possibility, came to Loretta. She put out a hand, touching his arm very gently. "You thought—did you think I was Toni? Antonia?"

"You know her?" he asked eagerly. "Ms. Stramiello?"

She nodded.

"You have the hair," he explained, pointing at her head, "and the dog so I thought . . . He said she walks a big, ugly dog every morning in the park next to her apartment block."

"Who?" she asked. "Who said that?"

"What's he say?" the deaf man in the crowd said loudly. Someone snapped back: "Shut the fuck up, grandad."

"Mr. Dunow. I paid him to—to find where she lived."

Loretta was beginning to see the resemblance to Toni, the similar bone structure and hollow cheeks. His, though, were smeared with blood, and he was trembling.

"Wait," said Loretta, looking round for the jogger who had initially taken control. He was talking to a black man with a perfectly bald head, gesturing with his hands and laughing, but when he saw Loretta getting unsteadily to her feet, he came to help her. She asked: "Has someone gone to call an ambulance?"

He shrugged. "I guess not."

"Where's the nearest phone?"

"A phone?" He considered. "West End Avenue and Seventy-eighth, there's a little café—"

"Please," she said, "get an ambulance. He needs a doctor."

He hesitated. "What about the cops? Didn't he just try and rob you?"

"No, it was a mistake. He thought I was someone else."

"You sure?"

"*Yes.* Hurry, please, he's losing blood." At this rate, she thought, they were more likely to get a TV crew on the scene, tipped off by a resident in one of the apartment blocks that overlooked the park, than the emergency services. To her relief, the jogger said a casual "OK" and set off at an easy run.

"Where's the nearest hospital?" Loretta asked, addressing

an anorexically thin teenage girl. She wondered where on earth all these people had come from, drawn to the scene as though it was free Sunday-morning entertainment.

"Dunno. Like—I live in Babylon."

Loretta closed her eyes, unable to bear it. Someone mentioned the Roosevelt, someone else St. Clare's, and an argument broke out. The nurse was questioning the boy again, asking about injections—tetanus, rabies, whether his shots were up-to-date. Loretta thought rabies was the least of their problems, compared to the risk of infection from Honey's saliva and loss of blood, and she crouched beside her: "You did say you were a nurse?"

The woman flushed. "I have some training, it was a while back but my brother-in-law's a dentist, couple days a week I help out in his office . . ."

Loretta rolled her eyes upwards. "There's nothing wrong with his *teeth*. Please, leave him to me."

The self-styled nurse withdrew and Loretta lowered herself gingerly onto the ground, taking the boy's clammy hand. "The ambulance'll be here soon," she said reassuringly, wishing she knew something about first aid. His leg looked a mess but at least it wasn't gushing blood. She didn't dare move him, thinking the bone might be fractured.

"Now what's she doing? What's going on?"

It was the deaf man again and Loretta lost her temper. "Why don't you all just . . . *go home?*" she demanded, having to restrain herself from putting it more rudely. People shifted and complained, not hiding their disappointment that nothing much was happening, and she was relieved when they started to drift away.

"Excuse me," said the woman who had spoken earlier, "but I have your dog . . ."

"Oh, I'm sorry," said Loretta, looking up. She felt the boy shudder and squeezed his hand. "Don't worry, she won't hurt you."

The woman said sympathetically: "You want me to walk her till the ambulance comes?" Loretta accepted the offer gratefully.

"Will she come see me?" Toni's son asked suddenly. "If they keep me in the hospital?"

In the distance, a siren wailed.

Loretta ducked the question. "What's your name?" she asked. "I've been staying in Toni's flat but I'm going home tonight, to England. I'll have to try and get hold of her before I go." She frowned, not relishing the prospect of informing Toni, on this of all weekends, that her grown-up son had turned up out of the blue.

"Frank," the boy said, a bit reluctantly. "Frank Ryan."

An Irish surname, Loretta thought, remembering that Toni's parents were Catholics. She was doing mental sums, working out that if the boy was eighteen, as she had guessed, he would have been born when Toni wasn't much more than that herself, presumably the result of a teenage romance.

"I tried to—I wanted to go up to her apartment but those guys on the desk . . . Mr. Dunow, he said it was better to contact her direct. I mean, not call her up first or anything."

The siren was getting louder.

"Not long now," Loretta said, and a moment later an ambulance swung onto Riverside Drive, coming to a halt against the curb. A couple of paramedics got out, running round the back and taking out a stretcher.

"Will she come see me?" he asked again, still holding her hand.

"I'll have to find her first," Loretta said evasively. She was about to say she'd come to the hospital herself, after she had taken the dog home, but she realised it might take her some time to get hold of Toni. "I mean, I know where she's staying, she's in the Hamptons for the weekend." His face fell and she added quickly: "She'll be home tomorrow. Where do you live?"

"Newburgh."

It meant nothing to Loretta and she thought she should write it down, if she could borrow a pen and some paper, but at that moment one of the paramedics touched her shoulder. "Are you hurt, ma'am? Do you need medical attention?"

Loretta got up stiffly. "No, not me." She gestured towards the boy, Frank. "He's been bitten, I'm afraid my dog . . . It wasn't her fault, she thought he was trying—"

"You have blood on your face," the woman said matter-of-factly.

"Have I?" Loretta was puzzled for a moment, then she remembered her hands. She looked down at the palms, which were scratched and bloody. The other paramedic was kneeling beside Frank, asking him questions, something about health insurance. The woman said: "You a relative?"

Loretta shook her head.

She turned and spoke to her colleague, and together they began preparing the stretcher, getting ready to move Frank onto it. It was a painful manoeuvre and he cried out, but in a surprisingly short time they were wheeling him towards the ambulance.

"Where're you taking him?" Loretta called after them.

"The Roosevelt. Tenth and Fifty-ninth."

"Do you have far to go?" It was the jogger, whose return Loretta had failed to notice.

She shook her head and pointed. "Just over there." The woman who had volunteered to walk Honey reappeared, and

Loretta took the lead from her. "Thanks," she said, meaning both of them.

"No problem," the jogger assured her. "Livens up a dull morning. You want me to walk you home?"

Loretta's eyes widened and she shook her head. He lifted a hand, gave her a mock salute and loped off.

"Miss? Is this yours?"

The dog-walker was holding out a manila envelope, A4 size.

Loretta stared at it, remembering something one of the porters had said, or written in the log-book, about the boy with the pony tail trying to deliver an envelope or package.

"Yes," she said, holding out her hand. "I mean, I'd better keep it for him."

She took the envelope, thanked the woman again and called Honey to heel. They left the park, using the shortest route to Riverside Drive, Loretta hurrying the dog along at an unusually fast pace which Honey seemed to enjoy, as she glanced up at Loretta from time to time and let out excited barks. It was not until they turned into Seventy-third Street, yards from home, that a thought occurred to Loretta: at no point, even when she believed she was being mugged, had she entertained the idea that her attacker might be Michael Lindsay. At some point during their recent confrontation, her fear of him had entirely evaporated.

She pushed open the door into the apartment block, ushered Honey inside and headed for the lift, bracing herself for a difficult conversation with Toni.

11

A woman moved about a vast, empty apartment overlooking the Hudson River, preparing an elaborate meal for someone who had so far failed to arrive. From time to time she looked out at the lights on the rippling black water, reflections from the New Jersey shore, saying nothing, revealing nothing. There was no phone, very little furniture, none of the habitual detritus of everyday life—magazines, books, CDs, discarded clothes—but the apartment was described in minute detail: hairline cracks in the high ceiling, every crevice in the old-fashioned kitchen, the monstrous dead roach on the stark white bathroom floor. Dale Martineau's prose was unadorned, without rhetorical flourishes, cinematic in its method of setting a scene; more like a director, Loretta thought, closing the book and remembering that he taught film studies, than a novelist. At first the style had reminded her of Bret Easton Ellis, without the trademark violence, but as she turned the pages and nothing happened another comparison came to mind, those sixties art movies in which someone set up a camera and left it rolling, regardless of whether there was anything to record.

The bus juddered to a halt and Loretta looked up from the novel in her lap. From Central Park West, where she got on, it had turned on to Broadway and was passing through the Theater District, familiar territory to her by now. Loretta fidgeted, wincing as her sore shoulder came into contact with the seat back, and thought how awkward it was going to be if she turned out not to like Dale's book. It wasn't holding her attention as she had hoped and she could hardly send him a note via his publisher saying how much she liked the cover—a detail of Leonardo's *cenacolo* with Jesus and two of the disciples blanked out—without mentioning the novel itself. Loretta had begun reading it in a little Moroccan café with outdoor tables on Amsterdam Avenue, not far from the bookshop where she'd bought it, propping it up against the salt cellar while she ate a plate of couscous and *merguez* sausages. She felt guilty about going out without speaking to Toni, passing on the shocking news that her son had turned up, but she had hung around in the flat for well over an hour after leaving a very insistent message on the minister's answering-machine in Sag Harbor. Perhaps Toni and Jay were staying at his grandmother's for lunch, in which case they might not return for hours; bruised and a little faint, dreading the uncomfortable night ahead of her on the plane, Loretta had finally decided she needed a meal herself and the last thing she felt like was rooting about in Toni's fridge. Before leaving the flat she had phoned the hospital to inquire after Frank Ryan but he was still in the emergency room, pushed to the back of the queue by a serious road accident; he had been given painkillers, she was told, but a dog bite, no matter how nasty, would have to wait until the survivors—that was the word the woman used—had been attended to.

By now she knew the whole sad story of Frank's birth and adoption, having pieced it together from the documents in the envelope he had dropped in the park. Curled up on the sofa, the phone in front of her on the coffee table where she could reach it without getting up, she had felt no compunction as she up-ended the envelope and allowed the contents to slide out, as though the intrusion was somehow balanced by the amount of damage she had sustained during the struggle in the park: her new white shirt ripped and smeared with blood, a painful gash on her left hand and a long abrasion running from her elbow to her wrist as well as minor scratches. The shirt was beyond repair and she had had to borrow one of Toni's, a bright turquoise that wasn't her colour at all but the only thing on the rail that went comfortably with her trousers. She changed into it as soon as she'd washed the ingrained dirt and blood from her hands, smearing them with antiseptic ointment from Toni's bathroom cabinet and covering up the two largest cuts with plasters. Her own shirt she screwed up in a ball and thrust into the waste bin, thinking she'd never owned anything for so short a time. She was going to feel quite aggrieved when it finally appeared on her Visa bill.

With Honey snoring on the floor, Loretta had quickly and efficiently examined the neat collection of papers Frank had clipped together: letters, photocopies, even some photographs. They began with a copy of his birth certificate which showed he'd been born in 1974, making him a year or two older than her hasty estimate in the park. His birthday was in August, the same month as Loretta's, and he'd be twenty next month. The mother's name was given as Antonia Annetta Stramiello, occupation student; Loretta wasn't sure whether this meant Toni was already at college when Frank was born, or still in high school. She had heard Americans use the same word for both. The space for the father's name was blank.

Attached to the birth certificate was a letter from an organisation called Right To Know, replying in detail to a letter from Frank asking how to go about tracing his natural mother. They had written to him at an address in Philadelphia, where he seemed to be at college. Loretta guessed that he'd gone home to his adoptive parents for the long vacation, travelling to New York to see Toni without telling them; Newburgh, she had discovered from an atlas on Toni's bookshelves, was in New York State, closer to Manhattan than Philadelphia. The letter was accompanied by a leaflet, a combative manifesto in which Right To Know insisted on the right of every adopted child to meet his or her biological parents; it was clear, in spite of the fastidiously inclusive language, that this meant the mother. Next came a couple of blurred ten-by-eights of Toni, one of her leaving the apartment building arm-in-arm with a man Loretta took to be Jay, the other of her walking Honey in Riverside Park. Jay was taller than Toni, wearing glasses, a bit nondescript, not at all Loretta's idea of a jazz musician, but the picture had been taken clandestinely, with a long lens, and it hadn't enlarged well. In the second photo Honey strained at the lead, staring angrily ahead as though she'd intuited the presence of the camera, while Toni's face was partly obscured by her hair. It was the same length as Loretta's and it wasn't really surprising that Frank, with only these poor images to rely on, had assumed that any blonde woman walking a bulldog in that particular park must be his real mother. The remaining picture was a snapshot, a colour photo of a chubby, fair-haired baby whom she took to be Frank at three or four months; it wasn't clear why he'd included it in the package, unless he had invested it with some talismanic power to bridge the gap between himself and Toni.

There was one more document in the envelope, a report from a private detective, Pete Dunow of Inside Investigations Inc., which supplied Toni's present address and phone number along with a startling quantity of other information. There was a schedule of her daily movements: the regular walks with Honey, her journeys to Columbia on Monday, Tuesday and Friday, where and when she did her shopping, the fact that Jay stayed over at the flat two or three nights a week. With a growing sense of outrage Loretta read that Toni had had an "intimate" relationship with Jay for almost a year and two boyfriends in quick succession before that; there were rumours, Dunow wrote, of an earlier, lesbian relationship with a female lecturer at Columbia, but he hadn't been able to stand them up. Loretta had been goggle-eyed, unable to believe that this degree of surveillance was permitted in New York, when a new and alarming idea gripped her: if Dunow had been watching Toni from a distance, always having to conceal himself, was it possible he had made the same mistake as Frank Ryan? That it was *Pete Dunow* she had glimpsed behind the statue in the Met, *Dunow* that the nutritionist had warned her about in the book shop? Loretta shook her head, refusing to take the idea seriously. The detective had done his job, written up what he'd found, and that was the end of his involvement. But his tone worried her, the lubricious interest he displayed in Toni's "intimate" relationships; there was a fine line between private eye and Peeping Tom and she couldn't help wondering whether he had overstepped it. It was just possible that Frank had innocently initiated this line of inquiry, he might well have wanted to know whether his real mother was married or single before he approached her, but this Mozartian catalogue of ex-lovers was something else.

Had Toni really noticed nothing while Pete Dunow was on his marathon trawl through her life? Either he was extremely skillful or he hadn't got really close to his target; at this point Loretta had put the papers to one side and dialled the Sag Harbor number again but there was the customary click and she broke the connection, in no mood to listen to that holier-than-thou voice reciting nonsense about prayers and credit cards.

She went back to the report, finding a garbled summary of Toni's academic career which apparently included a visiting lectureship at St. Frid's College, Oxford; there were also details of her bank account and the ownership of her flat. A final paragraph consisted of advice on how Frank should approach his mother: "Subjects do not generally respond well when the initial contact is made by phone," Dunow had written, "and letters may go unanswered for days or even weeks. For this reason, our recommendation is that the subject be confronted direct, at or near the home address. The subject's initial reaction may be defensive or hostile and for this reason, we also recommend that you carry full documentation with you at all times."

He might have been writing about a criminal, Loretta thought indignantly, a shoplifter or a drug pusher rather than an eighteen-year-old who, for reasons Dunow presumably knew nothing about, had given up her child for adoption. There was no acknowledgement that the sudden appearance of an adult son or daughter might cause turmoil in a woman's life, as Loretta suspected it was about to do in Toni's. Her own involvement, accidental though it was, had left her winded and aching but it was as nothing to the impact the affair was going to have on Toni, Jay, their unborn child . . . Loretta glanced at the resolutely silent phone, acknowledging her dread of the moment when it finally rang. On top of everything else, how would Toni feel, how would any woman feel, when she discovered her son had employed some quite possibly perverted private detective to *spy* on her? It was hardly a good omen for their future relationship.

Unable to quell her uneasiness about Dunow, Loretta had turned back to the first page of his report and read an office address on Lexington, a few blocks north of Tracey's hotel. He had told her the area was called Murray Hill and that it was rundown, a little seedy, and that was exactly how it had looked when she dropped him off the previous evening: drab buildings in brown brick, junk shops, the neon lights of cheap stores that stayed open all night. It was easy enough to picture a dark doorway between two shops, steps leading to a poky upstairs office, a glass door stencilled with the Inside Investigations logo; on the other side she imagined a thickset man with thinning hair, a phone in one hand and his feet up on the desk. Below the address was a column of telephone and fax numbers and without giving herself time to think, Loretta pulled the phone towards her and dialled one of them.

"Inside Investigations, Julie speaking. How may I help you?"

Loretta was unprepared, expecting an answering-machine.

"*Inside Investigations*, Julie spe—"

"Can I speak to Pete Dunow?"

"Mr. Dunow isn't in the office right now." She sounded wary. "Can I put you through to Mr. Delehanty?"

"No, I don't think . . . All I want to know is whether he's still working for one of your clients, his name's Frank Ryan."

She heard an intake of breath. "Client information is confidential, I'd better put you through to Mr. Delehanty, if he's free. Would you hold on one moment?" Loretta heard the soft tap of computer keys, a chair scraping back, voices conferring out of earshot. It didn't tally with the picture she'd formed of a shoestring outfit, a middle-aged man in a dirty mac and a part-time secretary. After a longish wait, Julie came back. "I'm sorry, Mr. Delehanty's with a client right now. Can he call you back?"

"There's no need, if you can just tell me—"

"I'm sorry, we're not allowed to give out client information over the phone." Julie was losing her temper. "If you leave your name and number Mr. Delehanty will call you back as soon as—"

Recognising an impasse, Loretta interrupted: "I won't bother, thanks very much," and put the phone down.

She frowned and looked down at her palms, wondering why they were hurting so much. It was a niggling pain, like a mouth ulcer, and it didn't seem to have been eased at all by the antiseptic cream. She realised she'd been digging in her nails while she was on the phone, making it worse.

"Oh, *God*," she complained, uncurling her legs and accidentally kicking Honey.

The bulldog growled, scrambled to her feet and backed away, teeth bared. Loretta did her best to pacify her, uncertain of the dog's temper after what had happened in the park, and eventually resorted to bribing her back into good humour with a plate of meaty biscuits. Looking at her watch and deciding she'd waited long enough for Toni to call, she stuffed Frank's documents back into the manila envelope and made

sure the answering-machine was switched on. Trying to remember the exact location of the Moroccan restaurant she'd
spotted the day before, she slipped quietly out of the flat while
Honey was too busy eating to protest. In the corridor she
glanced in both directions, still thinking of Pete Dunow, but it
was as quiet and empty as it had always been; Loretta wondered briefly what kind of people Toni's neighbours were, why
they never seemed to show themselves. As she rounded the
corner to the lift an impressive chorus of aches and pains
started up in her calves and ankles; Loretta shook each leg in
turn, not looking forward to the walk to the restaurant but
relieved to have a good reason for leaving the small and increasingly claustrophobic flat.

It was hot on the bus, sweltering, and it stopped with annoy-
ing frequency, letting in another blast of toxic air every time
someone got on or off. By the time it crossed Christopher
Street, way down in the Village, Loretta had read seven more
pages of *The Last Supper* and didn't feel any more engaged by
it; things hadn't improved much with the arrival of the long-
awaited guest, an elderly man in a dinner jacket who was carrying, for no obvious reason, a conductor's baton. She could
feel her leg muscles seizing up again and she longed to get off,
but her destination, Battery Park, was literally the end of the
line, a green blob on the map covering the southern tip of
Manhattan, with dotted lines marking the ferry routes to Ellis
Island and the Statue of Liberty. Loretta wasn't interested in
the statue and she was neutral about the immigration museum
on Ellis Island but a friend in California had recommended
the boat trip, saying the views from the ferry were fantastic.
She liked the idea of sea air, especially after sitting outdoors
on stuffy Amsterdam Avenue, but she hadn't realised the jour-

ney would take so long. Now they were trundling through TriBeCa, not far from the restaurant where she'd eaten with Tracey the previous night, and there was still something eerie about the quiet streets and flat-fronted commercial buildings, even in bright sunlight. Pete Dunow came unbidden into her mind and she grimaced, not wanting to think about him or his shabby activities; she closed *The Last Supper*, thinking she'd have another look at it on the plane, and busied herself looking up the times of the Ellis Island ferry in her guidebook. The boats left every half hour and she should just be in time for the three o'clock.

A band was playing in Battery Park when she finally got off the bus, the music drifting through trees that had the twisted, slightly stunted appearance caused by exposure to biting winds and salt spray. In winter the place would look bleak but on this hot Sunday afternoon the water glinted and glittered like mercury, boats bobbed under a serene blue sky, and Liberty presided over it all, in a commanding position at the harbour entrance. The statue was more affecting at a distance than she expected, Loretta thought, trying to imagine the feelings of immigrants who had travelled steerage, crowded into the bowels of a steamship for weeks on end without proper food or exercise, until the moment came when they were allowed up on deck for their first sight of New York. The statue must have seemed then like a promise, its arm raised both in greeting and as a pledge of protection. These days it was—what? A tourist attraction, a shorthand symbol for New York, having to compete with the ubiquitous green apple on postcards and guidebooks, a relic of a more innocent and hopeful past. Loretta turned away from the tranquil seascape, remembering she had a ferry to catch, and walked stiffly past stalls selling Liberty T-shirts and hats, visitors snapping each other with the statue in the background: "Left a bit, no, too far, come back, that's it, hold it *right there*."

As she drew near the queue for the Circle Line ferry, her path was blocked by a crowd with their backs turned to her, periodically cheering and breaking into applause. In between she could hear grunts and gasps, some sort of strenuous performance taking place, and when she edged round to a gap in the spectators she discovered that the attraction was a troupe of acrobats. They were all men, about a dozen of them, and they worked in groups of two and three, taking long cartwheeling runs and performing spectacular somersaults, leapfrogging over each other and forming human pyramids as though their bodies were spring-loaded. Fathers had hoisted toddlers onto their shoulders to get a better view, as though it was family entertainment, but Loretta was struck by the raw sexual power of the acrobats; they wore shorts and vests in shiny synthetic material, just this side of decency, and perspiration gleamed on their perfectly developed musculature. Her thoughts jumped to Michelangelo's *Battle of Lapiths and Centaurs*, a sculptural relief whose celebration of the male body was disguised in a not dissimilar way, the artist's excuse being a battle, whereas this was presented as a display of gymnastics. She happily handed a five-dollar bill to an older man, also in shorts even though he hadn't so far taken part in the show, who was working the crowd on their behalf.

"All currencies accepted," he called out, "dollars, pounds, cameras, wallets . . ." and there was a ripple of uneasy laughter at this ironic reference to the supposed criminality of black men.

Loretta turned away from the spectacle and joined the end of the ferry queue, discovering almost at once from someone just in front of her that she needed to buy a ticket from an office inside Castle Clinton, the stagey brown fort she had passed on her way through the park. Glancing nervously at her watch, she hurried back to the fort, found the ticket office and arrived back at the jetty just in time to board. Wrinkling her nose at the overpowering smell of engine oil, she shuffled through a long enclosed lounge and went upstairs to the top deck, looking for a seat that would give her an uninterrupted view of Manhattan when the boat pulled away. People were still coming upstairs, talking in half-a-dozen languages—the couple in front of her were Italian, the teenagers behind her Spanish—but the boat wasn't completely full, perhaps because of the broiling heat. It was even muggier on the ferry than it had been on land, the sun beating down on the shadeless deck and reflecting up from the water, trapping the boat like the filling in a toasted sandwich. Within minutes the seat of Loretta's trousers was damp with sweat and she got up again, pulling the clammy fabric away from her skin. To her relief the last passenger had filed on and the ferry started to move, pulling away from the landing-stage on the first leg of its circular route, the crossing to Liberty Island.

Its progress was rapid and a cooling breeze sprang up, the first time Loretta had felt comfortable outdoors all day. She closed her eyes, held on to the rail of the ferry with both hands and leaned back, sucking the fresh air into her lungs, her hair whipped away from her face by the wind, exhilarated beyond all expectation. On the quay they had just left she heard shouting, something to do with the acrobats perhaps, but it was quickly lost under the noise of the engines and the plangent cries of seabirds. Gulls wheeled between the boat and the shoreline and she stared across the water at the featureless twin columns of the World Trade Center, the tallest building in Manhattan but out of place there, dwarfing four gleaming blue towers which seemed to have been constructed on the opposite principle, with deliberately asymmetrical pediments. Over on the right, a slender art deco skyscraper peeped out from a cluster of older buildings, a ragged column of smoke floating mysteriously behind its conical verdigris cap. As the island receded the contrasting colours and shapes seemed to mellow and blend, honey-tinted by the afternoon sun, and the shoreline became very slightly concave, like the view through a wide-angle lens. The effect, thought Loretta, was almost a visual metaphor, the inanimate steel and glass columns seeming to strain upwards in a way that expressed the aspirations of their human designers . . .

She gave her head a slight shake, embarrassed by this flight of fancy. The Italian couple next to her were busily taking pictures and the man turned to her, asking in poor, heavily accented English if she'd mind taking one of himself and his wife on the other side of the boat, against the background of Liberty Island. Loretta assented in halting Italian and they fell into a ponderous, bilingual conversation as they struggled for words in each other's language. If Loretta understood them correctly, they were going to Ellis Island to look for an inscription commemorating the arrival of the woman's aunt Sinforosa, who had been brought to the United States as a child, on the wall displaying the names of immigrants who had disembarked there. The man added something in Italian that amused his wife, one of those North Italian honey-blondes, but which Loretta didn't quite catch. She smiled anyway and ushered them across the deck, realising that the boat would soon be too close to the statue to get the shot they wanted, and posed them against the rail, the man's arm encircling his wife's waist. Loretta stepped back, ignoring a shooting pain in her right ankle as she balanced herself on it; she pressed the shutter twice, from slightly different angles, and passed the camera back, shielding her eyes with her hand as she looked up at Liberty, now looming greenly over the ferry. Close up the statue was crude and rather masculine, especially the face, and weighed down by absurd, neoclassical draperies, but the Italians seemed genuinely excited by the prospect of exploring it. The man, who seemed more outgoing than his wife, suddenly asked Loretta if she and her friend would like to join them.

"Friend?" asked Loretta, beginning a confused explanation to the effect that she was on her own, *sola*, and anyway she didn't have time to see both islands.

"Ma c'era un uomo," the woman said, pointing to the other side of the boat where they'd been standing. They turned to look and she let her arm drop: *"E andato via."*

"Gone?" asked Loretta, groping for the right phrase in Italian. "Who're you talking about? I mean, *che tipo di uomo?"*

The woman made a moue of incomprehension, signalling she must have been mistaken. The couple said goodbye, wishing Loretta a nice journey of Ellis Island, and as soon as they'd gone downstairs she surveyed the deck. More than half the passengers were getting off and among those that remained there were no faces she recognised, but then she'd never seen Pete Dunow or, for that matter, Michael Lindsay. The man had used the word *amico*, definitely a male friend, prompting little rills of anxiety which she tried to repress by working out what could have given him the mistaken impression she was with someone. A man standing or sitting nearby, regarding her in a familiar or possessive way? She pushed her hair back from her damp forehead, thinking it always came back to the same thing: watching, spying, that sense of being observed. But this time she hadn't noticed anything, in spite of all the weird things that had happened in the course of the weekend. She recalled the sensual pleasure she had felt as the ferry left Battery Park, the way she had closed her eyes and thrown back her head, how much the skyline had excited her when she opened them. In effect, she had been oblivious of everything from the moment the boat left Battery Park until the Italian couple engaged her in conversation.

People were starting to come upstairs and in a moment the ferry hooted, announcing it would shortly depart. A few stragglers came down the path from the base of the statue, followed at a distance by a roly-poly couple, the woman unwisely wearing shorts, although this aspect of her appearance was as nothing to her head, on which wobbled a green rubber replica of the statue's crown. Its spokes quivered, Loretta thought, momentarily distracted, like the tendrils of some submarine animal unceremoniously plucked from its natural habitat.

"Wait for *me*," the woman called, holding the crown in place with her hand, and there was a round of sarcastic applause as she and her husband reached the gangplank.

The boat began to move again and Loretta sighed, thinking the strange weekend was almost over; in two-and-a-half hours she'd be checking in at Kennedy Airport. She had half an hour to go round the museum at Ellis Island, forty-five minutes if she had enough dollars left to take a taxi back to Riverside instead of the bus, and she drew out her purse, surreptitiously counting her dollar bills. She'd spent less than she expected, probably because she'd been paying for meals by credit card, and she could easily afford a taxi and something to drink on Ellis Island; she had yet to visit an American tourist attraction that didn't have a café *and* a gift shop. There might also be a phone and she could try Jay's parents again, just in case Toni had come back; the mere thought was enough to make her frown and she was relieved when the ferry swung round, distracting her with a broadside view of Ellis Island. It was closer to the Jersey shore than the Statue of Liberty and dominated by a single building, a grandiose red confection, stuccoed white round the windows and surmounted by four copper domes; more like a nineteenth-century town hall in southern Europe than a place where thousands of immigrants had queued to show their documents. It was nothing like the brutal concrete bunker near Heathrow airport which Loretta had visited with one of her students, an English woman whose Chilean husband had been arrested and threatened with deportation, just before she left Oxford for San Francisco. Shortly afterwards he had been put on a plane to Santiago and his wife had been trying to finish her D.Phil. thesis while her lawyer argued with the Home Office about whether he should be allowed back into the country.

Ellis Island, in contrast, was palatial. Her interest roused, Loretta went downstairs to the airless lounge, braving the engine fumes while the ferry manoeuvred and docked. She was surprised to see how many people had spent the crossing indoors, eating and drinking things they'd bought from the bar at one end; she glanced up and down, not quite knowing what she expected to see, and the result was exactly the same as it had been on the upper deck, no one who looked even remotely familiar. Near the exit, a girl with a harsh northwestern twang was describing to her friends how her grandparents had arrived at Ellis Island from Latvia and travelled by train to Seattle in one of the worst winters Washington State had ever known. Loretta followed them off the boat, along the glassed-over path to the main entrance, thinking how much bleaker the island must have seemed on a dark winter morning in the 1920s.

Inside was an airy, high-ceilinged room where, according

to the caption accompanying a series of blown-up photographs, immigrants gathered to collect their baggage. The grainy, black-and-white pictures showed men in collarless shirts and flat caps patiently searching among trunks and bundles and cheap suitcases for their belongings; women in voluminous late nineteenth-century clothes, babies cradled in their arms and peeping out from their skirts. The main section of the museum was on the next floor and Loretta went upstairs to another great hall with tall arched windows facing the southern tip of Manhattan, too high for anyone to see out. The pathos of this concealed proximity became apparent when Loretta entered a series of smaller rooms, once used for medical examinations and psychological tests, now devoted to lavish displays of documents and explanations of how the system functioned. For an unlucky minority, she read, Ellis Island was as near to New York and the rest of the United States as they got; the museum frankly admitted that the island's main function had been "to screen out those considered undesirable—the incurably ill, the impoverished, the disabled, criminals and all others barred by the immigration laws of the United States," sometimes as many as a thousand people a month. Three and a half thousand, too sick to go back to Europe, died in the island hospital. Doctors examined newcomers for as little as six seconds, chalking a mark on their clothes if they suspected some kind of illness or disability—L for lameness, E for eye conditions, X for suspected "mental defects"—and sending them off for tests. It occurred to Loretta that there weren't enough letters in the alphabet for this distasteful sheep-and-goats procedure, and she was reminded of a friend from London who'd been turned back at Kennedy Airport after customs officials found his supply of AZT, the anti-AIDS drug, and correctly inferred that he was HIV-positive. No one had actually scrawled P for plague on his shirt collar but he had felt humiliated just the same.

A chilling headline from the *New York Times*—500 REDS AT ELLIS ISLAND—revealed that by 1920 the island was being used for deportations as well as arrivals. Trade unionists, Wobblies, anyone suspected of being a Bolshevik or an anarchist, had been rounded up; during one of these mass arrests, a year earlier, Emma Goldman and Alexander Berkman had been picked up, taken to the island and deported to the Soviet Union. Loretta read that the ship they went on, a U.S. Army transport, was apparently nicknamed the "Soviet ark."

Feeling mildly depressed, Loretta went downstairs in search of the café. According to the signs she followed it was at the side of the building, beyond the gift shop, where the woman in shorts and the rubber crown was already looking for more souvenirs. Loretta stepped inside, wondering what it had to offer, and saw it was full of dolls in folksy costumes, supposedly representing the countries the original immigrants had come from, crudely carved wooden spoons, Statue of Liberty key-rings: knickknacks with only the most tenuous connection to the museum upstairs.

"Albie," the woman called across the shop, "come look at this cute ice-tray. You think Pammy would like it for her birthday?"

Loretta backed out of the shop and went into the café, ordering black tea and then changing her mind and asking for a large Coke with ice instead. She carried the full cardboard cup outside, sipping from it to avoid the risk of spilling it, and eyed the outdoor tables where she recognised half-a-dozen people who'd been on the same ferry as herself. She was about to sit down at an empty table when she realised it was possible to walk round to the rear of the building, where the sea wall faced Lower Manhattan. On the way she passed an elderly couple taking photographs of the commemorative wall the Italians had told her about, a simple grey monument in several curving sections which partially enclosed a sizeable lawn planted with shrubs and young trees. It was higher than she expected, around five feet, cutting off her view of the people from the ferry she'd just left behind, and there were hundreds of thousands of names; Toni's family, the Stramiellos, was probably there somewhere, Loretta thought, wondering where the S section began. She arrived at the sea wall and put down her Coke, shielding her eyes as she stared across the water to the green fringe of Battery Park; she ought to get the next ferry back, she realised, glancing at her watch, but first she wanted to fix the view in her mind. The light was softer now, the sun striking the skyscrapers at a gentler angle, colouring them pink even though it wouldn't set for hours. She pushed back her hair, which felt heavy and damp, lifting it and holding it away from her head, still not accustomed to the late afternoon heat. Then she took another sip of Coke, rested her elbows on the stone wall and gazed dreamily across the bay.

Hands sneaked round her waist, big, alien, masculine hands on Toni's turquoise shirt, crushing it like a belt. She started back with an intake of breath, colliding with their owner, and the hands gripped her waist, the stubby fingers splayed, digging into her flesh.

She let out a shriek but they were alone between the two walls, out of sight even of the people sitting outside the café. One of his hands jerked up, seeking her mouth, the other snaking further round her body. She bit his fingers and heard a startled cry: *"Shit."* He was unprepared for the ferocity of her counter-attack, her elbow thrusting into his chest, and he let go for a few seconds. "For Christ's sake," she heard him pant, "you're not—*stop,* you're hurting us *both.*"

He had her by the arms, pinioning them at her sides, and she lurched forward, unable to escape but twisting her neck until she got a view of his features. Her right arm hurt, her sore hands were agony, but before he averted his head, recoiling from her scrutiny, she registered a pudgy face, mottled complexion, wispy fair hair falling over a domed forehead. Even at this unnatural angle, she knew straightaway she had *never* seen him before in her life.

She had given him time to recover and although he was still out of breath, a smile twitched the corners of his lips.

"Loretta," he gasped, still not meeting her eyes, "can I— *phew*—is it safe to let go of you now?"

12

She didn't say anything but he released her anyway, took a couple of steps back and wiped his forehead with the sleeve of his jacket. Breathing heavily, in obvious discomfort, he panted: "Know who I am now, huh?"

She shook her head, breathing hard, studying her palms, the scratches from that morning reopened and dribbling blood.

He smoothed down his shirt, tucking it into his trousers, the waistband straining against the plump soft flesh.

"What'd you do to your hands?" He reached out, touched one of them and she snatched it back, moving out of range. "Look," he said defensively, coming after her. "I know I gave you a fright—OK, I was stupid, creeping up on you like that, but you didn't get *those* scratches from me." He felt in his jacket pocket and drew out a folded white handkerchief, holding it out to her. "Want to use this?"

She ignored the question, accepting the handkerchief reluctantly, only because she didn't want to ruin a second shirt with bloodstains. Dabbing at her palms, not looking at him, she said: "Pete Dunow, I suppose." She hesitated, troubled by his accent, which veered erratically between American and English. "You know my name so obviously you've realised I'm not Toni—"

"Pete? Toni? Who are all these people?"

She lifted her head and at once his eyes slid away, focusing somewhere beyond her right shoulder, on the wall with all the names. She said: "What do you mean, who are they?"

He started to fiddle with his jacket. "Bugger, I've lost a button. Can you see a button down there?" He crouched, patting the ground, gave a little crow of triumph and put it in his pocket.

"Toni," he said, straightening up, "I'm with you now, it's her apartment you're staying in. Old habits die hard, don't they, Loretta? No pun intended, of course, but wouldn't life be a lot simpler if you coughed up for a hotel instead of always doing it on the cheap?" She was staring at him, the handkerchief limp in her hand, but still he didn't look her in the eye. "So who's Pete?"

She didn't answer and he added, incredulous: "You really don't know who I am? You always forget guys you sleep with so easily?"

Her mouth fell open. "Sleep with? I've never seen you in my life before. *Never.*"

"Come *on*, Loretta." Indignation speeded up his voice,

which was light and distinctive, and he began to gabble. "You're not really going to keep this up? I know it was a long time ago, nineteen-eighty—nineteen-eighty-something, d'you remember the name of that café, it went right out of my head and I've never been back, I kind of avoid Paris. Not that I really think the French cops . . . I can't *believe* you've forgotten."

She stood very still, winding the blood-speckled square of fabric in and out of her fingers.

"Well go on, say something. Aren't you going to say *anything*?"

In a strained voice, as if she feared the answer, she whispered: "Jamie?"

He lifted a hand, silencing her, and she noticed that the fingers were a little swollen. "James, please. James Noel."

"Not—"

"No, it seemed . . . a sensible precaution to change it. You know, new life and all that." His vocabulary was eclectic, an unpredictable blend of American and upper-middle-class English. "Noel's my middle name, in case you wondered. I read somewhere, if you have to change your name, go for something familiar."

He was looking over her shoulder again, jumpy, not as confident as he sounded, unwilling to meet her gaze. She stared at him, confused by the voice, which had begun to stir old memories, and the astonishing change in his physical appearance. It wasn't just that he was older, he was *unrecognisable*.

As if he had guessed what she was thinking, he snapped: "You're no spring chicken yourself, Loretta. You're what, ten years older than me?" He folded his arms and caught sight of the hand she had bitten, a fading red semicircle extending over the knuckles. He thrust it at her and said satirically: "Love bites. How appropriate."

His eyes narrowed and for once he looked at her, making it clear he was assessing the physical changes in her face. He said spitefully: "Still on your own, I guess? Where're you living now, did you ever move from that poky flat? Islington, wasn't it?"

She said evenly, not rising to the provocation: "I found one of his books yesterday."

"Whose books?"

"You know." She was beginning to get over the initial shock of seeing him again after all these years but she couldn't bring herself to say Hugh Puddephat's name out loud.

He put his hands on the sea wall and heaved himself onto it, grunting with the effort. Thinking back to Jamie as she remembered him in the Café Costes—Loretta had never forgotten its name, it was the most fashionable place in Les Halles, all polished chrome and fake art deco—was almost physically painful. She had left him sitting at an upstairs table while she walked down the pale green stairs to the ground floor, then down more steps to the basement, to the ladies' loo. When she came back she glanced up at the balcony where they'd been sitting and he was gone. A completely irrelevant detail occurred to her now, she couldn't remember either of them paying for their drinks, which was laughable given what they'd just discussed. Loretta had never known where Jamie disappeared to but her last view of him, staring into space, without the energy even to stir his coffee, had stayed with her for years afterwards.

He had been thin, charming, his fair hair falling forward in a way that reminded her of a photograph of Rupert Brooke, though even then it embarrassed her to admit it. She had slept with him once, that was all, but it had been one of those rare nights when she voluntarily abandoned her habitual self-consciousness, giving in to the imperatives of desire to a degree which frightened and exhilarated her. She felt as if, in that brief time with Jamie, she had caught a glimpse of another, more instinctual self and the ache when the experience was not repeated was almost intolerable. The memory was so powerful that even now, scrutinising the man sitting on the wall in front of her, trying and failing to find a resemblance, she heard a distant echo of that unbearable longing and had to make a conscious effort to push it away. It helped that she was still unable to connect him with Jamie, not so much because of the fleshiness of his face, a bloated look which age all too frequently superimposes on youthful good looks, but because of the alteration in his eyes. She remembered them as wide and brown, he had a habit of glancing down as though he was afraid they might reveal too much, but now—now, she thought, they were watchful, shifty almost, looking out from behind his face as though through holes in a mask.

He had been distracted by something on the far side of the commemorative wall but now he said again: "Whose books?"

"You were *there*," she burst out, "didn't you see me pick it up? Someone else wanted it, we nearly came to blows."

"Some old bat was eyeing me up," he said, his expression darkening, "she didn't give me much chance. I must say, Loretta, you've led me quite a dance the last couple of days."

Realising she had allowed herself to be diverted, she brushed this aside and said bleakly: "You know perfectly well who I'm talking about. Hugh Puddephat."

Whatever reaction she had expected, it wasn't boredom. James Noel glanced down at his hands, turned and stared across the water at Manhattan. "Great view," he said.

She gasped. "Is that it? Is that all you've got to say? Don't you ever *think* about him?"

He lifted his right leg onto the wall and began to retie a shoelace. She wasn't consciously aware of it, but she remembered later that his shoes looked expensive, like his jacket. "Hugh?" he said casually. "No, why should I?"

"You *killed* him."

He finished trying a double bow. "It's not like you to go all coy, Loretta," he said petulantly. "Why beat about the bush? I *murdered* him."

The breath was knocked out of her and she began to stutter, unable to get a complete sentence out. "You said—you told me—it was self-defence, manslaughter, that's why I didn't—"

"Turn me in to the cops?" He swung his leg down, leaned forward and put his hand under her chin. "The reason you didn't turn me in, sweetie, is because you fancied me. Go on, admit it. You couldn't get enough of it."

She knocked his hand away. "*He* attacked *you*, that's what you said, you were only trying to defend yourself, he was bigger than you, you didn't—" Loretta hadn't actually witnessed the attack, it had taken place in the tiny Paris flat she had borrowed from an English friend; by the time she arrived Jamie was gone and she found the body. A phrase flashed into her mind from a newspaper report of the murder: *a frenzied attack . . .*

James Noel slid off the wall, brushing dust off his hands. "Hugh was scum, he deserved everything he got, the guy really fancied himself."

"Didn't you?" she retorted. In the café, when she accused him of being responsible for Puddephat's death, Jamie admitted luring the don into an affair. His sole motive, he said, was revenge for the suicide of his cousin, Melanie, a student who had been in love with Puddephat, not knowing he was gay. Jamie insisted he was heterosexual but said he knew he was attractive to men, and had used it to ensnare Puddephat, intending to teach him a lesson. But Puddephat had reacted furiously to Jamie's rejection, there'd been a struggle in the flat, the don had died—

James Noel said with satisfaction: "I never had any problem, there were always plenty of girls. Sorry, women. And men."

"Men?"

His eyebrows flicked up, mocking her. "Does bisexuality bother you, Loretta? That's not very PC."

"Not bisexuality," she said in a low, hurt voice. "You mean you were lying, that's what I can't stand—"

"You started it, you couldn't wait to get me into bed, you'd have done *anything*, you even asked me to write an article for that magazine of yours, what was it called? *Fem Sap*, poncey bloody title—I mean, for fuck's sake, did you really think I was a feminist? A new man?"

Her hand went to her mouth. "I can't—I've had enough of this," she mumbled, and started to walk away.

He slipped off the wall, moving quickly for a man of his bulk, blocking her path. In an entirely different tone of voice, he said: "Loretta, don't go, please, I'm sorry." He put his hand out and stroked one of her arms through her shirt, pleading with her. "I haven't had a chance—why d'you think I followed you all the way out here?"

She shook his hand off. "I don't know. I don't care."

"I saw you on Friday," he said rapidly, "in the Met, I'm an art dealer, I've got my own gallery in TriBeCa, I had a meeting with one of the curators, I've been trying to get a picture authenticated, it didn't take as long as I thought and I had some time left over. I couldn't believe it was you at first, it was the hair that made me think—"

"So it *was* you? Behind the *diadoumenos*?"

"The? Oh, the statue, yes. I was absolutely gobsmacked, I didn't know what to do, I followed you out of the Met and all the way down Fifth Avenue." His voice rose again. "I saw you go into a café, I waited awhile, I thought you hadn't recognised me—"

"I hadn't *seen* you, not properly."

"Loretta, I walked into the bloody café and sat down at the next table and you looked straight through me."

"That was *you*?" She was genuinely astonished.

He snorted. "Your friend even gave me my own matches back."

She remembered the matchbook. "I don't understand, why didn't you . . . I mean, why wait till this afternoon?"

"You're being a bit slow on the uptake, Loretta. You're the one person in the world who can tie me to an unsolved murder, I've been waiting to get you on your own, somewhere nice and quiet where there aren't any cops around. When you got on that boat, there was me thinking—oh, fuck, she's going to climb the Statue of Liberty. It was a hell of a relief when you didn't get off with those Italians, I can tell you."

She made an impotent gesture, responding to his remark about the police. "After all this time? In another country?"

"I don't know a lot about French law but I doubt if it has a statute of limitations, not for murder. Hugh was scum, certainly not worth doing life for." He looked grim. "For all I know they still have the death penalty in France."

Loretta said coldly: "You still haven't said what you want from me. What this is all about. I don't have much time."

He grinned. "Maybe I want to strangle you and throw your body over the wall, did you think of that?"

She felt a wave of contempt. "Unlikely, I think."

"How can you be so sure? No one's seen us together, you're going back to England tonight, you wouldn't be missed for days."

"Because you're a coward, that's why. You used a knife on Hugh."

"Ms. high-and-mighty, huh? You didn't exactly capture the moral high ground, letting me go because I gave you a good time in bed."

She flinched and he made another of his lightning reverses. "I'm sorry, I didn't mean—I'm nervous, I guess—I just wanted to tell you. I wanted you to know it worked out in the end."

"In the end? I don't know what you're talking about."

"Don't you want to know what happened?" he asked incredulously. "Didn't you ever think about where I went, after you let me walk out of that café?'

She looked down at her feet. "I know you didn't go back to Oxford. You didn't finish your degree."

"Who needs a degree? Don't be such a bluestocking, Loretta. What you did for me, it was *great*. I went to Italy, Turkey, Syria, met some people . . . I mean, it wasn't easy at first, there wasn't much money but look how it all turned out. I have my own gallery, I have a big apartment in the Village—"

She took a step back. "This is obscene. What am I supposed to do, congratulate you?"

He followed, trying to touch her. "I always liked you, Loretta, we nearly had something going, can't we be friends?"

"Friends?"

"Loretta—oh, *shit*."

She turned to see what he was looking at. Someone was on the other side of the commemorative wall, just a kid, seventeen or eighteen, dark-haired, sallow complexion, not very tall. Loretta saw feverishly bright eyes, a mouth working but no coherent sound coming out. She wasn't afraid until she looked back at James Noel and saw alarm and panic stamped all over his face.

"Johnny," he blurted out, trying to position himself behind Loretta, "I told you, I need a couple more days—"

The kid was moving from side to side, his dark head bobbing surreally above the columns of names. He was mumbling, Loretta caught occasional words, mostly obscenities but something about money, he wanted his *fucking* money, he had to get his shit, he needed it *now*. Abruptly he heaved himself up onto the wall, sat astride it for a moment, one leg hanging down either side, and Loretta suddenly felt his instability as a tangible, terrifying force. She started to move away, trying to put a gap between herself and James Noel, desperate not to draw the boy's attention to herself. It was Noel's problem, she wanted no part of it—

"Johnny," he pleaded, "one more day, that's all, I'll meet you at the usual place—"

"Gimme the money, I *fucking* told you." The kid slithered down the wall, making jagged tracks through the names with his trainers. Loretta saw he was wearing a long T-shirt, it came down almost to the knees of his baggy trousers.

"I don't have it on me, fifty bucks, a hundred at most—*Jesus fucking Christ,* don't point that thing at me." Noel threw up his hands, staring at the snub-nosed gun the kid had produced from under the T-shirt. "Johnny, listen to me, this is not what you think—"

"I *told* you not to fuck with me."

Noel backed away and the kid followed, passing Loretta as if she wasn't there. She eyed the gun, thinking fast, working out her chances of knocking it out of his hand without its going off. He was left-handed, that made it harder—

He fired. Loretta dived sideways, hit the sea wall, hardly felt the pain, cowered against it. The kid staggered almost comically from the recoil, recovered and walked towards James Noel, firing again, twice in quick succession, the gun leaping up each time. Blood spurted from Noel's chest, he threw up his hands and a hideous gurgling noise came from his lips, but he didn't fall, not yet. Pink foam flecked his mouth and he was trying to speak, his arms flailing, as if he still hoped to reason with the kid. Loretta saw the boy treading in Noel's blood, smearing it with his trainers, she dropped her head and vomited. There was another shot and she heard Noel collapse, several yards away from her by now, an odd, quiet, crumpled sound. She looked up, spitting bile from her mouth, and saw the kid standing in a kind of daze, as though he didn't understand the connection between the weapon in his hand and the man lying at his feet. The movement must have alerted him to her presence and he turned, staring down at her as though unable to work out what she was doing there. She saw him raise his gun hand, point it waveringly towards her, and for a few seconds she was paralysed, convinced he was going to fire. Then he blinked rapidly, grunted and tossed the gun over the sea wall.

Loretta let out an involuntary cry and for a moment the relief was so great she thought she was going to wet herself. She retched again, spewing out saliva this time, and when she raised her head from the ground an oldish man was running towards them, rounding the corner from the café. The kid saw him, muttered something and bolted in the opposite direction, towards the other side of the island.

"What's going on?" The man saw James Noel slumped on the ground, the widening pool of blood, and exclaimed: "Oh my God. Oh my God." He turned and threw his arms wide, blocking the view of a plump woman trotting after him. "Emily, don't look." Two men overtook them, one of them wearing the uniform of a security guard.

"Jesus. Is he dead?"

"You OK? Are you hit?"

"Which way'd he go? What'd he look like?"

Loretta pointed, still crouching against the wall. "Dark hair. T-shirt. Long."

They broke into a run. A woman was shouting over and over again: "A doctor, someone please go get a doctor—"

A man crouched beside James Noel, lifting his wrist, feeling for a pulse. He peered up at the rapidly growing crowd. "Sorry, folks, it's too late." He removed his jacket and placed it over Noel's head and chest.

"Did you see it, hon?" A head came down to her level and Loretta started back, flinching from the obscene rubber crown.

"Albie, where are you?" The woman looked round for her husband. "She's sick, I think she's gonna faint."

Loretta said: "No."

"You want me to help you up?"

Reluctantly Loretta took the woman's hand, struggled to her feet, clutching the strap of her bag. She walked unsteadily towards the crowd which by now partly obscured Jamie's body, mesmerised by the trail of blood which showed how long he had taken to go down. Someone had knocked her Coke off the wall, diluting the blood into a viscous brown puddle.

She felt a touch on her arm, saw the ludicrous green spokes nodding towards her again. "He a friend of yours, hon?"

No one else seemed to have noticed her. Loretta said in a small, cracked voice: "I—I've never seen him before in my life."

Someone called out: "He have any ID?"

"Try his wallet."

"Watch out, don't step in the blood."

Loretta edged round the crowd, still unremarked. She turned and stumbled towards the café, skirting the lawn and the wall, veering right onto the path between the tables. Another security guard appeared from the building and hurried towards her, seizing her arm.

"What happened? Someone get shot?"

"Yes," said Loretta, and he broke into a run.

She was at the café door when the ferry hooted at the landing stage. Without making a conscious decision, she wheeled round and began pounding across the grass, rounding the front of the building as the last passengers filed onto the boat.

"Hey, lady, no need to kill yourself, we won't go without you." A crewman put out a hand to steady her, regarding her with amusement, then his expression changed. "Are you OK?"

She nodded.

"Maybe you should sit down. Here, let me help you inside." He slipped an arm under her elbow and she sagged dizzily against him, thinking for a moment she was going to faint. He supported her into the lounge, leading her to an empty table next to a window. "What's up? Are you sick? You gonna be all right?"

She sank into a chair, shaking too much to speak.

"Maybe you should—" Someone called his name and he turned, not sure what to do.

Wanting him to go, Loretta got out: "The heat—"

He didn't look convinced but he was wanted on deck, the summons more urgent this time. "You take care now," he said, leaving her with obvious reluctance.

Loretta closed her eyes, leaned forward and slumped over her clasped hands. There was a grinding noise, the engines revved up and she felt the ferry move off, forcing herself to take long slow breaths because she didn't want to draw any more attention to herself. After a couple of minutes she got used to the gentle motion of the boat and something compelled her to turn her head to the window; Ellis Island was receding fast and she gasped, shocked beyond coherent thought by what had happened there. Her lips were dry and she licked them, tasting traces of vomit around her mouth, longing for a drink of water but too weak to do anything about it. She groped in her bag for something to wipe her mouth and drew out a crumpled handkerchief, dabbing at her lips and at the tears dribbling down her cheeks. Suddenly she remembered the crewman and glanced fearfully back towards the deck but there was no sign of him. Thankful for that at least, she began smoothing out the handkerchief on the table in front of her, doing it quite mechanically until the embroidered green initials leapt out at her and released a flood of memories almost a decade old.

Jamie—

Daily Telegraph,
Monday, August 8, 1994

Police in New York investigating the shooting last month of James Nowell, 29, a British art dealer based in Manhattan, say the dead man may have been killed after failing to deliver drugs which had already been paid for.

Nowell, who was co-owner of the Zenobia Gallery in fashionable TriBeCa, died from multiple wounds last month after a bizarre daylight shooting on Ellis Island, a popular tourist attraction in New York Harbour. Johnny McGrath, 18-year-old son of billionaire property developer Clay Studley McGrath, was seen running from the crime scene and has been charged with first-degree murder.

McGrath's defence team, led by top Manhattan lawyer Sidney Matousek, is lining up expert witnesses who will claim that the teenager was not responsible for his actions at the time of the murder because of his addiction to "crack" cocaine. McGrath claims to remember nothing about the killing but detectives from the NYPD say that Nowell had been using his gallery and the high-society contacts he made through it to supply drugs to a circle of rich kids which included McGrath and his friends.

They also believe that something went wrong with Nowell's usual line of supply just before his death, infuriating addicts who had paid in advance. Detectives have established that Nowell went to the Metropolitan Museum on the Friday before his death for a *bona fide* meeting with an expert on Indian art but they suspect he had also arranged a rendezvous with a courier who failed to turn up.

New Yorkers have been shocked by the fact that the murder happened on a site which has such a symbolic place in American history. Around half the country's present population have ancestors who arrived in the U.S. via Ellis Island, which has been turned into a very popular museum. Police have not yet established why Nowell went to the island but speculate he may have arranged to meet a drugs contact there.

Since his death Nowell has emerged as something of a mystery man, moving in society circles but apparently keeping himself to himself. He was unmarried and his business partner, Iranian-born Hazheer Fallahi, has told police he knows next to nothing about Nowell's private life. He vehemently denies any knowledge of his partner's alleged drug-dealing activities.

Nowell had lived in New York for six years but police have only the sketchiest idea of his movements before that date. People who knew him say he had a "cultivated" English accent and often talked about his time at a British public school; he claimed to have an Oxford degree but the university authorities have no record of him.

Detectives are working on the theory that Nowell was an assumed name and believe he may have entered the U.S. using skillfully forged documents, possibly obtained in the Middle East, although he is also believed to have had high-level contacts in Colombia. The dead man's fingerprints are being passed to Scotland Yard in the hope that they can help clear up the mystery.

Yesterday an NYPD spokesman said detectives were still hoping to trace a mystery blonde woman spotted near the body immediately after the shooting.

Among the first people to arrive on the scene were Emily and Albert Chessler from Tallahassee, Florida. Mrs. Chessler has told detectives she spoke to the woman, who seemed distressed, and asked her if she knew the murdered man. "She denied it," an NYPD spokesman said last night, "but we believe she may hold vital information. We think she may even have witnessed the crime, and we are appealing to her to come forward."

Mrs. Chessler said the blonde, who is believed to have left the island minutes before the alarm was raised and the ferry service suspended, spoke with an English accent. Police are working on the theory that she was a tourist who may already have returned to this country.

About the Author

JOAN SMITH was born in London in 1953. Formerly a journalist for the *London Sunday Times*, she is the author of four other Loretta Lawson mysteries: *What Men Say, A Masculine Ending, Why Aren't They Screaming?*, which have been filmed for BBC television, and *Don't Leave Me This Way*. She is also the author of two nonfiction books, including *Misogynies: Reflections on Myths and Malice*. She lives in Oxfordshire, where she is working on a new novel as well as writing articles and reviews for the *Guardian*, the *Observer*, the *Independent on Sunday*, and *Harpers & Queen*.